Kayla stuck out a hand. "Truce?"

Ry's smile was melting. "It's that easy?"

She shrugged. "I suppose I could go a few more rounds, if you want."

He quickly reached for her hand. "I'd just as soon avoid that, if you don't mind."

The moment their palms met, the air in the room seemed to change, grow warmer, closer, charged by a force he couldn't name.

"This has happened before, hasn't it?" he asked, his voice not quite steady.

She nodded.

How could she forget? It was the night that had changed her whole life....

PEGGY MORELAND

TANNER'S
MILLIONS

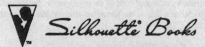

Published by Silhouette Books
America's Publisher of Contemporary Romance

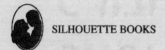 SILHOUETTE BOOKS

TANNER'S MILLIONS

ISBN 0-373-21805-2

Copyright © 2004 by Peggy Bozeman Morse

Chapter 1

In the days of the Old West, gunslingers usually chose to sit facing the door, rather than turn their backs to it, wanting to see trouble coming, before trouble found them. Twenty-first century lawmen often did the same and for much the same reason. Single men hanging out in bars preferred that position, as well, although safety had nothing to do with their preference in seating. On the prowl, all they cared about was seeing the available women who passed through the door.

Ry Tanner wasn't a gunslinger or a lawman, and he sure as hell wasn't interested in women, available or not. He sat with his back to the door because he wanted to be left alone. Period. He'd come to the River's End seeking oblivion and was damn close to finding it at the bottom of a glass of whiskey.

This was the fourth night in a row he'd spent in the rear booth at the River's End in downtown Austin,

Texas, a restaurant that promised corn-fed beef and liquor that wasn't watered down. Due to its proximity to the State Capitol and the University of Texas campus, the restaurant was frequented by legislatures and college students alike.

Ry had chosen it because it was within walking distance of the hotel he currently called home.

A month ago home for him was a Spanish-style villa, in Austin's exclusive West Lake Hills, an area inhabited by Austinites well able to afford the privilege of living in the prestigious community. Once owned by the CEO of a computer software company, the house came with a state-of-the-art media center, an Olympic-size swimming pool and a thermostatically controlled five-car garage, complete with an efficiency apartment above it, should the owner ever have need for a live-in housekeeper or nanny. His ex had gotten the house in their divorce settlement— along with just about everything else she could lay her hands on.

He didn't miss the house…or his ex-wife, either, for that matter. His discontent ran much deeper than that. He couldn't put his finger on exactly when the blue mood had settled over him, but it had slowly eaten away at him like a cancer, robbing him of his enthusiasm for life and his dedication to his profession as a plastic surgeon.

Desperate to find peace once again, he'd sold his surgical practice, a decision which had brought an abrupt end to his marriage, two radically separate areas of his life that he wouldn't have thought would have an effect on the other. He guessed it just proved that it was the money and prestige Lana, his ex, had loved and not him.

A flash of movement in his peripheral vision had Ry glancing to the left where a waitress was delivering the bill to a couple seated at the table next to his. The waitress was the same one who had kept a steady supply of whiskey coming his way for the past four nights.

He guessed her to be about twenty, judging by her youthful appearance, and more than likely a student at the University of Texas, which made him feel about as old as dirt, since he'd earned his bachelor degree from UT about the time she was starting first grade. But the wide gap in their ages didn't keep him from looking…or admiring. The woman was definitely easy on the eyes.

If standing, he could rest his chin on the top of her head, which would put her at about five-six or -seven, based on his own six-foot-two-inch frame. His brother Rory would call her a *hard body,* but Ry imagined all that well-toned flesh would soften quickly enough beneath the right man's hands. She had long, blond hair she'd pulled back in a ponytail that streamed halfway down her back, and big, brown eyes, a shade or two darker than the last finger of whiskey he swirled in his glass.

But it wasn't her looks that drew him back to the River's End each night. It was her smile. Bright, open, natural. She radiated a sense of happiness and exuberance that Ry hadn't experienced in a long, long time.

Though he'd like to believe she reserved her smile just for him, he'd be a fool to think so, as she shared it with all of her customers equally. What she found to smile about gave him something to puzzle over, while he drank. Night after night he'd watched her haul heavy trays back and forth from the kitchen, clean up messes a pig would've been proud to call its own and deal with cantankerous customers, who blamed her for everything, from the way their food was prepared to the noise level at the next table. And she did it without ever losing her smile.

Until now.

Though the change in her expression was there and gone in the blink of an eye, Ry caught it, having built his reputation as a renowned plastic surgeon on his ability to study the faces of his patients, noting each imperfection and variance in facial movement, no matter how minuscule. Intrigued, he watched her stare at the money the man had dropped onto the table. She was disappointed. Probably in the size of the tip the man had left.

To her credit, by the time the couple stood, she had her smile back in place and her call of "y'all come back and see us," sounded sincere to Ry's ear. She quickly cleared the table, stacking the remaining glassware and soiled napkins on her tray, with an efficiency and economy of movement that spoke of experience. Tucking the ticket and cash into her apron pocket for later tabulation, she headed his way, balancing the tray on her open palm.

Her smile brightened when her gaze met his. "Hey, cowboy," she called. "How's it going over here in the back forty?"

Ry didn't blink an eye at the nickname "cowboy." At the moment, he preferred the anonymity it offered over the title he'd worn for the last ten years. That of *doctor.*

He narrowed his gaze on her, as she stopped beside his booth. "He stiffed you, didn't he?"

She blinked, obviously unaware that anyone had witnessed the slight, then lifted a careless shoulder. "I guess he didn't like the service he received."

That she didn't attempt to shift the blame for the couple's discontent elsewhere, upped his opinion of the waitress another notch.

"Nothing wrong with the service," he assured her. "The guy's a tightwad. Pegged him the minute he walked through the door." He lifted his glass. "May he reap what he sows." He tossed back the whiskey, then shoved the empty glass to the edge of the table, his lips pressed together against the burn. "Bring me another whiskey."

"How about a cup of coffee, instead?" she suggested. "I just made a fresh pot."

Though he heard the concern in her voice, was even remotely touched by it, he shook his head. "Whiskey."

She hesitated a moment, as if she wanted to refuse, then smiled and picked up his glass. "Whatever you say, cowboy."

He watched her cross to the bar and let his gaze drop to the enticing sway of her buttocks, as she wove her way to the bar through the maze of tables squeezed into the restaurant's small lounge. A woman who obviously knew how to take advantage of every lull in activity, she set down her tray and stretched out muscles that had to be aching after the day she'd put in. With her arms lifted high above her head, she swayed to the left, to the right, then back, arching her spine.

Ry couldn't have looked away, if he'd wanted to. She had mile-long legs and a gentle curve at her waist, the perfect cradle for a man's hands. Her breasts, high and firm, strained against her shirt, the budded nubs of her nipples marking the center of each rounded mound.

But it was the expression on her face that his gaze locked on. Rapturous was the only word he could think of to describe her look—though he'd never be caught dead saying the flowery word out loud. Her smile was still there, but softer now, a whisper of contentment that curved the corners of her lips. He could almost hear her purr of pleasure, as she let her arms drift slowly down to her sides. Both the sound and the expression on her face made him think of a woman who'd just experienced a particularly satisfying climax.

The bartender, a barrel-chested guy sporting a dark mustache and goatee, stepped into view and sat Ry's drink on her tray.

"Since you worked a double shift yesterday and today," he heard the bartender tell her. "I'll cut you first tonight."

Relief washed over her face, as she picked up her tray.

"Thanks, Pete," she said gratefully. "As soon as I close out the tickets on my remaining tables, I'll clock out."

As she turned to deliver his drink, Ry quickly averted his gaze, fearing she would see the panic that had seized him at the mention of her leaving. He had to be drunk or crazy. He didn't know the woman, had no claim on her or her time. Sure, after his first visit to the bar, he'd made it a point to request the booth in her section. But that was because she'd respected his desire to be alone, yet kept the drinks coming, without making a pest of herself.

"Can I get you anything else?"

He glanced up as she placed his drink in front of him, saw the exhaustion behind her now familiar smile and decided right then and there to free her of her responsibilities, so she could go home and get some rest. From the hours he'd spent in the lounge, he knew which tables were her responsibility. She had only two left where customers were still seated. His and that of a couple of law students who were currently locked in a debate, arguing the fallacies of the judicial system.

He reached into the rear pocket of his jeans. "No. I'm about done. If you'll give me my bill and that of those two guys over there," he said, gesturing with his wallet at the law students, "I'll pay up."

"Are they friends of yours?"

He picked up his glass and drained it in two greedy gulps. Shuddering, he set the glass down and shook his head. "Nope."

She glanced over her shoulder at the two young men, then turned back to lay the two tickets on the table, her smile now warm and filled with admiration. "Then I'll let them know you picked up their tab. I'm sure they'll want to thank you."

"No need," he said, and stood. "Just tell 'em it's done."

He shrugged on his leather jacket, then reached for his cowboy hat, glancing down at the tickets she'd laid on the table, as he snugged it on...and wondered if he should've taken her up on the coffee she'd suggested. The numbers swam before his eyes faster than a school of minnows in a spring-fed pond. He peeled a hundred-dollar bill from his wallet and tossed it on the table, confident it would cover the two tabs and still leave a hefty tip for the waitress.

Stuffing his wallet back into the rear pocket of his jeans, he lifted a hand in farewell and headed for the entrance.

Kayla pushed open the alley door to the River's End and paused to draw in a deep breath, savoring the crisp, night air, as the door closed behind her. After breathing nothing but recycled air and cigarette smoke during her nine-hour shift in the bar, it felt wonderful to inhale fresh, clean air, despite its wintry bite. Hugging her jacket around her against the cold, she headed for the corner, sending up a heartfelt thanks to the cowboy who had left her the generous tip.

Prior to the start of her shift that day, she had been fifty dollars short of the rent due her landlord on Wednesday. But now—thanks to her cowboy, as the other waitresses had dubbed the man who seemed to have taken up residence in her section for the last few nights—she had the money to pay her rent, plus a little extra to send her mother.

Giving her pocket a satisfied pat, she quickened her step, anxious to get home. As she rounded the corner, she slammed into what felt like a brick wall. Dazed, she staggered back a step to find a man stood slumped against the restaurant's brick facade, his back to her. It appeared the building was all that was keeping him upright.

She squinted her eyes against the darkness and recognized the hat and jacket, as those of her cowboy. "I'm sorry," she said in apology, knowing the accident was her fault. "I wasn't watching where I was going."

When he didn't respond, she eased around him for a closer look. But his head was bowed and his hat brim blocked her view of his face. She laid a hand on his arm. "Are you okay?" she asked hesitantly.

He lifted a hand, as if in slow motion, and bumped his knuckles against the brim of his hat, pushing it farther back on his head. "Yeah," he said, a little shakily. He dragged a hand down his face, then grinned sheepishly. "Guess I should've taken you up on that cup of coffee you suggested. Looks like I might've had one too many."

"Just one of the many trials of being blessed with a large bladder."

He blinked, then blinked again. "What?"

She scanned the street for a cab to pour him into. "If you had a smaller bladder, you would've had to go to the rest room at some point during the evening, at which time you'd have realized, when you stood, that you'd had too much to drink." Not finding a cab in sight, she heaved a weary sigh. "Wait here and I'll call a taxi for you."

He peeled himself away from the building's stone facade. "No need. The Driskill's not far. Just a couple of blocks."

Her eyes sharpened at the mention of the hotel. Though she walked by the building almost every day on her way to and from work, she'd never been inside and was dying to see the changes made during the hotel's recent and much-publicized remodeling project.

She knew it was crazy to even think about offering to escort the cowboy to his hotel, but the opportunity to see the Driskill up close was a hard one to resist. Besides, she told herself. The guy seemed safe enough. If he'd wanted to make a pass at her, he'd certainly had ample opportunity during the hours he'd spent at the restaurant over the last few days.

"I could walk with you, if you like," she suggested.

"No need. I'm all right." He started off, weaving slightly.

Fearing he wouldn't make it to the end of the block, much less to his hotel, she quickly caught up with him and matched her steps to his. "It's not out of my way. I walk right past the hotel."

He stopped to stare at her. "You *walk* to work?"

She lifted a shoulder. "It's easier than trying to find a parking place downtown."

Hunching his shoulders to his ears, he stuffed his hands into his pockets and started walking again. "On a night like this, I'd take my chances."

She laughed softly, as she fell into step with him. "I don't mind the cold. It clears my mind for the studying I have to do when I get home."

"I figured you were a student."

"Really? How?"

"You…" He stumbled and his shoulder struck hers, knocking her off balance.

"Whoa," he said and grabbed her arm to steady them both. "Gotta watch those cracks in the sidewalk," he warned. "Those sons-of-bitches'll jump up and trip you every damn time."

Concerned that he was drunker than she'd originally thought, Kayla slipped her arm through the crook of his, offering him her support without making an issue of his need for it.

"So tell me how you knew I was a student," she said, anxious to keep him talking and hopefully on his feet.

His shoulder brushed hers in a shrug. "A lot of university students work at restaurants and businesses downtown. You're young. Figured you were one of 'em."

"I'm not *that* young," she said, then laughed. "In fact, I'm usually one of the oldest students in my classes."

He gave her a doubtful look. "If you're a day over twenty-one, I'll eat my hat."

She arched a brow. "Would you like salt with that Stetson? I'm twenty-six."

"Twenty-six?" He stopped and gave her a long look up and down, then shook his head and started off again. "Close, but not close enough."

She stared after him, then hurried to catch up. "Close enough for what?"

He puffed his cheeks, releasing a breath in a cloud of vapor the wind quickly shredded. "Juggling school and work must be pretty tough," he said, with a regretful shake of his head.

She wondered if he had purposely ignored her question or was too drunk to hold a thought longer than a nanosecond. Whatever the reason, she opted to let it drop. "Since I've never had it any other way, I wouldn't know."

He looked at her curiously. "Don't your parents help?"

"Parent," she corrected. "My father died while I was in high school. My mother would, if she could, but she has a tough time making ends meet, as it is."

He stopped, drawing her to a stop as well, and

frowned at the mass of people spilling from the Driskill's entrance.

Assuming it was the thought of fighting his way
through the crowd that drew his sour expression, she
tugged him toward a secluded side entrance. "We can
go in through here."

Once inside the hotel, she spotted the bank of elevators and guided him toward it, trying her best not
to act like the country-bumpkin she was and stare at
her surroundings. But it was difficult. She'd never
seen such grandeur outside the covers of a magazine
cover or a movie theater. Towering columns lined the
walls of the long lobby and intricate marble covered
the floor. Overhead, a stained-glass dome served as a
centerpiece for a hand-painted decorative ceiling that
must have taken years to create.

They reached the elevators much too soon, and she
drew her arm from his, disappointed that her tour was
officially at an end. "Think you can make it from
here?" she asked.

"Yeah." He stabbed a finger at the up button.

When he missed his mark by a good six inches,
she hid a smile and pressed the button for him.
"Maybe I better stick with you until you get to your
room."

"I'm not *that* drunk."

"Still," she said, and looped her arm through his
again, as the doors folded back. "What floor?" she
asked, as she urged him into the elevator.

He sagged against the rear wall. "The mezzanine."

She pressed the button then moved to stand beside
him, close enough to catch him if he crumpled, but
not so close that they touched. To fill the silence as

the elevator climbed slowly upward, she asked, "Will you be visiting in Austin long?"

"I live here."

She looked at him in surprise. "You live in the Driskill Hotel?"

The bell dinged, indicating their arrival, and the doors folded back.

Scowling, he pushed away from the wall. "Not by choice, I assure you."

His boot heel hooked on the elevator's metal threshold and Kayla made a wild grab, saving him from pitching forward and landing on his face. Determined to see that he made it safely to his room, she took him by the arm. "What's your room number?"

"Two fifty-five. The Cattle Baron's Suite."

At the door to the suite, Kayla held out her hand. He grudgingly passed her the card key, then propped a shoulder against the wall, his eyelids looking as if they were weighted with lead, as he watched her deal with the lock.

She pushed open the door and offered him the card and a smile. "Here you go, cowboy. You're on your own now."

He didn't make a move to take the key, only stared. "You sure are pretty."

Laughing, she tucked the card into his shirt pocket and gave it a pat. "That's the liquor talking."

"What liquor?"

That he would have to ask, only proved her point. "Have you ever heard the line in the song, 'women always look better at closing time?'"

"No," he said, then offered her a lopsided grin. "But you could come in and sing it for me."

She rolled her eyes and gave him a nudge toward the door. "Nice try, cowboy."

Grumbling, he staggered the two steps inside. Kayla strained to peer around him, trying to catch a glimpse of the suite's interior before he closed the door, robbing her of her one and only chance to experience such finery firsthand.

"Change your mind?"

She snapped her gaze to his and found him watching her. "No," she told him firmly, then glanced at the room beyond him and sighed. "It's just that, ever since the remodeling of the hotel began, I've been dying to see the changes they've made."

He motioned her inside. "No need in dying. Come on in and look around."

She wavered uncertainly on the threshold, watching him fight his way out of his jacket and toss it toward a chair. When his throw missed by a good three feet, she stepped inside, figuring she was safe. In his current state, if he tried anything, she knew she could be out the door and down the hall, before he made the first drunken step in pursuit.

She slowly circled the room, peering into a short hallway, noting the two bedrooms that opened off it. Stopping before the fireplace, she ran a hand over its ornate mantel and looked around.

"This is beautiful," she murmured, awed by the turn-of-the-century Victorian furnishings.

"It's just fluff."

She glanced over her shoulder and was surprised to find him sitting on the sofa, watching her.

"*Expensive* fluff," she corrected, then sighed wistfully, hugging her arms around her waist. "I can't even imagine what it would be like to own one piece of furniture as nice as this, much less a roomful.''

"Like I said, it's just fluff."

She stooped to test one of the sofa's cushions, and nearly groaned as her fingers sank into the leather's buttery softness.

He patted the spot next to him. "Give it a try."

Taking a step back, she shook her head. "No. I really should be going. I've got two chapters to read before I go to bed tonight."

"Those chapters'll still be there tomorrow."

She laughed softly. "Yes, and four more just as difficult to absorb." At his puzzled look, she explained. "I have two chapters of anatomy to read tonight and another four in statistics to outline before class on Monday."

"Anatomy and statistics? What's your major?"

"Nursing." She retreated another step closer to the door. "I really do need to go. Thanks for letting me see your room."

He stood, as if he intended to escort her out, but made only one step, before he threw his arms out to his sides, as if to stop the room from spinning around him.

"Can you make it to bed okay?" she asked, worried that he'd pass out on his way and knock himself unconscious.

His knees buckled and he fell back on the sofa. "Yeah," he said, and tugged at his collar, as if needing air. "I'll be fine."

She eased closer. "If you want, I'll help you to bed. But then I have to leave. Okay?"

He gulped, but didn't respond. Praying he wasn't about to be sick, she crossed to him and took one of his hands. "Come on, cowboy," she said, giving him a tug. "Time to hit the hay."

She managed to get him to his feet, then quickly ducked under one shoulder, supporting him, when his knees threatened to buckle again.

"This way," she instructed, as she urged him toward the short hallway and one of the bedroom doors she'd noticed during her inspection of the suite. At the side of the bed, she switched on the bedside lamp, then gave him a gentle nudge that sent him sprawling across the mattress. He lay with his arms flung wide, his eyes closed, his legs spread.

She frowned down at him a moment, debating whether or not she should remove some of his clothes. Shaking her head at the intimacy that would require, she decided the boots were as far as she would go. She closed her hands around the heel of one. "Let's get these boots off. Okay?"

If he heard her, he didn't respond, and he sure as heck didn't help. She grunted and groaned, straining to pull off the stubborn boot. When it finally gave way, the release in tension sent her stumbling backward, and she sat down hard on the floor.

Flattening her lips in irritation, she pushed to her feet, grabbed the other boot and yanked it off. Her rough-handling didn't seem to faze him, though. Throughout the tug-of-war, he hadn't moved so much as a muscle.

Satisfied that she'd done her duty, she started to turn away, but winced when she noticed the wide Western-style belt cinched around his middle. Knowing that the oversize silver buckle that adorned it had to be uncomfortable—and might possibly restrict his breathing—she leaned to unfasten it, then carefully pulled the wide strip of leather from the belt loops that held it in place. For good measure, she unfastened the first metal button on the fly of his jeans.

As she straightened, his hand snaked out and caught hers.

She snapped her gaze to his and found that his eyes were still closed. But he hadn't passed out, as she'd thought. She could tell by the strength of his grip that he was at least partially cognizant of his actions. When she tried to ease her hand from his, he tightened his hold.

"Stay."

What she *should* do was bolt and run, she told herself. But something held her in place. His grip wasn't threatening. Strong, yes. But not threatening. And the single word that had slipped past his lips wasn't an order, it was more like a…plea.

It was the despair in it that had her shifting to sit on the edge of the bed. "What's wrong, cowboy?" she asked quietly, as she drew their joined hands to rest on her knee. "Are you lonely?"

"My whole damn life."

The misery in his reply melted an already soft heart. "Don't you have family?"

"Brothers. Four of 'em."

Laughing softly, she gave his hand a reassuring squeeze. "With four brothers around, you couldn't have been all that lonely. I have two of my own, plus four sisters and there were times growing up when I would've killed for a little privacy."

He tightened his fingers around hers and she glanced down at their joined hands, jolted by the charge that arced from his skin through hers. She

looked up to see if he'd noticed the sensation, but
found his eyes still closed, his expression unchanged.

As she shifted her gaze back to their joined hands,
she found herself wondering who he was, what he did
for a living. His hands weren't those of a working
man, that was for sure. Though she sensed the
strength in the fingers laced through hers, his skin was
as smooth as silk and his nails neatly manicured. Noticing the band of paler skin on the ring finger, she
pursed her lips in irritation. "What about your wife?"
she asked dryly. "Doesn't she keep you company?"

"Divorced."

She eyed him, wondering if he was lying. She
knew men sometimes took off their wedding rings
when they went out for a night on the town. But his
marital state really didn't matter. It wasn't as if she
was planning on having an affair with him.

"How come you're so happy all the time?"

Startled, she glanced up. Though his eyes remained
closed, a frown furrowed his brow. She lifted a shoulder. "Why be sad?"

He snorted. "Like there's a choice."

"Happiness *is* a choice," she told him. "If you're
unhappy or sad, do something about it. Make a
change! Heck, life's too short to waste time being
miserable."

With a disagreeable grunt, he rolled to his side and
drew her hand to hold against his chest. "Easy for
you to say."

It was all Kayla could do not to laugh. *Easy?* she
thought. If only he knew! But why bother burdening
him with the trials she faced on a daily level? The
poor guy apparently had enough problems of his own.

Noticing that his breathing had grown rhythmic,

she carefully withdrew her hand from his and rose, thinking he would sleep now.

He groped blindly for her hand. "Stay. Please."

She smiled sadly down at him, wishing that she could. He looked like he could use a friend. "I can't," she said, and leaned to switch off the lamp. "Sleep well, cowboy," she whispered.

She'd almost made it to the door, when his voice stopped her.

"Hey."

She glanced back. "What?"

"I don't know your name."

She bit back a smile, doubting that he'd remember it in the morning. "Kayla. Kayla Jennings."

When Ry had checked into the Driskill, the desk clerk had warned him that the hotel was still undergoing renovation. But he'd never expected to be awakened by the ear-splitting sound of jackhammers. Prepared to kill whoever was operating the damn piece of machinery, he sat up...but melted back to the pillow with a groan, clutching his head between his hands. That was no jackhammer, he realized. It was a whiskey-induced headache trying to pound itself out of his skull one nauseating blow at a time. Sure that no one could feel this badly and live, he drew in a careful breath, then slowly released it. When his head didn't explode at the effort, he drew in another.

And caught a whiff of a feminine scent.

He frowned, trying to remember if he'd brought a woman back to his room. Though the details of the previous night were a bit fuzzy, he recalled its beginning well enough. He'd gone to the River's End, in-

tending to drink himself numb. Judging by the size
of his hangover, he'd succeeded.

The waitress, he remembered, as the memories began to gradually unfold. She'd walked him back to
the hotel, then insisted on escorting him all the way
to his room.

But he didn't remember her leaving.

He flipped open his eyes, sure that he was the vic-
tim of one of the stings he'd read about in the paper,
where a woman would slip a man a mickey, then rob
him. He lifted a hip, patted his back pocket and felt
the familiar lump of his wallet, then shot a sleeve and
found his Rolex still on his wrist. Pushing himself up
to his elbows, he looked around the room and saw
his boots in a jumbled pile on the floor, his belt curling around their tops like a snake.

He didn't recall taking off his boots, he thought,
frowning. Or his belt, either, for that matter. Had she
done it for him? What else had gone on? he wondered.

Groaning, he fell back against his pillow and
pushed his fingers through his hair, knowing it
couldn't have been much, since he was still, for the
most part, fully dressed. But he'd wanted to do more.
He distinctly remembered that.

He inhaled again, more deeply this time, savoring
her scent, willing more of the memories to the sur-
face. He saw again her smile and the wonder that had
filled her brown eyes as she'd prowled his room.
Heard the unabashed honesty with which she'd admitted never owning one piece of furniture as nice as
those in his room, much less a roomful. Saw her sitting on the side of his bed and felt again the comforting warmth of her fingers laced through his. Heard

the softness in her voice, the kindness when she'd asked, *What's the matter, cowboy? Are you lonely?*

He snorted a laugh at the absurdity of the question. Hell, lonely didn't come close to describing the misery that dogged his every step.

The telephone beside the bed rang and he winced, clamping his hands over his ears, to block out the abrasive sound. Before it could ring again, he snatched the receiver from the base. "Dr. Tanner." He snapped the formal greeting out of habit, after years of responding to calls at all hours of the day and night from patients and hospital staff.

"Good mornin', Dr. Tanner. Did I wake you?"

Frowning at the amusement he heard in his brother Ace's voice, he heaved himself up to a sitting position and dragged a hand down his face. "As a matter of fact, you did." He squeezed his eyes shut, then forced them wide, trying to shock his mind into alert. He glanced at the bedside clock and deepened his frown when he saw the time. "What in the hell are you calling me at seven o'clock on a Sunday morning for?"

"Business. We're having a meeting at the ranch today."

Stifling a groan, he pinched the bridge of his nose. He didn't want to go to the ranch today. He'd made more trips there in the months since their father's death, than he had in all the years since he'd left home. And each trip had proved more painful than the one before, dredging up memories and regrets that he'd kept buried for years.

But he was a Tanner and bound by the same sense of duty and family loyalty that had drawn his brother, Ace, as well as his other brothers, back to the family home. He couldn't leave them to deal alone with the nightmares their old man had left behind. He'd carry his share of the burden.

He opened his eyes to stare miserably at the wall opposite him. "What time?"

"Noon, if you can make it that soon. That's when the others are due. Maggie's cooking lunch."

His stomach roiled sickly at the mention of food. "Tell her not to make anything for me." He glanced at the clock again, gauging the distance against the time. "I'll be there by one."

"Good enough. See you then."

He dropped the receiver back onto the base and fell back against the pillow, shooting his fingers through his hair. A visit to the ranch wasn't on his agenda that day.

But, then, he didn't have an agenda any longer.

He had no home.

No wife.

No medical practice.

He had nothing to do and nothing to look forward to.

He could feel the darkness closing in on him, threatening to suck him down.

If you're unhappy or sad, do something about it. Make a change! Heck, life's too short to waste time being miserable.

He frowned, considering the waitress's advice, then snorted. She was young, he told himself. Hadn't experienced enough of life's disappointments to realize yet that happiness wasn't a choice. Shit happened, just like the bumper stickers and T-shirts proclaimed.

And even if he were to buy into her Pollyanna-outlook on life, it wouldn't help. He'd been miserable so long he couldn't remember what *did* make him happy.

But with no home, no wife and no medical practice, he had the time to find out.

And he had the money to stake him until he did.

Which was something the waitress didn't have.

He frowned again, remembering her telling him that her father had died when she was in high school and her mother was unable to help with her college expenses. So what did she have to be so damn happy about? he asked himself in frustration. Working to support yourself and going to the college at the same time couldn't be a stroll in the park.

But her happiness had seemed genuine and her smile sunny enough to warm a heart as jaded as his.

With a sigh, he heaved himself from the bed and headed for the shower, telling himself that the woman was either crazy or suffered delusions.

He snorted a laugh.

Or maybe he'd met Pollyanna in the flesh.

Chapter 2

A cold shower, a handful of aspirin, and Ry felt almost human again.

Though he dreaded like hell making the trip to the ranch, he couldn't complain about the day. It was perfect for taking a Sunday drive through the country. As he left Austin's city limits behind, he pushed on a pair of sunglasses, set the cruise control on the legal 65 and settled back to enjoy the scenery.

The highways that led to the ranch were as familiar to him as the hallways of the hospital he'd navigated for the past eight years and a hell of a lot more scenic. Winter had stripped the roadside of life, leaving it a dull, crusty beige, but he could envision it as it would look in a few short months, when wildflowers would carpet the area like a crazy quilt. The rich, royal-blue of bluebonnets, the eye-popping orange of Texas paintbrush, the egg-yolk yellow of dainty coreopsis.

He had Lady Bird Johnson and her "Beautify

America'' campaign to thank for the wildflowers that would soon appear and his mother for instilling in him an appreciation for them. He remembered, as a kid, in the springtime, his mother taking him and his brothers on walks through the pastures and woods that surrounded their house and making a game of seeing who could identify the most wildflowers. Ace usually won, which would bring a cry of "No fair!" from the others. But it only made sense that Ace would win. As the oldest, he had more experience than the others, had made more trips through the pastures with their mother. Yet, it still rankled. It didn't matter that they all received the same rewards as Ace for their efforts, usually homemade cookies their mother awarded from a sack she'd tucked into a pocket. Ace was still the winner.

Sibling rivalry was something Ry didn't like to admit that he and his brothers had suffered. But it was there for anyone with eyes to see. And it had all started with innocent childhood games.

Unfortunately it hadn't stopped there.

The Tanner Boys, as they were known around town, had carried their rivalry into their teen years, where they'd fought it out in classrooms, rodeo arenas and even in the dirt, rolling and punching, anxious to prove who was the smartest, the bravest, the strongest.

Who was the most loved.

That last bit came out of nowhere and had Ry gripping his hands tighter on the steering wheel, a defensive gesture he wasn't even aware of until his knuckles began to ache. He forced his fingers to relax and reminded himself that his mother had never played favorites. She'd loved each of her sons equally and was never shy about showing her love, showering their dirty faces with wet kisses or gathering them up in her arms for tight hugs. Unlike Buck, their father, who rarely even acknowledged his sons, much less offered them any affection.

At the thought of his father, Ry sat up straighter in the seat and narrowed his eyes on the road ahead. He wouldn't think about the old man. Buck Tanner didn't deserve his thoughts. He'd lived his life his own way, without a care for the sons he'd sired or the woman who had given birth to them. He'd cared even less about his second wife and the son she'd brought with her to the marriage. All that mattered to the old man was chasing skirts and throwing his weight around town. He was a Tanner, after all, a direct descendant of the family who had settled Tanner's Crossing and given the town its name. He'd felt his heritage alone entitled him to all the wealth and power associated with the name. Everyone in town had either hated him or loved him. But they'd all envied him.

Not that Buck cared how people felt about him. He did as he pleased and to hell with anyone who objected. And so what if he destroyed a few lives along the way, broke a few hearts? To him, people were like flies. Annoying nuisances easily dispensed with.

He'd certainly rid himself of his sons easily enough.

By the time Ry reached the end of the long, gravel road that led from the highway to his family home, he had his thoughts under control, and the memories tucked safely away.

As he pulled up to the house, vehicles already lined the driveway out front. Rory, his youngest brother's, Dodge Ram led the pack. Jet-black and sporting shiny chrome wheels and bumpers, the flashy truck fit his youngest brother's personality to a T, as Rory thrived on creating a stir, especially with the ladies. Woodrow's dually was parked behind Rory's truck and was, as usual, covered with mud, which surprised Ry. He had thought, after marrying Elizabeth—a city girl and a doctor, at that—Woodrow would've cleaned up his act a little. But it appeared Elizabeth had accepted Woodrow warts and all and hadn't made an effort to change him.

The beat-up truck behind Woodrow's belonged to their stepbrother Whit. As Ry passed by the trailer hitched to the truck's rear, he glanced inside, half expecting to find some green-broke horse pawing nervously inside. Whit made his living breaking and training horses and was always hauling one or more around. But the trailer was empty, as was the cab of the truck, which had Ry lengthening his stride, as he knew he'd catch hell from his brothers for being the last to arrive.

"Hey, Ry!"

He stopped and glanced toward the side of the house where Ace's wife, Maggie, and Woodrow's wife, Elizabeth, were pushing a baby in an infant swing hanging from the limb of a tree. *Laura,* he thought, catching a glimpse of the knitted cap protecting his half sister's head from the cold. He still couldn't believe that the old man had sired a child before he'd died, leaving it for his sons to raise, when the baby's mother had died, as well. Thankfully, Ace and Maggie had agreed to adopt the kid, which had saved Ry from assuming any responsibility for the infant but that of uncle…or half brother…or whatever

the hell relation he was to the kid now that Ace and
Maggie had adopted her.

He lifted a hand in greeting. "Where are the
guys?" he called.

"In the study," Maggie replied, then warned, "better hurry or there won't be any chocolate cake left for
you."

Ry pressed a hand to his middle, his stomach
threatening a revolt at the thought of the rich dessert
Maggie was famous for baking. He forced a smile for
her benefit, as he headed for the door. "Thanks, but
I think I'll pass. I'm trying to watch my weight."

Once inside, he plucked off his hat and dropped it
over a hook on the hall tree that had stood in the entry
since the day his great-grandfather had crafted it from
wood felled on Tanner land.

"That you, Ry?"

At the sound of Ace's voice, he sighed wearily,
wondering what bad news Ace had to share with them
this time. Since their father's death, it seemed every
time Ace called them together it was to inform them
of one problem or another that had surfaced.

"Yeah, it's me," he replied.

He crossed to the study, but stopped just inside the
door. They were all there. Ace. Woodrow. Rory.
Whit. The four brothers he'd grown up with, wrestled
with, grieved with, even defended when the situation
called for it…and eventually left behind. He stared,
emotion tightening his chest, as he wondered what
had happened to the five of them. What had broken
the tie that had once bound them all so closely together.

The old man.

The answer leaped to mind before he could stop it.

He quickly shoved it back, refusing to think about the man who had fathered them, the man who had turned his back on them and, eventually, turned them against each other.

"Have a seat and take a load off."

Ry gave Ace a tight nod. "Don't mind if I do." He dropped down onto the chair Ace had indicated. "So what tragedy brings us together this time?"

Chuckling, Ace shook his head. "No tragedy. Not this time." He hitched a hip on the corner of the desk and clasped his hands on his thigh, a sign that he was ready to get down to business.

"I called y'all together to let y'all know that I've been offered a photo assignment in North Dakota. Since it'll take a month or more to shoot, Maggie and the baby are going with me, which means, there won't be anyone on hand to take care of things around here. Up until now, as executor of the old man's estate, I felt it was my responsibility to put my life on hold and stay here to take care of things. But this photo shoot is an opportunity I just can't pass up."

Frowning, he rose to pace, rubbing a hand across the back of his neck. "If we had a foreman in place, I wouldn't think twice about leaving. But since we don't, and considering the work required to run a ranch of this size, I'd feel better if one of you was here to see after things."

Woodrow spoke up. "What is it you're wanting us to do? Take turns coming here to check on things?"

Ace shook his head. "No. What we need is someone here full-time. I know it's a lot to ask, and I wouldn't ask if I didn't feel it was necessary. But I'm hoping one of you can cut loose from your responsibilities for a month or so and come and live here."

Rory's eyes shot wide. "Are you kidding? Leave my Western stores to run themselves for a *month?*" He dropped his head back and hooted a laugh at the ceiling. "I might as well pull down the shades and lock the doors. In that length of time, my business would dry up faster than a stock pond during a drought."

"What about you, Woodrow?" Ace asked. "You live the closest. Think you could handle running the Bar T and your ranch, too?"

"When are you planning on heading out?"

"Tomorrow, if possible," Ace replied, then lifted his hands. "I know it's short notice, but that's the nature of my business."

Woodrow scrunched his mouth to the side, considering, then shook his head. "As much as I'd like to help out, this is the worst time of year for me to be away. I've got a hundred nanny goats due to start dropping their kids any day, plus cattle to look after." He shook his head again. "I just don't see how I could pull off running this place and mine, too."

Ace nodded in understanding and turned to Whit. "How about you?"

"Sorry, but I'm leaving Wednesday for Oklahoma. A guy up there hired me to break a half-dozen colts. I'll be gone longer than you."

While Ry listened to his brothers offer their excuses, he broke out in a cold sweat, knowing that eventually Ace would get around to asking him. And he didn't want to stay at the ranch. The brief visits he'd made to help out following their father's death were more than he could handle. Sleeping in the house he'd grown up in. Slamming into memories of the past at every turn. Having to face the people in town and know that the Tanner name they all looked up to and respected was nothing but a power tool his father had used to get what he wanted. Seeing the resentment in their eyes, every time they looked his way.

No. He couldn't do it. *Wouldn't* do it. He had enough problems of his own to deal with without taking on anything more.

Anxious to come up with an alternative, he quickly settled on the most obvious: a foreman to take over running the place. Coming up with the money for a salary and benefits certainly wouldn't be a problem. They could even offer a bonus large enough to lure a foreman away from one of the other ranches in the area. God knew they could afford it.

But finding someone qualified and trustworthy would take time and, from what Ace had said, a replacement was needed immediately.

While Ry struggled to come up with another solution, a chant started in his head, making it difficult for him to think.

Make a change! Make a change! Make a change!

The waitress, he thought irritably, and gave his head a discreet thump, trying to knock out her voice.

If you're unhappy or sad, do something about it. Make a change!

Living at the ranch wouldn't make him happy, he argued stubbornly. The thought alone was enough to send him into a major depression.

But living in Austin wasn't making him happy, either.

If you're sad or unhappy, do something about it. Make a change!

He could almost feel the waitress's breath on his

neck, as she urged him to volunteer. He wanted to tell her to shut up and mind her own business.

Instead he found himself saying, "I'll do it."

Ace whipped his head around to stare. *"You?"*

Ry lifted a brow. "What's wrong? You don't think I can handle it?"

Ace held up a hand to ward off a fight. "It's not your ability I'm questioning. It's your job. Don't you have surgeries scheduled and patients to see?"

Ry wished to hell he'd never opened his mouth. If he'd kept quiet, he could've avoided this question. None of his brothers knew he'd sold his practice. He hadn't told them. Hell, he never told them anything! But even if he'd wanted to, how could he explain the discontent that had driven him to walk away from a career that he'd trained for for years?

But he'd have to tell them now. There was no other way to justify his ability to drop everything to live on the ranch, without telling them what he'd done.

"I sold my practice."

Ace's eyes bugged. "You *what?*"

"Whoa," Woodrow said under his breath. "This is big. Really big."

"Why?" Rory asked, as dumbfounded by Ry's announcement as the others. "I thought you were making a killing doing boob jobs and face-lifts."

Ry gave him a sour look. His brothers' jokes about the surgical procedures he performed had worn thin years before. "Money wasn't the problem."

"Then what was?"

Unsure himself of the reason, Ry pushed to his feet and crossed to the window. Shoving his hands into his pockets, he stared out at the land he'd grown up kins toward her, anxious to get her side work done, before customers began to arrive. As she rolled the utensils into individual settings, Pete sauntered over and plunked his elbows onto the bar in front of her to watch.

"Your boyfriend came by earlier," he said, after a moment.

She sputtered a laugh. "I don't have a boyfriend and you know it."

"Yeah, you do. The cowboy."

Her smile turning wistful, she set the rolled napkin aside. "I feel sorry for him."

"Why?"

She thought for a minute, trying to put a finger on just what it was about him that drew her sympathy, then lifted a shoulder. "I don't know. He just looks sad, like he needs a friend in the worst sort of way."

"Looks like a drunk to me."

She shook her head. "No. I think he's just trying to drown his troubles." She pictured the cowboy slumped against the side of the restaurant, too drunk to stand, and wagged her head sadly. "Poor guy. I'll bet he woke up with one whale of a hangover this morning."

"Didn't look none the worse for wear to me." He reached beneath the bar, drew out an envelope and tossed it in front of her. "He left this for you."

She glanced at the envelope and recognized the Driskill Hotel logo in its upper left-hand corner. Her name was scrawled across the front. Wrinkling her brow, she picked it up, wondering why the cowboy would leave her a note. With a shrug, she slipped it into her apron pocket.

"Aren't you going to open it?"

on and eventually run from, trying to think of a way to explain his discontent to his brothers.

But it was impossible to explain something he didn't understand himself.

"I just got tired of it," he finally said, then glanced back over his shoulder at Ace. "Which means I've got time on my hands. So, unless you've got a problem with me taking over the reins for a while, it looks like I'm your man."

Ry didn't get it. Instead of kicking himself all the way back to Austin for offering to stay at the ranch, as he made the drive to collect his things from the hotel, he found himself almost looking forward to the change.

"Make a change," he muttered under his breath, then snorted a laugh, thinking the waitress would probably be turning cartwheels right now if she knew of his decision. But his amusement slowly faded, as he realized that he'd never see her again. Living at the ranch would put an end to his nightly visits to the River's End. Oddly, that saddened him, as he'd grown to look forward to seeing her and would miss her sunny smile.

He gave his head a rueful shake, at the thought of her smile. He had to give her credit. Whether this *Make a change!* advice of hers worked for him or not, it obviously had done wonders for her. He'd never met a more happy or well-adjusted woman. And how she managed it while working and going to school, he didn't know. Any other woman would be bitching and moaning about her plight in life, yet he'd never once heard the waitress complain about anything.

He remembered seeing a sign somewhere that claimed, Smiles Are Contagious. Give Someone One Of Yours. The waitress's smiles were definitely infectious. When blessed with one, a person couldn't help but walk away, feeling better about themselves and the world around them.

Except maybe the tightwad, he thought wryly, remembering the man who had stiffed her and how the slight had momentarily stolen her smile. It wouldn't have hurt the guy to have been a little more generous, he thought resentfully.

He tensed, his brain freezing on the word *generous*. He could make it up to her, he realized slowly. Not the tightwad, but *him*. Dr. Ryland Tanner. He was a wealthy man. Why not spread the wealth around? Make someone else's life a little easier? He could afford to be generous, and the waitress could certainly use whatever good fortune came her way.

But how could he give her money, without embarrassing her or hurting her pride? He suspected there was a strong chance he could do both, if he didn't handle this just right.

He'd think of something, he promised himself, as the traffic clogging I-35 forced him to focus his attention on the road.

The lady deserved a break.

When Ry spotted an empty parking space directly opposite the River's End's entrance, he accepted it as a sign that the plan he'd come up with while packing was the right one. As he pulled his Navigator into the space, he gave his jacket a pat, confirming that the envelope he'd tucked into the inside pocket was still there.

Anxious to bestow his gift and be on his way, he climbed from his SUV and entered the River's End. Waving away the hostess who approached, he headed straight for the bar, where he hoped to find Kayla.

But he found the bartender alone in the bar, busily pushing beer bottles into a cooler of ice. Ry braced his hands on the counter and peered over. "Excuse me. Is Kayla here?"

The bartender glanced up at Ry, then straightened, wiping his hands on the towel tucked into the waist of his jeans. "She's not due in until six."

Frowning, Ry rolled his wrist to check the time, then drew the envelope from his jacket pocket "Would you mind giving this to her?"

The man glanced at the envelope, then tipped h' head toward the giant screen television and the ba ketball game in progress. "Texas and Kansas playing. If you want to hang around and watch game, you can give it to her yourself. It looks li it's going to be a good one."

Shaking his head, Ry laid the envelope on the "Thanks, but I need to get on the road."

With a shrug, the bartender slapped a beefy on the envelope and dragged it from the bar. ' ever you say, mister."

With a nod of thanks, Ry turned and left.

Kayla hurried into the bar, struggling t apron strings behind her.

"Sorry I'm late, Pete," she said, out of b running. "My mom called just as I was the door."

She hopped onto a stool at the end o drew a tray of silverware and freshly l

She spread another napkin on the bar and aligned silverware in its center. "It's probably just a thank-you note. He was out front when I left last night, barely able to stand. I walked him to his hotel."

He waggled his brows suggestively. "And..." he prodded.

Pursing her lips, she bopped him on the head with the rolled silverware. "Get your mind out of the gutter, Pete. I walked him to his hotel. Period."

He folded his arms across his chest. "Prove it."

Huffing a breath, she tossed the rolled napkin onto the finished pile. "And how do you expect me to do that?"

"Read the note," he challenged, then added, "*Aloud.*"

"Oh, for pity's sake," she complained, but dug the envelope from her apron's pocket. She ripped open the flap and pulled out a slip of paper. Her eyes rounded as she stared.

"What is it?"

She opened her mouth, closed it, then tried again. "It's a check," she said weakly, then looked up at Pete. "For $30,000."

He snatched it from her hand. "Let me see that. It's probably a joke. If that cowboy has $30,000 to blow, I'll eat my—Holy Mary, Mother of God," he murmured, his eyes rounding as he read the endorsement. He lifted his gaze to Kayla's. "Do you know who this guy is?"

She reached for the check, but Pete held it up out of her reach.

"Dr. Ryland Tanner," he told her. "The plastic surgeon." He whooped a laugh. "Damn, Kayla, if you haven't landed yourself a millionaire!"

Pursing her lips, she plucked the check from his hand. "I haven't landed myself anybody," she informed him, as she smoothed the check open beneath her hands to look at it again. "Thirty thousand dollars," she murmured, sure that she'd never seen that much money at one time in her entire life. She looked up at Pete in confusion. "But why would he give me $30,000?"

"Hell, I don't know! But don't look a gift horse in the mouth. Take the money and run."

Firming her lips, she slid the check back into the envelope. "No way. I can't accept that kind of money. A fifty-dollar tip, yeah, I wouldn't think twice about pocketing that. But thirty thousand dollars?" She shook her head again. "I'm taking it back."

Pete looked at her in amazement. "Are you nuts? Keep it! The guy won't miss the dough, I promise you. He's got millions." Kayla hopped down from the bar stool. "I don't care how much money he has. I can't accept a gift like this." She untied her apron and tossed it onto the bar. "Cover for me, will you, Pete? I'll be back in a minute."

"Where are you going?" he called after her.

"To the Driskill."

Kayla stepped off the elevator and hurried to the door of the Cattle Baron's Suite, anxious to return the check and get back to work. She rapped her knuckles against the door, then folded her arms across her chest and waited, tapping her fingers impatiently against her forearms. When several seconds passed without a response, she rapped again. Louder.

A housekeeper rolling a cart down the hallway gave her a curious look. Kayla smiled politely, watched until the woman had disappeared around a corner, then pressed her mouth close to the door.

"Dr. Tanner!" she called in a loud whisper. "It's me. Kayla. The waitress from the River's End." She pressed her ear against the wood, listening for any sound of movement from the other side.

Praying he hadn't started drinking again and had passed out, she rapped her knuckles harder against the door. "Dr. Tanner!"

"He's not there, miss."

Startled, Kayla whirled to find the housekeeper was standing a couple of feet behind her. She pressed a hand to her chest. "Sorry. I didn't know you were there." She gave the woman a hopeful look. "Do you happen to know when he'll return?"

"Oh, he's not coming back. He checked out hours ago."

"Checked out?" Kayla repeated, panicked at the thought. "But…where did he go?"

"I don't know. I just clean the rooms. Someone at the front desk might be able to tell you, though."

Her shoulders sagging in defeat, Kayla murmured, "Thanks," and turned for the elevator, knowing it was futile to ask the hotel staff Dr. Tanner's whereabouts. Even if they were privy to the information, she doubted they were allowed to share it with every Tom, Dick and Harry who walked in off the street.

Kayla didn't care for mysteries. She didn't even watch the detective shows on television that were currently all the rage. But now she wished she had. If she'd watched them, she might have had a better idea of how to go about tracking down Dr. Tanner and

wouldn't have had to cut class trying to think of ways
to find him.

She'd tried the obvious. The phone book. She'd
found his residence listed in the white pages, but decided it wise not to call that number. Although he'd
claimed he was divorced, she wasn't at all sure she
believed him and wasn't anxious to explain to his
wife—or ex-wife, either, for that matter—why she
needed to speak with Dr. Tanner.

A flip through the Yellow Pages had turned up his
office number. She'd dialed it and asked the receptionist who answered if she could speak with Dr. Tanner. The woman had said that all of Dr. Tanner's patients were being referred to Dr. Martin and had given
her that number. Kayla had then explained that she
wasn't a patient and had asked for Dr. Tanner's private phone number or address. But the woman had
refused, stating that she wasn't permitted to give out
that information.

Frustrated by her inability to locate Dr. Tanner and
return his check, Monday afternoon Kayla trudged
down the sidewalk on her way to work. A half-block
away, she noticed that the parking spaces in front of
the restaurant were full, as were those in the lot along
its side. Wondering why the restaurant would be busy
this early in the day, she pushed open the door and
stepped inside.

Though the tables in the restaurant were empty,
people stood shoulder to shoulder in the bar. Curious,
she stopped at the hostess stand, where Jill, the hostess on duty, stood, watching the activities in the bar.

"What's going on?" Kayla whispered. "Is Pete
giving away free beer or something?"

Jill whirled, then clapped her hands to her cheeks.

"Oh, Kayla!" she cried. "You lucky dog! I'm so happy for you I could just scream!"

Kayla rolled her eyes, knowing only one reason why Jill would be happy for her. "I guess Pete told you about the tip."

"Of course he did! And it couldn't have happened to a nicer person than you." Tears welled in Jill's eyes and she darted from behind the stand to fling her arms around Kayla. "I'm going to miss you so much," she wailed.

Kayla drew back to look at her in confusion. "I'm not going anywhere."

Jill pulled a tissue from her pocket and dabbed at her eyes. "Yeah, right. Like you need to work anymore. Pete told us how much that doctor gave you." She gestured toward the bar. "Everybody's talking about it. Reporters have been crawling all over the place, waiting for you to get here."

Kayla's heart shot to her throat. "Reporters? From the newspaper?"

Jill nodded. "And camera crews, too." She flapped a hand toward the bar. "There must be a hundred people in there. They've come from all over. I recognized that hunky anchorman from one of the Dallas TV stations. You know the one. Don something-or-other. And Adrian Tyson, the lady who does that talk show where everybody on stage ends up in hairpulls or duking it out. She's here, too."

Kayla dropped her forehead to her hand. "Oh, no," she moaned. "I'm going to kill Pete!" She lifted her head to look at the people milling around in the bar. "I'm getting out of here," she whispered to Jill and turned to leave.

"Kayla!" Jill cried in panic. "You can't leave

now! These people have been waiting *hours* to talk
to you.''

Kayla broke into a run, sure that every one in the
bar had heard Jill and now knew that she had arrived.
Just as she closed her fingers around the door handle,
someone from the bar shouted, ''It's Kayla! She's
here!''

Before she could jerk open the door and make good
her escape, they were all over her, shoving micro-
phones in her face and blinding her with the flash of
their cameras.

''Tell us about your windfall, Kayla,'' someone
said.

''Yeah,'' said another. ''Tell us what it's like to
get a $30,000 tip?''

Knowing she was trapped, Kayla slowly unwound
her fingers from around the door handle and turned,
forcing a polite smile. ''I was stunned, to say the
least.''

''What are you going to do with all that loot?''
another asked.

She lifted a hand to shade her eyes from the glare
of a cameraman's lights, squinting to see the person
who had asked the question. ''Oh, I'm not keeping
the money,'' she called to the lanky man in the back
who had asked the question.

''Why not? Dr. Tanner gave it to you, didn't he?''

''Yes, but—''

''Is this the first time he's given you money?''

Kayla dropped her hand to stare at the woman who
stood directly in front of her. ''Well, yes,'' she replied, wondering why anyone would think Dr. Tanner
had given her money before.

"How about jewelry or furs?" someone shouted from the back.

She sputtered a laugh at the absurdity of the question. Imagine *her*, Kayla Jennings, decked out in diamonds and furs. "Sorry. I'm more a jeans and T-shirt kind of woman."

"What does it feel like to go from rags to riches?"

Kayla's smile slowly melted, her pride suffering a direct blow. "I wouldn't know," she replied. "I've never owned any rags, other than the cleaning variety."

The obnoxious woman with the microphone shoved it into Kayla's face again.

"Are you aware of Dr. Tanner's marital status?"

"No," Kayla replied, then remembered he'd told her he was divorced and amended quickly, "I mean, yes."

"Which is it?" the woman asked. "Yes or no."

Kayla pressed a hand to her temple and the headache that suddenly throbbed to life. The questions were coming so fast it was hard to think clearly. Dropping her hand, she said wearily, "I didn't know he was divorced until Saturday night."

The woman lifted a brow. "Oh? And what was so special about Saturday night?"

"Nothing. He had too much to drink, so I walked him back to his hotel room."

"And he told you then."

"Yes," Kayla replied, wishing the woman would quit hammering her with questions.

"Were you in bed together, when he told you?"

Kayla dropped her mouth open, then closed it with a click of teeth. "I hardly think that *where* we were when he told me is any of your business."

The woman pressed her lips together, to hide a smug smile, obviously enjoying herself, as well as Kayla's fury. "I take it you were in bed, then."

"I certainly was not," Kayla cried indignantly. "He was in bed. I was—" She stopped, suddenly aware that the crowd was pressing closer, hanging on her every word. Realizing too late how all this must sound, she clamped her lips together and offered a terse, "No comment."

But the reporter wasn't about to let her off so easily.

"Dr. Tanner's former wife was a guest on my show recently, discussing an art show she and several of her contemporaries were sponsoring to raise money for the children's wing of one of our local hospitals. When I asked her about her divorce, she intimated that there was another woman." She lifted a finely arched brow. "Would you know anything about that?"

Rage boiled up inside Kayla. She didn't deserve this kind of treatment. She'd done nothing wrong. It wasn't as if she'd *asked* Dr. Tanner to give her the money, and she certainly had no intention of keeping it.

But she knew by the way the reporters were hovering over her like vultures, waiting to pluck the juiciest morsels from her bones, that no matter what answers she gave them, they'd take her words and twist them and taint them and make them ugly. After all, what was destroying a woman's reputation, when compared to the number of papers they could sell or points they could gain in the ratings?

Though it took every ounce of her strength to do so, she forced a regretful smile. "I'm sorry, but I didn't see that segment. You see, I work for a living and don't have time to watch those trashy television talk shows.''

While the woman gaped, Kayla closed her index finger and thumb around the microphone. ''Now if you will excuse me,'' she said and moved it away from her face, as if it were a particularly disgusting bug. ''I need to speak with my employer.''

Ignoring the chorus of ''You go, girl!'' called to her from the cooks on duty, Kayla stormed through the restaurant's kitchen and into Pete's private office.

Slamming the door behind her, she planted her fists on her hips. ''How could you?'' she accused angrily. ''You knew I had no intention of keeping that money.''

Looking pleased with himself, Pete reared back in his chair and stacked his hands behind his head. ''Well, of course you're not.''

''Then why did you tell all those reporters that I was?''

''I never said anything about you keeping the money. I merely told them he'd given it to you.''

''Why tell the media, *anything*?'' she cried. ''It had nothing to do with them or *you*.''

''It happened in my bar,'' he reminded her, then dropped his head back with a lusty sigh. ''Just think of all the free advertising the restaurant's gonna get as a result of this story. We'll be packing 'em in the place. I'll probably even have to hire more waitresses to keep up with all the business this'll draw.''

Kayla stared, unable to believe what she was hearing. She took a step closer to his desk. ''Do you mean to tell me that you alerted the media, just to get free advertising?''

He lifted his head to frown at her. ''Well, of course. Why else would I tell 'em?''

''Did you ever think about what would happen to *me*, when you told them?'' She flung out a hand in the direction of the bar. ''Those people are going to crucify me! They're talking as if Dr. Tanner and I were having an affair. As if I'm the reason his wife divorced him. My reputation will be ruined!''

He waved away her worries. ''Hell, a couple of days and nobody will remember your name, much less associate it with his.'' He shot her a wink. ''And just think of all the tips you'll earn, when business picks up around here.''

She swelled her chest. ''If I cared more for the money than I did my reputation, I would've kept Dr. Tanner's check and quit this lousy job.'' Reaching behind her, she untied her apron.

''Hey!'' he cried, jumping to his feet. ''What are you doing? You can't leave. You're on the schedule tonight.''

She whipped off the apron and threw it on his desk. ''I'm not leaving. I quit.''

His eyes shot wide. ''What?''

''I quit. I refuse to work for someone who thinks so little of me that he would sacrifice my reputation for his own personal gain.''

''But you can't quit now! A radio station will be here any minute to do a live broadcast. They're going to interview you, even take calls from listeners, just like Howard Stern does on his show.''

''Too bad you didn't think to ask me first.''

He hurried around the desk. ''Kayla,'' he begged,

stretching his hands out to her. "Please. You can't do this to me. I'll look like a fool."

She lifted a brow. "And it would be better that I look like a whore? A home wrecker?" She turned her back on him. "Sorry, Pete," she said, as she jerked open the door. "You're the one who got yourself into this mess. You'll have to get yourself out."

Chapter 3

The apartment Kayla rented was originally the dining room, kitchen and butler pantry of a two-story, single-family residence. Nestled on a tree-lined street near downtown Austin and the University of Texas, the Victorian-style house had changed ownership several times over the years, its deed currently held by a retired university professor and his wife. With its original gingerbread trim, turrets and fluted columns intact, the house was a classic example of nineteenth-century Victorian architecture and a prime candidate for designation on the National Register of Historic Homes.

Unfortunately, as the University of Texas had grown, the demand for student housing had increased, and the home's owners, like many of their neighbors, had opted to cash in on the investment opportunity open to them, rather than preserve their home for the sake of posterity. With dollar signs gleaming in their eyes, they'd subdivided the house into five apartments and rented out four, reserving the largest of the five to live in themselves.

After several years of suffering the inconveniences—and many times nightmares—of serving as onsite-landlords to a rowdy bunch of college students, they'd packed their bags, rented out the fifth apartment and hightailed it for Santa Fe, New Mexico, where they now lived a quieter and much more relaxed existence, thanks to an unlisted telephone number.

Out-of-sight, out-of-mind, as the old saying goes, and that was certainly true of the homeowners' attitude toward what they considered their little cash cow. Requests for repairs from their renters were tossed out with the sale-flyers and unsolicited credit card applications they received in the daily mail. The house quickly deteriorated from their neglect. Doors stuck. Plumbing clogged. Paint peeled. Appliances died a natural death of old-age. The one thing the apartment house had going for it over others in the area was its low rent, as the owners hadn't raised the price since converting the house into apartments.

It was the location of the apartment house that first attracted Kayla to the property, but it was the low rent that sold her on the place.

The constant aggravation of clogged plumbing and broken appliances was an inconvenience, but nothing she felt she couldn't deal with. Give her a plumber's snake and a Phillips screwdriver, and she figured she could fix just about anything. She'd developed her handyman skills early on—out of necessity, not desire. Raised in a home with seven children and no father around to handle what crises arose—and no

money to hire someone else to take care of them—
she'd tackled the needed repairs herself. Giving herself a crash course in home repair from a "Do-It-
Yourself" book she'd checked out from the public
library, she dug out her father's toolbox from the garage and dug in, enjoying a smug sense of satisfaction
at her accomplishments, as well as, surprisingly, a
sense of pleasure.

But that night when Kayla returned to her apartment after resigning from her job and found frost
building up on the inside of her windows, she didn't
whip out her trusty Phillips screwdriver and go to
work on the ancient heating system. Instead she
flopped down in the middle of the floor, hugged her
coat around her and cried like a baby.

In a matter of hours, she'd received an insane
amount of money, had her reputation ripped to shreds
by reporters and quit her job. The first should have
had her soaring with joy, but knowing she wasn't
keeping the money kept her feet fixed firmly on the
ground. The second was humiliating, at best, but a
temporary state of affairs, something she prayed she
would heal from in time. It was over the third that
she wept buckets of tears.

With no job and no income, how would she survive? After she paid her rent on Wednesday, with
what cash she had on hand, she could last maybe two
weeks. And that was only if she kept the money she'd
planned to send her mother and subsisted on a diet of
peanut butter and beans.

She yanked her coat around her, with a resentful
sniff. This is all Pete's fault, she thought. She could
just wring his selfish neck for getting her into
this mess!

And when she finished with him, she was going gunning for Dr. Ryland Tanner.

She scowled at the reminder of her absentee benefactor. The jerk. Dropping $30,000 on her, then disappearing off the face of the earth. Didn't he know what kind of trouble a gift like that would cause a woman? Even the most naive would think the worst of her when they heard about her unexpected windfall.

Especially if they heard Adrian Tyson's twisted version of the story.

And who could blame them? she asked herself miserably. She hadn't trusted his motives, either, which was exactly why she'd tried to return his stupid check. A man didn't give a woman a gift of that size without expecting something in return.

Her eyes narrowed in suspicion. And what exactly *did* he expect in return for his gift? A mistress? An affair? If so, he'd picked the wrong woman. Kayla Jennings wasn't interested in becoming some wealthy man's plaything. She had goals, ambition. Dammit, she had her pride!

And she had a temper—not that she was necessarily proud of it. Over the years, she'd learned to control it, though it still reared its ugly head on occasion. And when Dr. Tanner showed up to claim whatever it was he wanted from her...

Well, it wasn't going to be pretty.

Ry stood on the back porch nursing his first cup of coffee for the day and watching the sun rise higher in the sky. Ace and Maggie had pulled out a half-hour earlier, headed for Kerrville and Ace's home, with Laura tucked safely into her carrier in the rear seat and Daisy, Ace's dog, riding in back, her ears pinned to her head by the wind.

Which left Ry with the place all to himself.

He looked around, wondering what chore he should tackle first that day. The night before, Ace had given him a brief rundown on the state of things at the ranch: where the cattle were currently pastured; the breaks in the fences that needed mending; which horses needed shoeing and the phone number of the farrier he could call to do the job. The rest, Ace had told him, Ry could figure out on his own, just as Ace had.

Ry didn't doubt for a minute that he would find plenty to keep him busy. A ranch the size of the Bar T didn't come without its share of work. Much more than Ry and the three ranch hands left under his supervision could handle.

But for the moment, he was content to sip his coffee and watch the cattle graze in the pasture behind the house.

For the first time since selling his practice, he was actually looking forward to the day. Maybe because he actually had something to do, other than stare out a hotel window and brood. Or maybe it was because he was more suited to ranch work than the duties of a surgeon.

With a shrug, he turned for the house. Whatever the reason, he didn't have time to dawdle over his coffee, psychoanalyzing himself. There were three ranch hands on the payroll who were probably sitting on their thumbs at that very moment, awaiting his instructions for the day's work.

As he reached to open the back door, the sound of an engine had him glancing around the side of the house. Seeing Ace's truck approaching, he dropped his hand and went to meet him, wondering what item of the kid's Ace had forgotten to load. The truck was already stuffed from floorboard to headliner with enough baby gear to outfit a set of quintuplets. He couldn't imagine how his brother could squeeze in one more item.

As he watched Ace climb down from his truck, he tucked his tongue into his cheek to hide his smile. "If you came back to get something of the baby's," he called to him, "you're going to need a trailer to haul it. There's barely room to breathe inside the truck, as it is."

Ace didn't crack a smile at the teasing, but kept coming.

Ry's smile faded at his brother's somber expression. "What is it?" he asked, his stomach knotting in dread. "Did something happen?"

Ace drew a newspaper from beneath his arm and held it out. "I saw this when I stopped for gas. Thought you'd want to see it."

Puzzled, Ry took the paper and snapped it open. An image of the waitress all but leaped from the front page to slap him in the face. Positioned dead center, the photo took up almost a quarter of the space. Surrounded by reporters and cameraman, she stood with her back to the restaurant's front door, her eyes wide, her expression stricken.

With a groan, he dropped his gaze to read the accompanying headline and blurb.

Sugar Daddy?
Over the weekend, Kayla Jennings, a waitress at the River's End restaurant in downtown Aus-

tin, received a $30,000 tip from local plastic surgeon, Dr. Ryland Tanner. When asked her reaction to receiving such a large gratuity, Jennings replied, "I was surprised, to say the least." But subsequent questions regarding her relationship with Dr. Tanner were met with, "No comment."

Jennings' reluctance to answer questions about her relationship with Tanner, leaves one to wonder why a recently divorced surgeon would bestow such a generous gift upon a single and unquestionably attractive young woman.

Only the obvious answer comes to this reporter's mind.

Swearing, Ry crumpled the paper in his fist.

"Well?" Ace asked. "Is it true?"

Ry shot him a contemptuous look. "What? That I left the waitress a tip? Or that I'm her sugar daddy?"

Ace lifted a shoulder. "Essentially they're one and the same."

"Like hell they are!" Ry spun furiously away, took two angry steps, then swung back. "Yes, I gave her $30,000. But the money was nothing more than a scholarship. She's a nursing student, working her way through college. The kid deserved a break, so I gave her one."

Ace lifted a brow. "Kid?" he repeated. He gestured to the paper Ry held fisted in his hand. "Doesn't look much like a kid to me."

Ry bristled defensively. "She's twenty-six. In my book, that makes her a kid."

Ace shrugged. "Whatever her age, it looks like your good intentions have caused her some trouble."

Swearing, Ry flung the newspaper away. "Damn nosy reporters," he muttered. "What business is it of theirs anyway? The woman needed money, so I gave her some. They ought to be applauding my generosity, instead of trying to twist this into some sordid love affair."

Ace gestured toward the crumpled pages the wind had caught and swept along the grass. "It won't stop there," he warned. "The press will milk this for all it's worth. They'll dig, then dig some more, in hopes of finding something to base their assumptions on, more dirt to put into print." He shook his head sadly. "You're a Tanner, Ry. Buck Tanner's son. It won't take them long to find more to write about. The next headline will probably be, 'Like Father Like Son?'"

Groaning, Ry dropped his head back, knowing what Ace said was true. The media would have a field day, once they made the connection that he was Buck Tanner's son, a part of his heritage he'd thought he'd left behind when he'd left home.

"The sad part is," Ace continued, "the waitress's name will get dragged through the dirt right along with yours."

Ry balled his hands into fists. "Dammit! She doesn't deserve this."

"No," Ace agreed. "But then, neither do you."

None of the Tanner brothers deserved to suffer the sins of their father. But Ry didn't bother to remind Ace of that. Didn't need to. As the official head of the family now, Ace knew better than anyone what kind of nightmares came with being Buck Tanner's son.

Ry dragged a hand through his hair. "There's got

to be something I can do to stop this before it goes any further.''

"Like what?"

"Hell, I don't know!" Slapping a hand against the back of his neck, Ry paced away, rubbing at the tension at his nape, as he struggled to come up with a solution, a way to put an end to this before it spun out of control.

With a sigh, he dropped his hand, knowing there was nothing he could do to stop the media from reporting what they considered news. "I'll go and talk to her," he said wearily. "The least I can do is warn her about what might lie ahead."

Ace shook his head. "I don't know, Ry," he said doubtfully. "She might not want to see you."

Ry scowled. "Yeah, well, the feeling's mutual. I wish to hell I'd never laid eyes on the woman."

Ry didn't waste any time in leaving for Austin. After giving the ranch hands their orders for the day, he climbed into his Navigator and headed for the city.

At a convenience store near the campus, he stopped to fill up his tank with gas. While the fuel was pumping, he borrowed a phone book from the cashier and looked up the waitress's name. Finding the listing, he quickly jotted down the address and phone number on the back of a scrap of paper, then asked for directions.

Realizing he was only a couple of blocks from where the waitress lived, he quickly topped off his tank and climbed back into his Navigator. Within minutes, he was pulling up in front of a house, the faded numbers painted on the curb matching those of the address he'd written down.

He stared out the passenger window, sure that he'd made a mistake. Nothing but termites would willingly live in a place like that. To call the house a dump would be much too generous a description. Chips of yellow paint clung to the wood siding, a fading testament to its original color. The roof that covered the wraparound front porch sagged between decorative columns, sorely in need of a jack and shoring up.

But there was evidence that humans occupied the space, as well. A hodgepodge of mailboxes were nailed haphazardly to the wall beside the front door and a minimum of four vehicles were parked on the cracked driveway that ran alongside the house. Another two were parked on the front lawn. The grass— what little was left of it—was tramped down to dirt. Two bicycles were chained to one of the porch's leaning columns. A third, minus its rear tire, lay rusting under a magnolia tree.

With a woeful shake of his head, he climbed down from his truck and strode for the front porch. Unsure which of the two visible exterior doors marked the entrance, he searched the fronts of the mailboxes for the waitress's name. Just as he located it, noting the number 1-B below, the door beside him swung open, releasing a deafening blast of rock music. A young man seemed to float out on its swell.

Ry was sure the stocking cap the kid had pulled down over his ears was worn more to contain the tangled mass of dreadlocks than to protect his ears from the cold. His coat looked to be about three sizes too big for his lanky frame and hung down to his ankles, its hem brushing the tops of a pair of scuffed army boots.

Spotting Ry, the guy lifted his chin. "Hey, dude. How's it going?"

Ry cringed at the word "dude," but managed a tight smile. "Fine. And you?"

His eyes dreamy—a state of mind Ry suspected was induced by drugs—the guy looked off into the distance. Giving his backpack a hitch higher on his shoulder, he started down the steps. "Smokin', dude. Really smokin'."

Ry stared after him. *Smokin'?* What the hell was that supposed to mean? Painfully aware of a generation gap he hadn't realized he'd crossed over, Ry stepped through the door the guy had left open. The music was louder inside, the walls of the small entryway seeming to pulse with its metallic beat. Directly in front of him a hallway trailed off into darkness. Along its side, a stairway stretched upward to a second floor. The door to his left—which seemed to be the source of the loud music—was marked 1-A. The one on his right 1-B.

Anxious to get his business with the waitress over with and get back to the ranch, he crossed to the door and knocked. A door slammed overhead and he glanced up, to find two girls clattering down the wooden stairs, laughing and talking. One of the girls' hair was dyed a shocking pink and spiked up from her head in stiff-looking clumps. The other's was sheared within a quarter-inch of her scalp. Their conversation died the moment they saw him.

Feeling conspicuous, he stuffed his hands in his pocket. "I'm here to see Kayla," he said, feeling as if he needed to explain his presence, then shrugged. "But it doesn't appear she's home."

The girls looked at each other, then burst into laughter.

He glanced down to make sure his zipper was zipped, then frowned. "What's so funny?"

The one with the pink hair tapped an ear that was pierced with at least six studs. Ry self-consciously touched his own ear, wondering if he had left a streak of shaving cream on his lobe when he'd shaved that morning.

The bald-headed one laughed. "Not you. Earplugs. Kayla wears them. You'll have to knock really hard, if you want her to hear you."

Scowling, Ry mumbled a thanks, waited for the girls to leave, then doubled up his fist and pounded on the door.

Ramming his hands into his pockets, he glanced out the sidelight beside the door and watched the girls stroll down the walk. He wondered what kind of fashion statement the two were trying to make. Goodwill wouldn't accept as donations the rags they were wearing.

"What do you want?"

He snapped his head around to find a woman standing in the open doorway of the apartment. It took him a second to recognize her as the waitress. Instead of the ponytail he was accustomed to seeing, her hair hung down past her shoulders, and she was wearing a sweat suit rather than the T-shirt-and-jeans uniform she wore at the restaurant.

But the most radical change in her appearance was the absence of her smile. Which proved that Ace had been right, he admitted miserably. She wasn't happy to see him.

He dragged his hands from his pockets. "I'd like to talk to you, if you've got a minute."

Rolling her eyes, she snatched the earplugs from her ears. "What did you say?"

He raised his voice to be heard over the loud voice. "I'd like to talk to you."

Her eyes narrowed to slits. "I'll just bet you would," she snapped then spun back into the room.

Ry hesitated, wondering if the open door was an invitation for him to follow her inside.

She glanced over her shoulder. "Well?" she said impatiently. "Do you want to talk or not?"

He quickly stepped inside and closed the door behind him, cutting the volume of music by half. "Yeah," he said, dragging off his hat to hold in his hands. "I do."

"You've got exactly five minutes. Starting—" She rolled her wrist to check the time. "Now."

The woman was definitely sporting an attitude and Ry had had about all of it he was going to take.

"Look, lady," he said, struggling to hold on to his temper. "I saw the morning paper, so I think I have a pretty good idea why you're upset. But if you—"

"Upset?" she repeated shrilly, cutting him off. "Buddy, you don't even know the half of it." She lifted a hand and began ticking off items. "First, Pete gives me the check you left for me, which," she added and gave him a look that would melt paint off a wall, "I have no intention of keeping." She tapped a second finger. "Then I go to the hotel to return it, and I discover that you've checked out." She hit a third finger. "Then, Monday, I cut my classes and spend the day trying to get in touch with you, which turned out to be a total waste of my time." She struck a fourth finger hard enough to make Ry wince. "*Then* I go to work and I'm all but attacked by a herd of bloodsucking reporters, who all but accuse me of wrecking your marriage, and I'm forced to quit my job, which means I can't afford to pay my tuition or my rent or buy groceries or *any*thing!"

Out of fingers and out of breath, she balled her hands into fists, dragged in air through her nostrils and finished furiously, "And all because of *you!*"

With each tap of her finger, she'd hammered the guilt Ry already carried a little more solidly onto his shoulders. But when she got to the part about quitting her job and it being his fault, he held up a hand.

"Now wait just a damn minute," he said angrily. "How do you figure you quitting your job is my fault?"

She stamped her foot. "Because it is! If you hadn't asked Pete to give me the check, he never would've known about it, and he wouldn't have come up with the idea of using it to cash in on free publicity."

"Pete's the one who alerted the media?"

"Do you think *I* would tell them?" she asked incredulously, then rolled her eyes at the ceiling. "Please. Like I would ask for that kind of grief."

Ry dragged a hand down his mouth, trying to make sense of what she'd told him, then dropped it to frown. "I still don't understand what Pete's wanting free publicity has to do with you quitting your job."

"Would *you* work for someone who would sell your soul to the devil at the first opportunity?"

He blew out a breath. "I see your point."

"Lucky me," she muttered sarcastically, then marched across the room and yanked open the door. Turning to face him, she folded her arms across her chest. "Your five minutes are up. You can leave now."

Ry didn't blame her for kicking him out. In her place, he'd probably do the same damn thing. But he'd come to warn her, and he wasn't leaving until he had. He snugged his hat over his head. "This may not be over."

She tossed up her hands. "And what more could they possibly do to me? They've already destroyed my reputation and forced me to quit my job."

Ry didn't want to tell her about his father and how, if the press discovered that relationship, it would open up a whole other can of worms for them to explore.

"I'm not saying that anything else will happen," he hedged. "But it might be wise if you laid low for a while. Avoided reporters."

"And how do you suggest I do *that?* I can't stay holed up in my apartment forever. I have to go to class, and I have to find a job."

He crossed to the door, as anxious to leave, as she was for him to go. But in the doorway, his conscious stopped him. He glanced her way. "I'm sorry, Kayla," he said quietly. "I never meant for any of this to happen."

Tears filled her eyes, but she jerked up her chin, stubbornly forcing them back. "I'm sure you didn't, but the fact is, it did." Reaching down, she snatched a piece of paper from a table beside the door and thrust it at him. "Here's your check."

He held up his hands, refusing to take it. "Keep it. You're going to need it now more than ever."

Pursing her lips, she stuffed the check into his shirt pocket, then gave him a nudge that sent him over the threshold. "Sorry, cowboy, but I don't need or want a sugar daddy."

The next thing Ry heard was the slam of the door at his back.

Before she could leave for class, Kayla had a phone call to make, one she dreaded like heck making. Her mother had enough problems to worry about, without Kayla dumping more on her. But she had to tell her mother what had happened. With Kayla's face plastered all over the newspaper and the television screen, her mother was bound to hear about it eventually.

And better to hear it from Kayla, than at the beauty shop where her mother worked.

Steeling herself, she picked up the phone and dialed the number. Her twelve-year-old brother, Jimmy, answered on the second ring.

"Hey, Jimmy," she said, surprised to hear his voice. "Shouldn't you be in school?"

"Nope. Strep throat."

"Poor, baby," she sympathized. "Does it hurt?"

"Yeah. Every time I swallow, it feels like a wad of rusty razor blades are sliding down my throat."

Wincing at his graphic description, she asked, "Did Mom take you to the doctor?"

"Yeah. Dr. Andrews stuck one of those swab thingies down my throat and did a test. Made me gag. He said to tell you hi."

"Tell him I said 'hi' back." She threaded a strand of hair behind her ear, wanting to stall but knowing she couldn't put off the inevitable any longer. "Is Mom there?"

"Yeah. Just a sec."

She heard the phone clatter down and then Jimmy

yell "Mom!" at the top of his lungs. Holding the phone from her ear, she frowned at it, thinking his throat couldn't hurt that badly, if he could let out a blood-curdling yell like that.

"Kayla? Are you there, honey?"

Kayla quickly drew the phone back to her ear. "Yes, I'm here."

"Why are you calling so early in the day?" her mother scolded. "The rates are cheaper at night."

"I know," she said, wishing she didn't have to tell her mother what had happened. "But I need to tell you something and it couldn't wait."

"What? Have you been in an accident? Are you hurt?"

Kayla heard the panic rising in her mother's voice and quickly put her fears to rest. "No. I'm fine. It's just that—" She paused, trying to think of a gentle way to prepare her mother. "Well, I thought I better warn you that you might see my name mentioned in the paper or on the television news."

"Television? You?"

Kayla bit back a smile at the surprise in her mother's voice. "Yes, me," she said, then went on to explain about the wealthy plastic surgeon leaving her the check, Pete alerting the media and the circus that had followed.

"Oh, Kayla," her mother said, sounding distressed. "You can't keep the money. That just wouldn't look right. Not right at all."

"I didn't keep it," Kayla said in frustration. "I gave it back to him. I even told the reporters I wasn't keeping it, but it didn't seem to matter to them whether I was or not. All they seemed to care about was *why* he gave it to me."

"Why did he?"

Kayla flipped her hair up over the back of her head and paced, holding the receiver to her ear. "I don't know," she said miserably, "but the media is referring to him as my sugar daddy."

"Oh, no."

Kayla heard the horror in her mother's voice, could imagine the stricken look on her face. "I know. It sounds really awful."

"But...what are you going to do?"

"What *can* I do? He came by this morning to apologize and suggested that I lay low for a while and avoid reporters."

"But you can't stay at home! You have to go to work and to school."

Kayla winced, at the mention of work. "Uh, Mom," she said hesitantly. "There's something else I need to tell you." She took a deep breath and said in a rush, "I quit my job."

"Oh, Kayla," her mother moaned. "Why? Jobs are so hard to come by these days."

"I know," Kayla said, dabbing at the tears that filled her eyes. "But I couldn't work for Pete anymore. Not after what he did." She gulped back the tears, then added, "Mom, I'm sorry, but I won't be able to send you any money this week."

"Oh, honey. Don't worry about us. We'll be fine."

"But Jimmy said he had to go to the doctor, and I know that Jen is wanting a new dress for the prom."

"We'll manage," her mother assured her. "We always do. You just concentrate on your studies and finding a new job. Don't worry about us. We'll be fine."

But Kayla did worry. While she loaded her backpack with the items she'd need for her classes that day, she fretted and stewed, wondering how her mother would make it without her help. Keeping a family of eight going was hard, a fact that, as the oldest, Kayla was only too aware. Ever since her father's death, she'd tried to help out as much as she could, tried not to be a burden. She'd felt guilty, when she'd left home to pursue a degree in nursing, leaving her mother to handle everything alone, and had tried to ease the burden by sending home every penny she could spare. She lived a frugal life, focused her energy and time on her studies and on her work. With a degree in hand, she knew she could get a real job, one that would enable her to help her family out even more.

But things had changed. Her *life* had changed. Now she had no job, which meant she wouldn't be able to send money home, as she'd done in the past. And she could almost feel the degree she yearned for slipping through her fingers. Without any income, she wouldn't be able to pay the next installment on her tuition that was due in less than a month. She'd have to withdraw from her classes. Possibly even move back home.

And it was all Dr. Ryland Tanner's fault.

The jerk.

Frustrated—and more than a little resentful—Kayla pulled on her jacket, slung her backpack over her shoulder and headed out the door, aware that she had just under twenty minutes to make it to class without being late.

Once outside, she paused a moment to let her eyes adjust to the bright sunlight, then jogged down the steps, her head down, her mind focused on thinking of a way out of this mess.

"Kayla!"

She glanced up, fitting a hand at her brow to shade her eyes from the sun's glare. A man stood at the curb, a camera held before his face. Before she could duck and run, he snapped a picture, then dropped the camera to swing from a strap around his neck and fumbled a notepad and pen from his pocket.

"You've been quoted as claiming that you and Dr. Tanner have no relationship, yet I saw Dr. Tanner leaving your apartment earlier this morning." He held the pen poised above the pad. "Would you tell me the purpose of his visit?"

That night, Ry sat behind his father's desk, holding the phone to his ear, filling Ace in on his trip to see the waitress. "You were right," he admitted reluctantly. "She wasn't too happy to see me."

"Did you warn her about talking to the press?"

"Yeah," he said, then sighed. "Or at least, I tried to. The only way she can avoid them is to stay holed up in her apartment, which she refuses to do."

"Have you considered bringing her to the ranch? The press couldn't get to her there."

Though he hadn't thought of that particular solution, Ry shook his head. "Wouldn't work. She's got classes, plus she needs to find another job."

"What about the money you gave her? Surely she can live on that for a while."

"She could, if she'd kept it. But she gave it back. Said she doesn't need or want a sugar daddy."

"A sugar daddy, huh?" Ace said, then snorted a

laugh. "Sounds as if the press isn't the only one questioning your motives."

"This isn't funny."

"No," Ace agreed, sobering. "It's not."

Silence stretched along the phone lines, as both tried to think of another solution to the problem.

"What if I offered to meet with the press?" Ry said, thinking aloud. "I could explain my purpose in giving her the money, answer whatever questions they might have and put an end to all the speculation."

"It might work," Ace said thoughtfully. "But it would be even better if you could persuade her to take part."

"Yeah," Ry agreed, seeing the wisdom in his brother's suggestion. "It would, at that. I'll give her a call and see if she's willing."

"Let me know how it goes."

After replacing the phone, Ry sank back in the chair and frowned. *Sugar daddy,* he thought contemptuously. The tag was insulting at best. Just to be sure of the term's meaning, he rose and crossed to the bookshelf. He scanned the spines of the books until he found the dictionary and pulled it from the stack. Holding the book open on his palm, he quickly flipped pages until he found the listing.

> *sugar daddy n (1926) 1: a well-to-do usu.*
> *older man who supports or spends lavishly on a*
> *mistress or a girlfriend*

He slammed the book closed, refusing to read anymore. Hell, the waitress wasn't his girlfriend, and she sure as hell wasn't his mistress. He'd never supported her or spent lavishly on her. He'd given her a gift, dammit. A one-time, this-is-it scholarship!

But that first part? The reference to *older?* That much was at least true.

It also royally pissed him off.

Chapter 4

Though Ry had agreed that Kayla's presence and participation at the news conference he planned to request was crucial to its success, he put off making the call until the next morning. Before heading out to help the ranch hands repair some downed fences, he tried her number, but got her answering machine. He tried again when he came in for lunch, with the same result. That night he dialed her number a minimum of four times. At each attempt, after the fourth ring, her answering machine had clicked on. Frustrated, but not overly concerned, he'd left a message for her to call him and had gone to bed.

Just after six the next morning, he'd dialed her number again, sure that he'd wake her, but figured she deserved the disruption for not returning his calls. When he heard the canned, "Hi! This is Kayla. Sorry I can't take your call right now," he'd slammed down the phone, without listening to the rest of her recorded message. He hadn't bothered to call her again, until that evening. That time he didn't wait to hear the recording, but slammed the phone down, after the fourth ring, knowing the tape was about to click on.

On the third morning, he woke up before daylight in a bad mood, one spawned by his inability to get in contact the waitress. With a glance at the clock, he noted it was just after four. His smile smug, he picked up the phone and punched in her number. This time when the answering machine clicked on, he listened to her recorded message, the click, then shouted into the receiver, "Why don't you answer your damn phone?" then slammed down the receiver and swore some more.

His bad mood stuck with him like a fly on stink throughout the day, worsening when he hammered his thumb, instead of the fence staple he'd aimed at. It took another dive late that afternoon, when he realized that he'd forgotten to order diesel for the tractors. Knowing the hands would need the fuel the next morning to haul the round bales of hay out to the cattle in the pastures, he loaded every gas can he could find into the back of the ranch truck and headed for town.

It was after he filled the cans and went inside the service station to pay for the fuel that his mood took another swing, this time toward panic. In the newspaper rack placed strategically beside the register, a headline screamed the question, Foul Play? Below the bold type was a photo of Kayla—or he assumed the woman pictured was Kayla. It was hard to know for sure, since the photographer had snapped the picture with her running in the opposite direction, a jacket pulled up over head.

Dragging the newspaper from the rack, he paid for it, along with his gas, and returned to his truck. Once inside, he opened the newspaper over the steering the wheel to read the accompanying article.

Less than a week after receiving a $30,000 tip from Dr. Ryland Tanner, waitress Kayla Jennings has disappeared. Her apartment windows remain dark; her car parked in the same spot on the driveway beside her apartment house; her ringing phone goes unanswered. When questioned, neighbors who share the apartment house with Jennings, claim they haven't seen her since Tuesday morning when she left for class. But students enrolled in Jennings's classes report that she never showed up for class that day.

Oh, God, Ry silently prayed. Please don't let anything have happened to her. Gulping, he swiped at the cold sweat that had popped out on his forehead, then read on.

A source at the University, who wishes to remain anonymous, is quoted as saying, "Her professors are naturally concerned, as this kind of behavior is totally out-of-character for Ms. Jennings. She's a diligent student. Turns her work in on time. She's never been late for class, much less missed one."

When a person turns up missing, usually the police are notified. But in a telephone interview, Detective Harry Combs of the Austin Police Department stated, "As of this date, the Austin Police Department has no record of a missing per-the spaced-out kid. "You come to lay some cash on us, too?" He glanced over at the other kid and they both laughed, then went through a complicated hand slapping routine that Ry was sure had some meaning for them, but meant nothing to him.

Near the end of his patience, he pulled out his wallet. "As a matter of fact, I might." He removed a crisp fifty, then looked up at them over his brow and added, "*If* you can tell me where I can find Kayla."

The two looked at the fifty-dollar bill, then at each other and shared an uneasy glance.

"Why do you think we'd know where she is?" Chris asked suspiciously.

Ry flicked a finger, flipping the bill around so that they could see the president's face on the other side. "You live across the hall," he said, stating the obvious.

"Yeah. So what if we do?"

He pulled out another fifty, then slid his wallet back into his pocket. "Must be nice living across the hall from such a good-looking woman."

The two shared another glance, then Chris said cautiously,

"It has its perks."

Chuckling, Ry nodded. "I imagine it does. I know lived across the hall from Kayla, I'd be watching door night and day, hoping to catch her going out er mail in her nightgown—" he waggled a brow r less." Noticing that they had begun to squirm y, he lifted his hands. "Hell, what red-blooded ican male wouldn't sneak a peak?"

glanced at Chris, then turned to Ry and said sh, "She sleeps in a T-shirt, not a nightgown." !" Ry slapped one of the fifties across Joey's

son report filed on Ms. Jennings." Combs went on to explain that, "Before the department can actively pursue a missing person, a report must be filed." Ms. Jennings has been missing since Tuesday morning, nearly forty-eight hours, yet no one has bothered to file a missing person report.

Ry glanced at the date on the paper's masthead and paled when he realized the paper was a day old.

Prior to her disappearance, Pete Gulley, owner of the River's End Restaurant and Jennings' former employer, refused to respond to questions about Ms. Jennings. But today, after learning that she was missing, Gulley, visibly shaken by the news, said, "I don't know where she is. I haven't seen her since she left the restaurant Monday afternoon." Gulley, like others who are aware of Jennings and Tanners' relationship, suggested that Dr. Ryland Tanner might know of her whereabouts.

"Oh, that's right," Ry muttered darkly. "Stick the blame on me."

Attempts to reach Dr. Tanner for comment were unsuccessful. A guest at the Driskill since moving out of the Westlake home he shared with his former wife, Lana Drummond Tanner, Tanner checked out of the hotel on Sunday and left no forwarding address.

With both Jennings and Tanner missing, one has to wonder if this a case of Foul Play...or simply a couple Playing Around?

Ry tossed the paper aside in disgust. "Playing around," he muttered under his breath. Why not *Going to Ground,* which is exactly what he prayed Kayla had done. Lay low for a while, he'd told her, the suggestion he'd offered as a way for her to avoid reporters. Though she'd claimed that was impossible for her to do, he figured she'd changed her mind, seen the wisdom in his advice.

Or maybe she hadn't.

He gulped, as the thought gelled into a strong possibility in his mind. She hadn't answered her phone in, what, three days? That, in itself, was strange. What woman could resist answering a ringing phone? He gave himself a shake and reached for the key, started the engine. She wasn't answering her phone for the same reason she wasn't leaving her apartment, he told himself. She was avoiding reporters.

Or maybe she'd met with foul play.

Swearing, he jerked the gearshift down and, with a squeal of tires, spun out onto the highway, setting the gas cans rocking in the back, as he pointed the nose of the truck toward Austin.

His heart racing, Ry jogged for the front porch of the apartment house, shouldered open the door and strode inside. Music blasted from behind the door of 1-A, but not a sound came from 1-B. Swallowing back the fear that wanted to grip him, he strode to the door and pounded his fist against the wood. He waited, muttering, "Come on, come on. Be there," impatiently under his breath.

When he lifted his hand to pound again, the door behind him swung open. He whirled, the blare of mu-

sic striking his face like a slap. The spaced-out kid he'd met on his first visit to Kayla's apartment stood in the open doorway.

The kid held up his hands. "Whoa, dude. Don't go ballistic. I was just checking out the noise."

Realizing that he still had his fist raised, Ry lowered his hand. "I wasn't going to hit you," he muttered irritably, then snapped, "Would you turn that damn music down! I can't even hear myself think."

The kid called over his shoulder, "Hey, Joey! Cut the volume. We've got company."

Seconds later, silence fell over the small entry and a second kid—obviously Joey—joined the first at th[e] door.

"What's up?" he asked, glancing from Ry to [ ] friend.

The spaced-out kid gestured at Ry. "This [ ] dude I told you about. The one who came [ ] Kayla the other day.

Joey looked at Ry. "You're the knife? [ ] who slammed Kayla with all the green?"

Ry had to assume that by "the knife" [ ] "the surgeon." As to the rest, he could [ ] Joey was referring to the money he had [ ] Kayla. Though he was tempted to pin h[ ] the wall and pound the information h[ ] them, he feared a show of force w[ ] clam up. Instead he crossed the hall[ ] hand.

"Dr. Ryland Tanner. And you[ ]

Instead of shaking his hand[ ] bumped his knuckles against R[ ] dude. And this is Chris," he [ ]

palm. "I knew you guys were the type who'd know your neighbors." He caught the other fifty between two fingers and held it up. "Now who wants to tell me where she is?"

"Hey!" Chris cried. "That's not fair. Joey got a fifty and he didn't tell you nothin' but what she sleeps in."

Ry lifted a brow. "Is there something else you'd rather share with me?"

The kid gave his oversize jeans a cocky hitch. "To get a fifty, sure."

"Then let's hear what you've got."

Chris gave Joey a smug look. "She doesn't sleep in panties."

Joey gave Chris an angry shove. "Man, you never told me that! How do you know?"

Chris swelled his chest and preened. "One morning when she went out to get the paper, the wind was kickin' pretty good." He lifted a shoulder and rocked back on his heels. "Took her a second or two to jerk her T-shirt back to her knees."

"And you didn't tell me so I could look?" Joey gave Chris another shove. "Man, that's low."

Ry wanted to knock the two young hoods' heads together, just for the sheer pleasure of it, but managed to restrain himself. He needed what information they might have too badly to take a chance on alienating them.

Remembering a congratulatory hand gesture he'd seen a teenager make on one of the reality TV shows, he slapped his hands down on Chris's palms, leaving the fifty there, turned his up for the kid to reciprocate, then bumped chests and said, "Way to go, dude."

The kid gave Ry's now empty hands a pointed look. "Looks like we broke the bank, Joey."

Ry pulled his wallet out. "Not quite." Raking his thumb over the bills lining the inside, he selected a one-hundred-dollar bill and held it up. "Now for the big question. Winner takes all. Where's Kayla?"

The two eyed each other suspiciously.

"Down the middle?" Joey suggested.

Chris nodded, then turned to Ry. "Upstairs. First door on the right."

Before Ry could thank them, Joey had snatched the bill from his hand and the two were inside the apartment with the door closed, probably already making plans to spend their loot.

Praying the two hadn't played him for a fool, Ry took the stairs two at a time and knocked on the door to 2-B. The girl with the pink-spiked hair opened it. She took one look at Ry and slammed it.

Ry stopped it from closing with a well-placed boot.

She glared at him through the narrow opening. "What do you want?"

"Who, not what. Tell Kayla I'm here."

"She doesn't live here and you know it. Her apartment's the one below."

His patience gone, he shoved his face up close to hers. "I know where she lives," he growled. "And I also know that she's hiding out up here. Now, are you going to let me in, or do I have to bust down the door?"

"It's okay, Shanda," he heard Kayla say from the other side of the door. "I'll talk to him."

Her gaze fixed on Ry's, Shanda curled her lip in a sneer, but stepped back and opened the door.

"Kick ass," she muttered to Kayla, as she strode past her.

Folding her arms across her chest, Kayla narrowed her eyes at Ry. "This is beginning to feel like harassment."

Unfortunately she was wearing a T-shirt, which was a real distraction for Ry, considering what Chris and Joey had just shared with him.

Scowling, he stepped inside and peeled off his hat. "You're a hard woman to get a hold of."

"'Lay low for a while,'" she said, quoting him. "Weren't those your instructions?"

"I didn't mean for you to quit answering your damn phone!"

"That *damn* phone, as you referred to it, never quit ringing. Rather than let it drive me crazy, which was a distinct possibility, I turned off the sound."

"Reporters," he said, with a snort of disgust. "I should have known they'd start calling you."

"Oh, it wasn't just reporters," she informed him. "It seems every con man and pervert in the state now has my phone number."

"Con men?"

She pressed a hand to her chest and batted her eyes. "Why, yes," she gushed, in the same southern drawl he'd swear Scarlett O'Hara had used on Ashley Wilkes. "Since it's a well-publicized fact that I'm just swimming in money, all these wonderfully, generous men keep calling, wanting to help little ol' me invest my sudden windfall.

"Why, I've been offered deeds to land off the coast of southern Florida and leases on oil wells in countries I've never heard of." She fanned her face, as if about to swoon. "And there was this one particularly tempting offer to purchase the patent on a formula for a paint guaranteed not to chip or fade.''

Flapping a hand, she batted her eyes. ''But those were nothing compared to the call I received from the CEO of a cosmetics company who wanted to hire me to endorse his company's new line of cosmetics.''

He lifted a brow. ''Really? How much did he offer you?''

She dropped the Southern Belle act to scowl. ''We didn't get that far. I hung up on him, before he started talking money.'' Deepening her scowl, she began to pace. ''But the perverts were the worst.'' Shuddering, she hugged her arms around her waist. ''Real sickos, who called at all hours of the day and night, promising me jewelry and money, if I'd let them be my sugar daddy. One of them even offered me a condo in Aspen and my own bank account.''

''You didn't agree to meet any of them, did you?''

She turned, throwing her arms wide. ''Do I *look* stupid?'' Before he could respond, she dropped her arms limply to her sides. ''What does it matter, anyway?'' she said miserably. ''They know my name. My phone number. They even know where I live.''

She looked up at him and he was stunned to see that tears filled her eyes. ''Now do you understand why I don't answer my phone? Why I hide out in Shanda's and Lulu's apartment?''

Ry felt lower than a snake. ''I'm sorry, Kayla.''

Even as he offered the apology, he realized how empty the words were, how useless. There was nothing he could do to wind back the clock to the previous Sunday, nothing he could say or do that would erase all the humiliation and inconveniences she'd suffered, as a result of him and his well-intentioned gift.

But he could hopefully put an end to all this, before she suffered anymore.

"I've come up with an idea," he told her.

"If it includes me, forget it."

He set his jaw. "Would you at least hear me out?"

She folded her arms across her chest. "All right. But make it fast. *Survivor* is on."

"I thought if I agreed to meet with the press, explain to them why I gave you the money, then answer whatever questions they might have, it might put an end to this nightmare."

She turned up a palm in invitation. "If you're willing to subject yourself to that kind of persecution, to that level of public exposure, be my guest."

He drew in a deep breath, before telling her the rest. "I think it's important that you be there, too."

She dropped her arms to gape, then pushed out her hands and backed away. "Uh-uh. No way. I'm not going through *that* again."

He took a step in pursuit, desperate to convince her. "But this will only work if we're both present. We need to answer questions, verify each other's statements, dispel any more rumors before they get blown out of proportion."

"I said, no. Now, leave."

"If you don't do this with me, you know they're going to come after you again. Squeeze you to find out if what I've told them is the truth, see if you have anything to add."

She pointed a finger at the door, her hand shaking in fury, her face red with it. "Out."

"But, Kayla, I—"

"Out!" she screamed.

"Why are you being so damned stubborn about this? I'm only trying to help you."

"She said, out, mister."

Ry glanced beyond Kayla to find Shanda had returned. She stood in front of the beaded curtain that separated the small entry from the living room, a pistol in her hand, its barrel aimed at a spot somewhere between his eyes.

He lifted his hands, a trickle of sweat working its way down his spine. "Look. I didn't come here to cause any trouble. I only wanted to make sure that Kayla was all right. To offer her a way out of this mess."

There was a loud click, as Shanda drew back the hammer. "Don't make the mistake of thinking I don't know how to use this," she warned. "My daddy gave me this pistol and taught me how to shoot it, so I could protect myself from perverts like you." She waved the barrel of the pistol toward the door, then leveled it on his nose again and repeated, "Kayla says she wants you out, so go."

Ry went.

Ry sat on the side of the bed, an elbow braced on his knee, his head in his hand, the phone held to his ear.

"It didn't go very well," he said, in answer to Ace's question about his meeting with Kayla.

"What do you mean by 'not well'?"

Ry dragged himself to his feet. "As in no way in hell will she take part in a press conference with me."

"I guess that nixes that idea, then, huh?"

"It looks that way."

"I don't suppose the press has backed off any?"

Ry huffed a breath. "Hardly. Now they're suggesting foul play."

"Foul play?"

"Kayla's been hiding out in one of her neighbor's apartment, so now the press is running stories suggesting that she's either met with foul play or run off with me, who, by the way, they've also listed as missing in action."

"Oh, man. This is getting worse by the day."

Ry flopped down on the side of the bed again. "Tell me about it."

"So what do you do now?"

"Hell, if I know. I'll tell you one thing, though. I'm not stepping foot in that apartment house again. Nothing but a bunch of crazies live there. This one chick even pulled a gun on me."

"A gun! Are you serious?"

Ry shuddered just thinking about it. "Believe me. Having a pink-haired punk queen hold a gun on you is nothing to joke about. And if you laugh," Ry warned, "I'll personally deck you the next time I see you."

"I'm not laughing," Ace assured him, though Ry would swear he heard amusement in his brother's voice.

"I'm fresh out of ideas," Ry admitted in defeat. "Have you got any other suggestions?"

"I still think the best thing to do is bring her to the ranch."

"She can't come here," Ry reminded him. "Remember? She has to work."

"Has she found a job yet?"

Ry rubbed at the headache that had gathered between his eyes. "I doubt it. From what she told me, it sounds like she's been hiding out all week."

"Why don't you offer her a job?"

Ry choked on a laugh. "Doing what?"

"When we were living at the ranch, Maggie took care of cleaning the house and cooking meals for the hands. Why not hire the waitress to take over those duties?"

Ry considered a moment, then shook his head. "That would resolve the problem of her needing a job, but she would still have school. I doubt she'd be willing to quit."

"Couldn't you pull some strings at the university? God knows, you've donated enough money over the years. They ought to be willing to do something for you in return."

Ry started to shake his head, the suggestion sounding too much like arm twisting to suit him, then stopped. "The Internet," he said, snapping his fingers.

"What?" Ace asked in confusion.

"The university offers all kinds of classes over the Internet. And even if they don't offer any of the ones she's taking, I could talk to her professors and see if they would agree to let me tutor her and allow her to turn in her assignments by e-mail."

"Sounds like a plan to me," Ace said, putting his stamp of approval on it.

Ry groaned, realizing that this would require another trip to Austin and a visit to that hellhole of an apartment house where she lived, in order to present Kayla with the idea. "Got a bullet-proof vest you can loan me?" he asked wryly.

"No, but I've got a better idea. Send Woodrow."

"Woodrow?" Ry fell back on the bed and laughed. "Are you crazy? One look at that big lug of a brother of ours and the woman will run and hide." He popped right back up. "No, wait a minute," he said, imagining the expression on the pink-haired chick's face when she got a look at Woodrow. He dropped his head back and hooted a laugh. "You're right! Woodrow's the perfect man for the job."

Kayla paced back and forth across the worn carpet like a caged cat, the only deviation in her course, a slight swerve to dodge the old chicken coop she used for a coffee table. With the blinds drawn tight and the lights turned off, the room was like a tomb. Dark. Confining. Suffocating. After less than twenty-four hours back in her own apartment, she was tempted to chance discovery and sneak back up to Shanda and Lulu's. At least up there, she could switch on a lamp. Watch a little TV.

But she wouldn't do that to her friends. As her mother frequently said, house guests, like fish, began to smell after three days. Besides, after the scene Ry had created in their apartment the night before, Kayla was reluctant to subject her friends to that kind of drama again.

She sputtered a laugh, picturing Shanda standing there with a gun aimed at Ry's head. Even funnier was Ry's reaction. And wouldn't he feel like a fool, if he were to find out that the gun was only a toy? She'd pay good money for a ticket to see that show.

Chuckling, she crossed to the window and lifted a blind to peek out. Her smile faded. The Mercedes she'd spotted earlier was still parked a few doors down. She'd never seen the car on the street before, which in itself was enough to make her suspicious. It was unlikely that it belonged to any of her neighbors. Most of the students who lived in the area drove clunkers or didn't drive at all, opting to ride bikes or walk where they needed to go, rather than fight the downtown traffic.

She dropped the blind with a frustrated groan. Much more of this cloak and dagger lifestyle and she was going to go insane!

And it was all Dr. Ryland Tanner's fault, she thought bitterly.

The jerk.

Unable to bear the confining apartment one more second, she snatched her jacket from the sofa and headed out. On the front porch, she pulled her hood up over her head to conceal her identity, just in case the Mercedes did belong to a reporter, as she feared. With a quick look left and right, she hopped off the porch and ducked around the side of the house. Once she reached the alley at the back, she shoved back the hood and shook out her hair, confident that she'd given the reporter the slip.

Just as she inhaled her first greedy breath of freedom, a hand closed around her arm. She whirled, and her heart shot to her throat, when she found herself facing a man big and mean enough looking to star as a starting linebacker for the Dallas Cowboys.

"We need to talk."

The guy's voice was as deep as he was tall and gruff to the point of intimidation. Judging on his size alone, she knew she'd lose if it came to a fight.

But she wasn't about to let him see her fear.

Curling her lip in a snarl, she shoved her face up close to his. "Look, buster—"

A movement had her whipping her gaze to the left, where a woman stepped from the shadows.

The woman laid a hand on his arm. "Woodrow," she scolded gently. "Let her go. Can't you see that you're frightening her?"

Kayla looked from one to the other, wondering if reporters, like policemen, used the good-cop-bad-cop routine to get the information that they wanted from a person.

But she didn't intend to hang around long enough to see if that's what they had planned. Taking advantage of the distraction the woman's appearance had created, she jerked her arm free and quickly stepped back out of reach.

"You reporters are nothing but a bunch of scumbags," she accused angrily. "I ought to call the police and have you both arrested for harassment."

"Oh, we aren't reporters," the woman said in dismay, then offered Kayla a regretful smile. "How rude of us not to introduce ourselves. I'm Dr. Elizabeth Tanner," she said and offered a hand.

Wary, Kayla took the woman's hand and shook it.

"And this," Elizabeth said, giving the muscle beside her an adoring look, "is my husband, Woodrow."

Kayla stuffed her hands into her pockets to avoid having to shake Woodrow's, as well. She wasn't at all sure she wouldn't come away from the experience without a few broken bones.

"Tanner," she repeated and eyed the two suspiciously. "You wouldn't happen to be any relation to Dr. Ryland Tanner, would you?"

"Woodrow and Ry are brothers," Elizabeth explained, then laughed softly. "But please don't hold that against us. We're here to offer you our help."

Kayla sized Woodrow up, noting the muscled arms his heavy jacket couldn't hide, the large, wide hands that appeared strong enough to crush bone. "If your offer includes him as a bodyguard," she told Elizabeth, with a jerk of her head toward Woodrow. "I might be interested."

Laughing, Elizabeth tucked her arm through Kayla's and urged her toward the house. "My husband may look like a grizzly, but I assure you he's nothing but a big, cuddly teddy bear."

Kayla glanced back at Woodrow, who trailed along a few steps behind. Stifling a shudder, she turned back. "Could've fooled me."

Woodrow sat on Kayla's sofa, an arm stretched along its back, looking bored. His wife, Elizabeth, sat primly beside him, a model of calm, as she watched Kayla pace back and forth across the small room.

"Let me get this straight," Kayla said, trying to absorb the plan Woodrow had laid out for her. "You're asking me to pack up my things, move to a ranch I've never heard of and cook and clean up after a bunch of cowboys?"

Woodrow lifted a shoulder. "That's about the gist of it."

Elizabeth laid a hand on his knee. "It isn't as bad as Woodrow makes it sound," she assured Kayla. "The cowboys live in a bunkhouse and only come to the ranch house for their meals. The remainder of the time, you and Ry will have the house to yourselves."

Kayla stopped pacing to look down her nose at the

woman. "And that's supposed to make me feel better?"

"Oh, no, I—" Elizabeth glanced at Woodrow, then down at her lap, a blush staining her cheeks "I—I didn't mean to insinuate that you and Ry...well, that you would—"

Woodrow heaved an exasperated breath. "What she's trying to say," he said to Kayla, "is that you aren't expected to keep house for a bunch of cowboys. You're only expected to cook their meals."

"And I'll get paid for this?"

Woodrow nodded and named an amount.

Kayla choked at the number he tossed out. "You're kidding me, right?"

Woodrow folded his arms across his chest. "Serious as a heart attack."

Kayla pressed the heel of her hand against her forehead, her mind reeling at the thought of making that kind of money. And all she had to do was cook for a bunch of cowboys? There had to be a catch.

"What about my classes?" she asked. "Is the ranch close enough for me to commute to the university?"

Woodrow and Elizabeth shared a glance.

"I suppose she could," Elizabeth said uneasily, then turned back to Kayla. "But that may not be necessary, as Ry is working on an alternative."

"An alternative?" Kayla repeated, then narrowed an eye. "What kind of alternative?"

"He'll have to explain the details," Elizabeth replied, obviously hedging.

Frowning, Kayla shook her head. "I don't know. This all sounds like a setup to me."

"A setup?" Elizabeth repeated, her face flushing

with anger. "I'd say you're darn lucky that Ry's offering to help you at all!"

Kayla stared, stunned by Elizabeth's unexpected burst of anger.

Pressing a hand to her chest, Elizabeth drew in a breath, then slowly released it. "I'm sorry. I know that was harsh. Ry really does want to help you, but with you refusing to take part in a press conference with him, you've left him with very few options in which to do so. And it isn't as if this is forever," she added. "Once it's safe for you to return to Austin, you will be free to return to your home."

"Wait a minute," Kayla said, at the mention of Austin. "What about Ry? How can he stay at the ranch? Won't he have to be in Austin to see his patients?"

Elizabeth and Woodrow shared another uneasy glance.

"Well, no," Elizabeth said reluctantly. "You see, Ry's not practicing medicine any longer."

That news all but floored Kayla. She couldn't imagine anyone willingly giving up practicing medicine. She took her commitment to nursing very seriously and doubted, once she received her degree, that she'd ever willingly give up her career. And she certainly couldn't imagine ever losing her desire to help people. That need had been with her for as long as she could remember.

"Well?" Elizabeth asked expectantly. "Will you agree to give this a try?"

Kayla didn't know what to do. Woodrow was scary, but Elizabeth seemed like a nice person. She had a kind face, sympathetic eyes. If not for her, Kayla wouldn't even be considering this insane plan.

But what other choice did she have? The alternative—staying in her apartment and hiding from the press—was anything but appealing.

She lifted her hands, then dropped them in defeat. "I guess so."

Elizabeth popped to her feet. "Great. Shall I help you pack?"

Ry glanced up from the pile of hay he was forking into the stall for the horses' evening meal to find Woodrow standing in the barn doorway, watching. He quickly rammed the tines of the fork into the stack of hay, spearing it there, and crossed to Woodrow, peeling off his work gloves. "Did she agree to come?"

With a sigh, Woodrow shoved his cowboy hat back on his head and hooked a thumb over his shoulder. "Yeah. She's up at the house with Elizabeth."

"Did she give you any trouble?"

"Depends on what you call trouble," Woodrow muttered, then shook his head. "I swear, if George W. Bush himself knocked at that lady's door, she'd demand to see his driver's license and birth certificate as proof it was him before she'd let him in."

Amused that the waitress had given Woodrow a hard time, Ry slung a companionable arm along his brother's shoulders and headed him toward the house. "I take it she didn't believe you when you told her you were my brother? You can't really blame her. We don't look all that much alike."

Woodrow snorted. "It wasn't our relationship she questioned. The fact that I'm kin to you at all was what set her off." He gave Ry a sidelong glance. "What did you do to that woman, anyway?"

Ry dragged his arm from Woodrow's shoulders

and stuffed his hands into his pockets, irritated that everyone seemed willing to cast him as the villain. "I didn't do anything to her. It happened just like I told you. I gave her some money to help her out, and when the press got wind of it, they tried to turn it into something that it wasn't."

"So why does she hate you so much?"

Ry snapped his head around. "She told you she hates me?"

Woodrow lifted a shoulder. "Not in so many words. But she doesn't care for you. She made that clear as a glass." He wagged his head sadly. "I feel for you, bro. I sure as hell wouldn't want to live with a woman who felt that strongly about me."

"I'm not living with her," Ry reminded him drolly. "She's just staying here until all this blows over."

"Same damn thing, if you ask me," Woodrow grumbled, then warned, "I'd be careful, if I were you. I wouldn't put it past her to sneak in while you're sleeping and put a knife in your back."

Ry tensed at the suggestion, then forced his shoulders to relax. "You're just trying to spook me," he said, trying to make light of what he feared was a very real threat. "She doesn't despise me that much."

"Oh, really?" Woodrow lifted his chin, indicating the house ahead. "Take a good look, then tell me that again."

Ry followed Woodrow's gaze. Though it was dark out, the front porch light cast enough illumination for him to see Kayla standing on the front porch, her arms folded across her chest, her eyes narrowed on him. If looks could kill, he'd be pushing up daisies from six feet underground.

"It isn't me she dislikes," he said, as much to convince himself as Woodrow. "It's the fact that she had to come here."

Woodrow clapped a hand on Ry's shoulder, gave it a sympathetic squeeze. "You just keep telling yourself that, bro. After a couple of hundred years, you might even begin to believe it." He gave Ry a push that sent him tripping forward. "But in the meantime, you've got a houseguest waiting."

Chapter 5

Ry stood on the front porch staring down the drive long after the red taillights of Elizabeth's Mercedes had disappeared from sight. He wasn't staying outside to avoid Kayla, he told himself. He was simply enjoying the cool night air.

He'd no sooner made the defensive claim, than a gust of wind swept around the side of the house to challenge him on it. Hunching his shoulders against the cold, he set his jaw to keep his teeth from chattering. Who was he trying to fool? he asked himself in disgust. He was freezing his butt off out here.

But he wasn't going inside. No way. And it wasn't because he feared what bodily harm Kayla might inflict upon him—a suggestion he had Woodrow to thank for planting in his mind. He just wasn't in the mood to deal with her right now.

And who would blame him? he asked himself in frustration. His previous attempts at conversations with her had ranged from teeth-grinding tests on his patience to full-blown nightmares. The first time he'd tried to talk to her, he'd spent the five minutes she'd allotted him, listening to her rant and rave, blaming him for every bad thing that had happened to her seemingly since the day she was born. The second time, he'd almost gotten himself shot. What man in his right mind would purposely seek that kind of grief?

The front door opened behind him and he swallowed a groan, knowing the choice was no longer his to make.

"Do you always have other people do your dirty work for you?"

It was the same as calling him a coward, fighting words on any other occasion. Ry merely spared her a glance. "Would you have agreed to come, if I was the one who'd asked?"

She gave her chin a haughty lift. "What do you think?"

With a shrug, he turned and brushed past her. "That's why I sent Woodrow and Elizabeth."

She wheeled to follow him inside, slamming the door behind her. "Not so fast, cowboy. We need to talk about this."

"There's nothing to discuss. You're staying here, until this nightmare is over. Sounds simple enough to me." He stepped inside the study, caught the door in his hand and gave it a shove intending to shut her out.

She slapped a hand against it, threw it wide, then marched in after him.

"Well, I happen to disagree. I think we have plenty to talk about."

Ry sat down behind the desk and picked up a folder from the stack Ace had left on the corner. Flipping it open, he focused his gaze on the papers inside. He didn't know what he was looking at it, but it didn't matter. It saved him from having to look at her.

"Such as?" he asked, hoping he placed enough annoyance in his voice to make her believe he had things to do and didn't have time for idle chitchat.

"We can start with my purpose in being here. I think I've made it clear that I don't want or need a sugar daddy. In case I haven't, I want it understood that I have no intention of becoming involved in a physical relationship with you now or at any time in the future."

Without looking up, he turned a page. "I don't recall asking you to."

"Just because you didn't, doesn't mean that isn't what you have in mind."

He spared her a look. "Trust me. A physical relationship with you is the last thing on my mind." He drew a pen from the holder on the desk. "Now that we've got that cleared up," he paused to make a notation in the margin, "I've got work to do." He started to turn yet another page, but she slapped a hand down on it.

"I'm not through yet."

With a sigh, he pushed back in his chair and laced his fingers over his chest. "All right. What else is bothering you?"

"School. Elizabeth said that you were working on an alternative, so that I wouldn't have to drive back and forth every day. If your alternative is *you* driving me back and forth, you can forget it. I wouldn't be caught dead riding in the same car with you."

Her eyes were dark with resentment, her lips tight with it. Without her having to say the words, he received the message she was sending loud and clear. *This is all your fault. I'm the innocent party here.*

And Ry was a little tired of having all the blame heaped on his shoulders. Especially when she was doing the shoveling.

Pushing back his chair, he stood and leveled a well-aimed finger at her nose. "Let's get one thing straight right now. I don't like this arrangement any more than you do, but until this nightmare blows over, this is the way it's going to be. So you might as well suck in that lower lip, because pouting isn't going to change a damn thing."

He watched the color crawl up her neck and recognized the red stain as fury a split second before she unleashed it on him.

"Pouting?" she repeated, and took a threatening step closer to the desk. "I'll have you know I haven't pouted since I was three years old. But if I should choose to pout," she informed him and slapped away the finger he still held before her face, "I will. So don't make the mistake of thinking that, just because I agreed to come here, that I will let you rule my emotions, as well as my life." Out of breath, but obviously not out of steam, she swelled her chest, slapped her arms across it and finished with a curt, "So put that in your pipe and smoke it, cowboy."

That last jab was so juvenile, so childish, he wanted to laugh. But he found he could do nothing but stare. What had happened to the bubbly and vivacious waitress he had found so enchanting? The woman whose sunny smile had drawn him back to the River's End night-after-night just for another chance to experience its warmth?

"Was it all just an act? A way to get tips?"

"Was *what* all an act?" she snapped impatiently.

He hadn't intended to ask the question, but now that he had, dammit, he wanted an answer. He felt cheated, victimized, lied to. He deserved an explanation and by God he was going to get one.

"The smile!" he shouted, tossing up a hand, as he rounded the desk. "You sashayed around that bar like Little Miss Merry Sunshine, beaming smiles left and right, as if you alone held the key to happiness."

She dropped her head back and laughed.

That she found this amusing, angered him all the more. "What's so damn funny?"

She flung out a hand. "You are! Imagine you, a doctor no less, and a rich one, at that, so desperate for a friendly face that you have to hang out in bars to find one."

"That wasn't why I went to the River's End! I went there because I...because I..."

She lifted a brow.

Scowling, he turned away. "Okay," he grumbled, dragging a hand over his hair. "Maybe I was a little lonely." He burned her with a look over his shoulder. "But you try living in a hotel room for three months, with no one but yourself for company, and see how much you like it."

"Just give me the word, cowboy, and I'm there."

He furrowed his brow in confusion. "You're where?"

"The Driskill. I'll take it and you can have the dump I live in."

He shuddered at the thought of spending even one

night in the spook house she called home. "You ought to draw combat pay for having to live in that place."

"Oh, it's not so bad." She tucked her tongue against the inside of her cheek to hide a smile. "At least I don't have to hang out in bars when I need a good laugh. All I have to do is step outside my door."

He wanted to hold on to his anger, lash back with something cruel and demeaning, but couldn't. Not when an image of the spaced-out kids who lived across the hall came so easily to mind, as well as one of the gun-toting, pink-haired punk queen who lived above her. In spite of his anger, he found himself chuckling. "No, I guess you wouldn't."

She stuck out a hand. "Truce?"

His smile melting, he stared at the offered hand, then up at her. "It's that easy?"

She shrugged. "I suppose I could go a few more rounds, if you want."

He quickly reached for her hand. "I'd just as soon avoid that, if you don't mind."

The moment their palms met the air in the room seemed to change, grow warmer, closer, charged by a force he couldn't name. He watched her face pale, even as awareness flared in her eyes, and knew she was as conscious of the change as he.

"This has happened before, hasn't it?" he asked, his voice not quite steady.

She gulped. Nodded.

"That night in the hotel room."

She dropped her gaze and nodded again.

"I was drunk," he said, shamed even now by the memory. "But not so drunk that I don't remember your kindness, your concern." As he said the words, he was struck again by all that she'd suffered as a result of her kindness.

He squeezed her fingers within his, wanting to make it up to her somehow. "I'm sorry this happened, Kayla. All of it."

When she lifted her head to look up at him, he saw the tears that filled her eyes. More, he saw the misery, the resignation behind them. The gold flecks that had once danced in her brown eyes were gone, as was the smile that had produced them. He wanted to haul her into his arms and simply hold her. Offer her the comfort she'd offered to him.

But, if he did, he was afraid she would misconstrue his actions, think he was coming on to her.

I don't need or want a sugar daddy.

Sugar daddy, he thought contemptuously, remembering looking up the term. The definition was insulting, at best, but it was that *older* part that had rankled the most, and still did, if he were honest. He didn't need to be reminded that he was older than Kayla…or maybe he did.

She was an attractive woman, one he was ashamed to admit he'd caught himself weaving sexual fantasies around during the lonely nights he'd spent in the hotel room. And now here they were living in the same house, a form of cohabitation that presented its own unique set of problems, if not handled properly.

Cognizant of the temptations they might face, he dropped his gaze and picked up a paperweight from the desk to fill his hand with something other than her.

"I know that coming here is an inconvenience for you," he said, as he rubbed a thumb thoughtfully over the cool stone. "But I want you to know that I intend to do everything within my power to see that you are able return to Austin, as soon as possible.''

Heaving a sigh, he set the paperweight down and looked at her. ''And to respond to your initial concern, yes, I've made arrangements for you to continue your classes, while you're here at the ranch.''

Her eyes narrowed suspiciously. ''How?''

He gestured at the computer on the credenza behind the desk. ''Via the Internet. I spoke with your professors and they've agreed to e-mail your assignments to you. Once you've completed them, you'll return them in the same manner. Whatever tests you're required to take, I've agreed to monitor, sign for authentication and fax to the appropriate professor.''

''It must be nice to be so rich that people will jump through hoops to do whatever you ask of them.''

Though he doubted she'd meant the comment as an insult, it stung like one. Using money as a power tool was something the old man had done. But not Ry. Never Ry.

Scowling, he rounded the desk and sat behind it again. ''Wealth had nothing to do with the arrangement. I merely made a few calls. You could've done the same, if you'd thought of it.'' He opened the file again, a sign of dismissal he'd used effectively on his office staff. ''Now, if you'll excuse me.''

''What is it with you, anyway?''

He kept his gaze down. ''I don't know what you mean.''

''Look at me when you're talking to me!''

Though he would prefer looking anywhere other than at her, he set his jaw and looked up.

She flung out a hand. ''One minute you're bending over backward doing nice things for me and the next you're stiff-arming me, like I've got some kind of communicable disease.''

He lifted a brow. ''Do you?''

She slapped her hands down on the desk and pushed her face to his, her eyes cold with fury, her face red with it. ''Would it matter, if I did?''

He'd thought her beautiful when she smiled, but anger added a whole new dimension to her beauty. It was a test of his self-control to keep his gaze fixed on hers, his face free of the conflicting emotions that swirled inside him. ''If you're asking if a communicable disease would provide you a one-way ticket back to your apartment, the answer is no. You're stuck here the same as I am.''

She glared at him a full three seconds, then shoved away from the desk and turned for the door. ''You're nothing but a spoiled, rich kid,'' she tossed over her shoulder.

He rose to go after her, to set her straight, then dropped back down on the chair. Let her think what she would, he told himself. He knew who and what he was. He might be a Tanner, but he wasn't like his old man. He didn't use the Tanner name or his wealth to manipulate people for personal gain. He'd made his own way in the world and would continue to do so.

In spite of both.

Ry stepped into the kitchen bright and early the next morning, hoping to get a fix of caffeine into his system before he had to deal with Kayla again.

It appeared he would have to make do without it.

Dressed in sweatpants and a hooded jacket worn to a dull pewter, she stood before the kitchen sink, her legs crossed at the ankles, the toe of one scuffed running shoe propped against the floor. Her stance was insolent, her expression sullen.

So much for the olive branch she'd offered the night before, he thought. But at least she'd made coffee. For that alone, he was willing to put up with whatever aggravation she was obviously anxious to dump on him.

"You're up early," he said, as he poured himself a cup.

"You didn't mention what time I was to have breakfast ready. I assumed cowboys like to get an early start."

He nodded, sipped, ignoring the temper in her voice. "You assumed right." He shot a sleeve to look at his watch. "You've got about an hour. They usually show up about seven."

"What am I supposed to cook?"

He shrugged. "Whatever strikes your fancy. Maggie didn't have time to stock the refrigerator before she and Ace left, but there should be plenty to choose from."

"Maggie," she repeated sourly, as she crossed to the refrigerator. "Is this someone I'm supposed to know?"

"Maggie's my brother Ace's wife. She cooked for the cowboys, while she and Ace were living here."

He watched her select a carton of eggs and a pound of bacon from the items stored in the refrigerator. "Better grab another package of bacon," he warned. "These guys are hearty eaters."

She gave him a withering look, but retrieved another pound of bacon. Bumping her hip against the door, she crossed to the island. "Mixing bowls?" she asked tersely.

He fished one from one beneath the island and set it on top. "Skillets are in the drawer under the range. Utensils in these drawers," he said, tapping a finger against the row of drawers that lay below the granite island's top. He crossed to the cabinets flanking the sink and pulled open a pair of doors. "Dishes are kept up here. Everything else you'll need, you'll find in the pantry." He turned and lifted a brow. "Any questions?"

Jutting her chin at a stubborn angle, she began cracking eggs. "Not at the moment."

She wore her resentment like a cloak hugged tightly around her body, but he'd decided during the night—a decision reached after hours of frustrated tossing and turning—that he wasn't going to let her goad him into another fight. He would be as polite as humanly possible and prayed she'd return the favor.

"If you want," he offered, "I could help. Just until you get the feel of things."

She used an elbow to nudge the packages of bacon toward him. "I suppose you could start the bacon."

As he pulled out the frying pan, he glanced over his shoulder, determined to give conversation another try. "Been for a run this morning?"

She lifted a shoulder. "I always run in the morning." Holding an egg poised over the rim of the bowl, she looked over at him. "Or I *did* until you robbed me of that pleasure, along with my reputation and my job."

He slapped the frying pan over the burner. To hell with Mr. Nice Guy, he thought. Two could play this game as easily as one.

but he hadn't returned a one of her smiles, and had stubbornly ignored all of her attempts to draw him into conversation. He'd simply sat in the booth, one corner of his mouth dipped down in a scowl, and brooded. She hadn't known then who or what was responsible for his scowl, but she knew that the one he wore now was her fault.

Kayla had always believed that things, good or bad, happened for a reason. There was a purpose for Ry choosing the River's End to do his drinking. A reason for him ending up in her section. A reason for him wanting to give her money, and a reason for all the nightmarish publicity his gift had drawn.

She had no way of knowing why the events leading up to Ry bringing her to his family's ranch had taken place, but she had a feeling she knew why she and Ry were destined to meet. Kayla cared about people. Truly cared. She had an uncanny ability to sense their moods, their needs. More, she cared enough to try to help them.

Maybe that's why she was here, she realized slowly. Maybe God had sent her here to help Ry.

Squaring her shoulders, she straightened. And if that was the case, she was going to have to do better, try harder to get along with him, make an effort to show her gratitude for all that he was doing for her. She couldn't help him as long as she hung on to her resentment toward him.

She wasn't normally so disagreeable, so difficult to get along with. She was a happy person. Cheerful. Optimistic. It was this maddening situation that had put her out of sorts.

But she was changing her attitude, her disposition, starting right now.

And, in the process, hopefully she could change his.

"Well, there's no one to bother you here," he told her, "and there's plenty of room to run." He adjusted the flame beneath the pan, then added, "Although you might want to carry a gun. We've had trouble with coyotes in the past." He glanced over his shoulder and gave her a slow look up and down, then turned back to the stove and began laying thick strips of bacon in the pan. "But I'm sure they won't bother you. One look at that sour face of yours and any varmint with a half a brain will turn tail and run."

Thus began their first day together as roommates— or housemates, as Ry preferred to think of them. Seasoning the food they prepared with their resentment and animosity and serving it up to the cowboys with sugar-coated barbs they zinged back and forth at each other from opposite ends of the table.

Though he was an active participant in the verbal war, Ry secretly hoped the tension between them would eventually ease. Not that he particularly cared about establishing a friendship with the woman.

It was just a nuisance having a sourpuss around all the time.

After breakfast, they both worked in tight-lipped silence, with Ry helping Kayla clear the table and load the dishwasher, then drying the pots and pans she washed.

His duties finished, he spread the damp dish towel over the drainer to dry. "I'll be out on the ranch all morning, working with the hands."

She lifted an indifferent shoulder. "Whatever."

He crossed to the door and retrieved his coat from the rack and slipped his cell phone into the pocket. "I'll call the local grocery in town and place an order.

They usually make their deliveries before noon. I'll tell them to leave the bags on the back porch.''

She gave the dishcloth an angry twist, wringing the water from it. "I suppose that means I'm to be a prisoner here, if you won't even let me go into town to pick up the groceries."

"I won't let you go into town, because you might be recognized. As to being a prisoner, you don't have to stay inside the house. There are thousands of acres here for you to roam."

He plucked his hat from the rack and rammed it down over his head. "Feel free to use the computer in the office. The Internet connections and passwords are saved. All you have to do to get online is click an icon."

Since his statement didn't require a response, she didn't bother to offer one, but snatched the plug from the sink, wishing it were his hair, and drained the water from it.

"You're welcome."

She spun at his sarcastic remark, ready to lambaste him, but the slam of the door cut her off before she could utter the first word of rebuttal. She wanted to run after him, throw something at him, bang him over the head with the frying pan he'd dried.

Instead she dropped her chin to her chest and squeezed the bridge of her nose between her fingers, knowing she'd deserved the cutting remark. It wouldn't have hurt her to acknowledge his offer to let her use his computer, she told herself. And he was certainly due her thanks for his help in the kitchen. She was the one getting paid to cook and clean up after the cowboys. Not him. But rather than offer him the thanks he was due and acknowledge his gener-

osity, she'd let her temper overrule her good manners, which left her feeling small and petty, two traits she despised finding in other people.

Ashamed of her behavior and herself, she turned back to the sink to stare miserably out the window. As she did, Ry strode into her line of vision, headed for the barn. He walked with his shoulders stooped, his hands shoved deeply into his pockets. Something in the way he carried himself reminded her of the first time she'd seen him. Dropping an elbow to the edge of the sink, she rested her chin on her hand and watched him, letting herself remember that night.

The minute he'd walked into the bar, the other waitresses had stopped what they were doing to stare, later claiming that he had the tortured good looks o Antonio Banderas. But Kayla hadn't noticed h looks. At least, not at first. She'd been only aware his expression, the discontent that shadowed eye startling shade of blue. From the moment the hos had seated him in the rear booth in her section, s wanted to bundle him up and take him home her. Not to make him her sex slave, as the other resses had whispered that they'd like to do wit She'd wanted only to fix whatever it was th him, smooth away the glower lines that fann the corners of his eyes and mouth, chase a shadows that clouded his eyes.

When he'd shown up the second nigh quested a booth in her section, the other had given her a hard time, referring "Kayla's cowboy." Kayla hadn't minded ing. In fact, she'd kind of liked thinking "hers." During the hours he'd spent at t done everything within her power to c

* * *

Kayla connected to the Internet with a simple click on an icon, just as Ry had said. Within seconds of sitting down before his computer, she was downloading her e-mail.

She scrolled through the long list of messages, grumbling as she was forced to weed her way through spam that promised cheaper mortgage rates, larger penises, free admittance to porno sites. She'd just deleted a request from the widow of a foreign dignitary, who wanted to deposit millions of dollars in her bank account, if she'd just send the woman her account number, when she spotted a message from one of her professors. Excitement pumped through her, at the thought of being able to resume her studies.

After carefully reading her professor's instructions, she opened the file he'd attached to the e-mail and printed off the assignments he'd sent. With her books spread out on the desk before her, she scrubbed her hands together and dug in.

She had just finished the first assignment and was double-checking her work, before moving on to the next, when she heard a loud pounding. Frowning, she lifted her head and realized that the sound was coming from the back of the house.

Remembering the groceries Ry had told her he was having delivered, she jumped up and ran for the kitchen. She peeked out the window over the sink and saw a gray-haired woman standing on the porch, stooped beneath the weight of the grocery bags she held.

She wavered uncertainly, wringing her hands, wanting to help the woman, but remembering Ry's warning about the danger of Kayla being recognized. When the woman kicked a foot at the door, Kayla dropped her hands and ran to pull open the door.

"Here," she said, reaching to take one of the heavy bags. "Let me help you with that."

Scowling, the woman surrendered the bag, then clomped into the kitchen behind Kayla. She plopped her bag onto the counter and surprised Kayla, when she began pulling out items.

"Mary Garner," she said by way of introduction. "But most folks call me Maw. My grandsons usually make the deliveries." She rubbed a gnarled hand at the middle of her back. "Me having a bad back, and all. But when I heard Ry Tanner had placed an order for groceries, I had to see it for myself, 'fore I'd believe it was true." She pulled a gallon of milk from a sack and shoved it at Kayla. "Put that in the fridge before it starts to clabber," she ordered, then picked up two large cans of vegetables and headed for the pantry.

Eyeing the woman warily, Kayla did as she was instructed. "I'm sorry you missed seeing Ry. He's out working with the men."

The woman humphed. "Guess it's true, then. He's come back to stay." She wagged her head. "I can't believe that boy would have the nerve to show his face around here, after what he did. 'Course he was here for his daddy's funeral a few months back," she went on. "Saw him with my own eyes. But, then, who didn't see him? The whole dad-blamed town turned out for Buck's funeral, all of 'em wantin' to see the Tanner boys and what kind of men they'd become, as much as to show their respect for ol' Buck.

"But you expect a son to come home for his daddy's funeral. It's a child's responsibility to see that his parents receive a proper burial. But Ry comin' back to Tanner's Crossing to make his home here?" She snorted a breath. "Now, that takes some nerve."

Kayla stared, unsure what to say. "I don't know the Tanners very well," she said carefully. "Only Ry, and I haven't known him that long. I have met Woodrow and his wife Elizabeth, though."

"And didn't that Woodrow catch himself a fine one?" The woman slapped a thigh, chortling. "Who'd've ever thought Woodrow would marry, much less hitch himself to a doctor."

Kayla smiled weakly, again unsure what to say. "Elizabeth does seem awfully nice."

The woman looked at her askance. "Nice? Why, that woman is pure gold!" She tucked a roll of paper towels under her arm, scooped up bags of flour and sugar and held them against her ample bosom, as she waddled for the pantry again. "That girl set herself up in practice the minute she moved to town, filling a need that Tanner's Crossing has been suffering for a long time.

"Most doctors won't move to the smaller towns, once they finish their schooling. Think they can make more money in the big cities, I guess." She glanced over at Kayla and pursed her lips. "'Course you probably know all about that, since you and Ry are so close. I've seen the papers," she added, lifting a brow.

Kayla's cheeks burned in embarrassment. "I hope you don't believe everything you read, because nothing that was printed about me held a word of truth."

Maw lifted a doubtful brow. "You're here, aren't you?"

"Well, yes!" Kayla cried, then pushed her hands into fists at her sides, trying to get a hold on her temper. "But this isn't what it appears to be. The press was making my life a nightmare. Following me everywhere I went and shouting questions at me. And the phone calls," she continued, gulping back the tears that threatened. "People were calling night and day, pressuring me to let them invest my money. But the perverts were the worst." She shuddered, remembering. "Dirty old men, who wanted to be my sugar daddy."

The tears swelled higher, as every injustice she'd suffered wrapped itself around her chest and squeezed. "I had to quit my job, because I couldn't work for Pete anymore. Not after what he did. And I couldn't go to class, because the reporters followed me everywhere I went." She hiccuped a sob. "And all because Ry gave me that stupid check!"

Her face creased with concern, Maw bustled over to Kayla and looped an arm around her waist. "Now, now, sweetheart," she soothed, as she guided her to the table and eased her down onto a chair. "There's no need to get yourself all worked up like this. We all make mistakes from time to time."

"But don't you see?" Kayla cried in frustration. "I didn't do anything! I was a waitress, working my way through school, then along comes Ry and gives me that check. I didn't even know who he was! I thought he was just some lonely cowboy who needed a friend.

"And I didn't have an affair with him and ruin his marriage like everybody is saying I did," she added, furiously swiping at the tears. "He was drunk and I was afraid he'd fall and hurt himself, so I walked him back to his hotel room. And that's all I did!" she cried. "I swear, that's all. Then he leaves me that big check."

The woman pulled out a chair and sat down, then reached over and patted Kayla's hand. "Maybe you better start over from the beginning, sweetie," she suggested gently. "This is all so confusing, I'm having a hard time wrappin' my mind around all the facts."

Drawing in a deep breath, Kayla started over, filling the woman in on every detail that had led up to Ry leaving the check for her, then followed with everything that had happened to her since, including her reason for being at the ranch.

When she had finished, the woman sat back in her chair and folded her hands over her lap, shaking her head. "You poor thing. No wonder you're a bundle of nerves. I would be, too, if I'd been through all that."

Kayla dabbed at her eyes with the napkin Maw had shoved into her hand, while she was telling her story. She offered Maw a watery smile. "Thank you. It's nice to know someone believes me."

"Oh, I believe you, all right," Maw assured her. "I just don't know how you think that coming here is going to put an end to all the gossip."

Realizing that Maw could easily blow her cover by placing one call to the local newspaper, Kayla grabbed her hand. "Please promise that you won't tell anyone that I'm here. Please," she begged. "If the reporters find out, they'll hover like flies."

Maw pursed her lips and furrowed her brow, as if

a pledge of silence was a difficult one for her to make. "All right," she said reluctantly. "You have my word." She bent forward and looked Kayla square in the eyes. "But if Ry Tanner starts putting pressure on you to…" Her face reddening, she flopped back in the chair and fluttered a hand. "Well, you know what I mean." She narrowed an eye at Kayla. "But if he does, you just call me, and I'll come a runnin'. My husband and I use to raise cattle, and I still know what to do with a bull calf that tries puttin' his business where it don't belong."

Chapter 6

After Maw left, Kayla returned to the study and the
homework she'd abandoned. She knew that Ry was
going to be mad at her, when he found out that she
had answered the door and let Maw in, after he'd
specifically told her not to. But she refused to feel
guilty about what she'd done. She'd made a friend.
How she could feel guilty about that, when she was
virtually a prisoner in the house, with no one to talk
to but a bunch of men?

He'll just have to deal with it, she told herself, then
opened her book again and focused on her assignment.

Some time later, she heard the back door open and
the sound of heavy footsteps. She glanced down at
her watch and was horrified to see that it was almost
noon. Having totally forgotten about lunch, she rock-
eted from the chair and ran for the kitchen, where she
found Ry standing at the sink, washing his hands.

"I'm sorry," she said breathlessly, as she yanked open the refrigerator door. "I forgot the time."

"You haven't cooked anything for lunch? What the hell have you been doing all morning? The men will be here any minute!"

Kayla kept her head buried in the refrigerator and counted slowly backward from ten. When she was sure she could open her mouth without biting off his head, she said, "Talking to Maw Garner. But don't worry. I can throw together some sandwiches for y'all in nothing flat."

"Maw Garner was here?"

Ignoring the fury in his voice, she pulled a package of bologna from the meat drawer, then grabbed a loaf of bread and jar of mayonnaise. "Yes," she said, and headed for the island. "She's such a nice lady. She promised to come back and visit again soon."

Ry stalked her to the island. "Maw Garner's the biggest gossip in town!" he shouted, then slammed a fist down on the island, making Kayla jump. "I told you not to answer the door! That I'd arrange for the groceries to be left on the back porch. Why in the hell did you let her in?"

"I couldn't just leave that poor woman standing on the back porch holding those heavy sacks all day, now could I? Not with her bad back."

Groaning, he dragged his fist from the counter and hammered it against his forehead. "Now everybody in town will know that you're here."

"She won't tell anyone."

"How do you know she won't?"

"Because she promised she wouldn't, and she seems like a woman who keeps her promises."

"She's a gossip," he repeated.

"I happen to think she's nice. In fact, I enjoyed her visit and look forward to her seeing her again." She pulled slices of bread out of the bag and hid a smile, as she laid them out on the corner, unable to resist digging at him a little. "She said something, though, that I didn't understand."

"What?"

"She said that if you ever give me any trouble, I'm to call her, because she knows what to do with a bull calf that tries to put his business where it doesn't belong." She angled her head to look at him curiously. "What did she mean by that?"

He opened his mouth, let it hang there a minute, then snapped it closed. "Never mind," he growled and stomped from the room.

After watching the cowboys devour the two dozen sandwiches she'd thrown together for their lunch, then file out the back door looking as hungry as when they'd first walked in, Kayla knew that, in the future, she was going to have to put more thought and effort into the meals she prepared. She was no stranger to a kitchen, but cooking for a family of eight had in no way prepared her for cooking for four grown men. Even her brothers, whom she'd often accused of having hollow legs, couldn't hold a candle to the amount of food a working cowboy consumed in one sitting.

Determined to earn the money Ry was paying her, as well as satisfy the appetites of the men she was responsible for feeding, she spent the afternoon in the kitchen, preparing a seven-pound roast and peeling a five-pound bag of potatoes and two pounds of carrots.

The mindless chore of peeling vegetables allowed her time to think about ways to find out what was troubling Ry. She considered the obvious method of asking him outright, but quickly discarded that idea. Ry didn't strike her as the type who would willingly and openly share his emotions and feelings with a woman. What man would?

But there were ways to draw a man out, to poke and prod at the gray matter in his head, to massage his heart and find the soft spots inside.

She snorted a laugh.

Yeah, and if given a couple of years, she might actually come up with a way that would work.

By the time the cowboys trooped into the kitchen at six for their evening meal, Kayla was exhausted, but the kitchen was filled with mouthwatering aromas and the table piled high with food.

Best of all, she'd come up with a plan to get Ry to talk about himself, one which the cowboys—without their knowledge or prior consent—were going to help her implement.

After washing their hands at the sink, the cowboys hurried to the table and took their seats, hungrily eyeing the platters and bowls of food spread before them. With Ry taking the seat at the head of the table, Kayla sat down at the opposite end, which she considered the best position to keep a watchful eye on him.

She picked up the platter of roast beef and offered it to the man on her right, along with a smile. "You're Luke, right?"

Accepting the platter, he gave his chin a jerk. "Yes, ma'am. Luke Jordan."

She peered around Luke in order to see the man seated on his other side. "And you are—" She held up a hand. "No, don't tell me. It's on the tip of my

tongue." Wishing she'd paid closer attention when
Ry had made the brief introductions, she searched her
brain for the man's name. "It starts with an M," she
said, frowning. "Matthew—no," she said, shaking
her head, then cried, "Monty!"

Blushing, Monty accepted the platter Luke passed
to him. "Yessum. Short for Montgomery."

"Montgomery," she repeated, testing the sound of
his name. "I like that. Is it a family name?"

He raked a couple of slices of roast onto his plate,
his blush deepening. "No, ma'am. My granny had a
thing for Montgomery Clift. Made my mother name
me for him."

She laughed. "Well, whatever the reason. Montgomery is a beautiful name. Strong. Dignified. It suits
you perfectly."

His chest swelling a bit, Monty passed the platter
on to Ry. Kayla glanced toward her left at the third
cowboy. "And you're Slim," she said, then teased
him with a smile. "It's easy to remember your name,
because it fits you so well." She titled her head and
looked at him curiously. "How tall are you, anyway?"

"Six-six." He took the platter of meat Ry passed
to him and forked a thick slice onto his plate. "I was
the runt of the litter. All my brothers stand six-eight
or more."

"Oh, my," Kayla said, then laughed again. "I'll
bet your high school basketball coach loved having
y'all on his team."

"Oh, no, ma'am. My brothers and me didn't play
any basketball. No time for it. Our parents were farm-
ers and we had to work the fields."

Kayla's smile wilted a bit, as she was saddened at

the thought of Slim and his brothers missing out on what she considered an important part of growing up. Having fun. She quickly pushed her smile back into place and leaned to give his hand a pat. "Well, I'm sure you and your brothers would've all been stars, if you'd had the opportunity to play. You've certainly got the height for the sport."

"If you're through interviewing the men, would you mind passing the potatoes?"

Kayla glanced down at the end of the table to find Ry scowling at her. Wrinkling her nose at him, she picked up the bowl. "Sorry. Just trying to get to know the guys a little better." She passed the potatoes to Luke, then turned her attention to Ry. "How about you? Did you play any high school sports?"

He lifted a shoulder. "Some."

"Basketball?" she prodded helpfully.

He took the bowl Monty passed on to him. "Yes."

Getting the man to talk was like pulling teeth, but Kayla was determined. "What position?"

"Center or guard." He scooped a heaping spoonful of potatoes up and slapped it to his plate. "Depended on where they needed me."

"Football?"

"Yes."

"Position?" She held up a hand before he could answer. "You were the star quarterback."

He picked up his fork, one side of his mouth tightening in irritation. "My senior year."

Slim looked at Kayla in amazement. "How'd you know Ry was the quarterback?"

Her gaze on Ry, she smiled smugly. "A woman's intuition." Shifting her gaze to Luke, she asked, "What did you do before you became a ranch hand?"

Caught with his fork halfway to his mouth, Luke slowly lowered the utensil to his plate. "Nothin'. I've worked on ranches for as long as I can remember."

"What if you weren't a ranch hand, and you could work at any job you wanted, what would it be?"

He frowned a moment. "Well, when I was a kid, I wanted to be a vet. I s'pose I'd have to say that. I have a way with animals. Can usually tell just by lookin' what's ailin' 'em."

Kayla propped her chin on her hand, fascinated. "Really. Then why didn't you become a vet?"

Luke stole a glance at Slim, then dropped his gaze to his plate. Picking up his roll, he pinched off a chunk. "I don't have much book learnin'."

Kayla nudged the butter dish his way, thinking he'd want some on his roll. "But that's what school is for. You learn what you don't already know and how to apply what you do."

His gaze on his hands, he continued to pluck bits of bread from the roll. "I never cared much for school. All that readin' and such. What I know about animals was already inside my head. What wasn't, I learned by doin'." He shook his head. "I ain't never learned nothin' from no books."

By the time he'd finished his explanation, his roll was a pile of breadcrumbs on his plate. With nothing left to occupy his big, clumsy-looking hands, he curled his fingers against his palms and dragged them to his lap. "I guess I'm just dumb," he mumbled, "just like my teachers said."

Kayla reached over her and laid a hand on his arm. "No two people learn in the same manner," she said quietly. "Some people learn visually, by reading. Some are auditory learners, which means they learn best by hearing. Others, like you, by doing. Just because a person learns one way over another, doesn't mean he's dumb. It simply characterizes the method in which he best processes and retains information.''

When she noticed that his eyes had glazed over, she laughed and gave his arm a reassuring pat. ''I know that probably sounds like a bunch of mumbo-jumbo, but what I'm saying is, you aren't dumb. You just learn in a different way than someone who reads.''

''Oh,'' he said, his forehead smoothing.

''I'm audi—audi—'' Frowning, Monty looked at Kayla for help. ''What's the one you said that means you learn by hearing?''

''Auditory.''

''Yeah,'' Monty said, gesturing with his fork. ''I'm that. I can hear a song and sing it right back to you word for word. But give me the lyrics to read and, five minutes later, I can't remember the first dang line.''

Chuckling, Kayla looked at Slim. ''What about you, Slim? What method best typifies the way you learn?''

He lifted a shoulder. ''Hearing, I guess. Though I enjoy reading a good book, every now and then.''

''He likes writin' 'em, too,'' Monty threw in.

Slim half rose from his chair, his hands doubled into fists. ''Have you been pryin' in my bunk again?''

Hoping to distract the two before a fight broke out, Kayla quickly shifted the conversation to Ry. ''What about you, Ry? Which one are you?''

He slammed his fork down on his plate and glared at her. ''Is there a point to any of this?''

Kayla didn't flinch so much as a muscle at his angry outburst. ''Yes, there is. We're discovering things about each other that we didn't know before.'' She gestured at Luke. ''Take Luke, for example. If we hadn't had this discussion, I would've never known that he wanted to be a vet.'' Bracing her forearms on the table, she leaned forward and offered him an encouraging smile. ''But if you'd rather not discuss your learning method, then share something else with us. Tell us what you'd do with your life. If you were free to do anything you wanted to do, what would it be?''

Shoving back his chair, he threw his napkin down onto the table. ''I sure as hell wouldn't be sitting here, that's for damn sure.''

Ry grabbed a six-pack of beer from the refrigerator and headed straight for the barn, where he spent the next couple of hours shoveling out the feed room and chugging beer. It was colder than a well-digger's butt outside, but heat from the horses stalled in the barn kept the temperature inside at a bearable level.

But he'd have locked himself in a walk-in freezer rather than remain at the table with Kayla.

He didn't know what she'd been up to with all that touchy-feely dinner conversation, but he wasn't about to join in. He wasn't laying his life open on the table for all of the cowboys to gawk at and poke through like it was a cadaver. He was their boss, their leader. Or he was for a time, anyway. They didn't need to know his dreams, his aspirations. And they sure as hell didn't need to know his weaknesses. Revealing them would give the cowboys a certain power over him. Something to use as leverage against him, if the need ever arose.

And there was no way in hell he'd spill his guts to

Kayla. He'd already shared more about himself with
her than he had with any other woman, including his
ex-wife. His only excuse in having done so was that
he'd been drunk at the time and the liquor had loos-
ened his tongue.

Which was reason enough to never take another
drink.

He eyed the half-empty bottle of beer he held, then
turned it upside down, watching as the gold liquid
splattered onto the barn's hard-packed dirt floor.
Tossing the bottle aside, he picked up a fifty-pound
bag of oats and hefted it up to his shoulder.

No sense in taking any chances, he told himself, as
he strode for the first stall and the horses waiting on
their evening meal.

Drunk or sober, he wasn't baring his soul to her
ever again.

Ry groped blindly for the portable phone on his
night stand and dragged it to his ear. "Dr. Tanner,"
he mumbled into the receiver.

"Have you seen the Austin paper?"

Ry opened an eye to squint at the digital clock
beside his bed. Groaning, he slammed it shut. "For
God's sake, Ace. It's four-thirty in the morning. What
in the hell are you doing up reading the paper?"

"The baby's cutting teeth and Maggie sent me to
the all-night pharmacy for some of that teething gel.
I picked up a copy while I was there. Have you seen
it?"

Rolling to his back, Ry sighed wearily. "No, I
haven't seen the paper."

"Well, don't. It'll ruin your day."

Ry scowled. "If you don't want me to see it, then why in the hell did you call me and ask me if I had?"

"Because Kayla needs to call her mother."

"And how would you know that? Did her mother run an ad in the classifieds?"

"Funny. But, no. The reporters tracked her down. There's a story about it in the morning paper. The woman's distraught. Claims she hasn't talked to her daughter in five days and has no idea where she is."

Ry swore.

"My sentiments exactly."

Ry dragged himself up to a sitting position. "All right," he said wearily. "I'll tell Kayla to give her a call."

"Better do it quick. The woman looked pretty upset in the picture they printed of her."

Swearing again, Ry broke the connection, then swung his legs over the side of the bed. Muttering curses under his breath, he scooped his jeans from the floor, tugged them on, then palmed the portable phone and marched down the hall. Without bothering to knock, he threw open the door to Kayla's room and flipped on the overhead light. .

"Why the hell didn't you call your mother and tell her you were staying out here?" he shouted at her.

She moaned pitifully and dragged a pillow over her head. A split second later, she popped up, her eyes wide, her face as white as a sheet.

Ry wished he'd knocked first. The bright orange T-shirt she had on proved that Joey had earned the fifty bucks Ry had paid the kid to get information about Kayla. Unfortunately, now he was wondering if the spaced-out kid had earned his fifty, as well.

Did she really sleep without panties?

"My mother?" she asked, then gulped. "She called here?"

Scowling, Ry tossed the phone at the bed, where it landed beside her hip. A hip that, thankfully, was covered by a sheet. "No. Ace did. It seems some reporter tracked her down and interviewed her. Ace saw it in the morning paper."

She dropped her face to her hands. "Oh, no," she moaned.

"Why the hell didn't you call her?" he asked in frustration. "Didn't it occur to you that she would worry?"

She lifted her head and curled her fingers around the phone, as if she considering throwing it at him.

"No, as a matter of fact, it didn't occur to me," she shot back at him. "I talk to my mother once a week. On Sunday. I'd planned to tell her then."

"Don't wait until Sunday." He flung out a hand, indicating the phone. "Call her now. Ace said she looked upset in the picture they printed of her."

"Picture?" she repeated, then fell back against the headboard with a groan. "That means they went to my hometown. Were probably even in our house."

That she was more upset about the reporters visiting her family's home than she was about Ace calling him at the butt crack of dawn and awakening him irritated the hell of him. "So what's the big deal, if they did?"

She jackknifed to a sitting position. "I'll tell you what the big deal is," she said furiously. "I don't want reporters stalking my mother or my sisters and brothers like they have me and turning their lives into a living nightmare. You might not care about your family or what happens to them, but I happen to love mine, and I don't want them hurt.''

Ry's stomach did a slow nauseating flip at the mention of his family. He'd never considered how the publicity might affect his brothers, obviously hadn't cared enough about them to worry about protecting them. No, dammit, he thought angrily, he'd all but hand-delivered trouble and dumped it right on their doorstep.

Disgusted with himself and the whole damn mess, he turned away. "Call her," he snapped. "Let her know you're safe."

Safe?

Why had he told Kayla to tell her mother that she was safe? Ry asked himself later that day, as he stopped the tractor and released the lever to lower the round bale of hay to the ground. He didn't know if Kayla was safe or not. Based on the call he'd received from Ace that morning, it didn't appear the press had backed off any, which made him wonder if his decision to bring her to the ranch had been the wrong one to make. For him, it was the perfect hideout. They wouldn't think of looking for him there, as no one in Austin knew of his connection to the Tanners of Tanner's Crossing. He'd cut his ties to his family at eighteen and had never once looked back. He'd thought, with its remote location and gated entry, the ranch would be the perfect hideout for Kayla, too.

Was it her welfare you were worried about? Or your own?

He tensed at his conscience's prodding. Hers, he thought defensively. The press was giving her a hard time. By bringing her to the ranch, he was saving her from any more harassment. With both of them out of the limelight and unavailable for comment, he figured the press would eventually grow bored with the story and find something else to write about.

And hopefully never uncover the fact that you're Buck Tanner's son.

He scowled. That hadn't been his goal. A side benefit, maybe, yeah. But so what? He was taking care of her, wasn't he? He'd made arrangements for her to continue with school, had even given her a job.

Oh, yeah, you're Mr. Nice Guy, all right. You set her up for Internet classes, which you said yourself, she could have done just as easily. And you gave her a job, one in which she'll earn every penny you pay her and then some. Now be honest, Ry. Weren't you thinking that, by getting her to the ranch, you could nip this media frenzy in the bud before the reporters found out your relationship to Buck? Wasn't that just the tiniest bit selfish on your part?

Selfish? Him? Setting his jaw, he released the brake and drove on, dragging the heavy forks from beneath the bale of hay. There was no way he could be selfish. Not when the old man had kept all the selfish genes for himself. Unlike his father, Ry had always tried to be fair in his dealings with other people, gave generously to a hundred or more charities. Even tossed bills into the hats of every beggar and homeless person he passed on the street corners between his office and the hospital.

Every check you wrote to a charity was a tax deduction and the money you tossed was nothing but a salve for your guilty conscience. Remember the kid who dreamed of saving the world? The kid who wanted to make up for all the bad his father had done? Remember him, Ry?

Ry stomped on the brake and clapped his hands over his ears, trying to shut out the voice that had haunted him for months. Years, if he bothered to think about it. He didn't want to remember that kid. He didn't want to be reminded of the dreams and ambitions that had once guided his steps and fired his soul. He didn't want to think of his failures, his father. He just wanted…peace. Was that too much to ask? It wasn't as if he was asking for wealth or fame or power. He'd had all those things and they'd never given him the one thing he wanted most.

Peace.

Ry had forgotten how boring it was to drive a tractor. Back and forth to the barn, loading up round bales of hay, then hauling them out to the pastures. It gave him way too much time to think, and thinking did nothing but depress him. And, God knew, he was depressed enough.

Desperate for a distraction, he reached up to turn on the radio. He twirled the dial left and right, but picked up nothing but static. Grumbling under his breath, he gripped his hands firmly on the wheel and focused his gaze on the rutted path. What he needed, he told himself, was a good zone. His high school football coach had taught him about zoning, as Ry had always had trouble tuning out the crowd during a game. Listening to the jeers and cheers that came from the stands was suicide for a quarterback, as they distracted him from the game, broke his rhythm, sometimes even destroyed his confidence. Zoning was all about finding a focus and blanking the mind to everything but it.

Reminded of his coach and the year he'd played quarterback on his team, Ry sank back with a smile. He'd been the official stud on campus, with every girl in school chasing after him, wanting his letter jacket. It was amazing, but he hadn't thought about his high school years in…. Groaning, he closed his eyes, then opened them to slits to glare at the rutted path he followed. Since the night before when Kayla had pumped everyone at the table for information about themselves, he finished angrily. Gripping his hands more firmly on the wheel, he searched for that focus, the zone he needed to blank out thoughts of her.

But the only image that arose was one of a bright orange T-shirt, a longhorn emblazoned across its front.

In his mind, he saw Kayla as she had looked that morning, sitting up in bed, her hair mussed from sleep, and wearing nothing but the orange T-shirt.

Or, at least, he assumed that's all she'd been wearing.

"Damn," he swore under his breath, wishing to hell he'd never pumped those kids for information about her. If he'd left them alone, he wouldn't be sitting here now, wondering whether or not she wore panties to bed.

Or maybe he would.

He swallowed hard, recalling how she'd looked during those few seconds before she'd awakened. One hand buried beneath the pillow, the other resting on the pillow below her slightly parted lips. Her body curled in a long, lazy S beneath the covers. She'd looked so innocent lying there. So sexy.

Then she'd sat up and proved Joey to be an honest man. To Ry's shame—or credit, depending on how he chose to look at it—he had noticed the swell of her breasts beneath the longhorn logo, the nub of nipples evident beneath its thin fabric. He hadn't intended to, wouldn't have if he had it to do over again, but he'd dropped his gaze to her lap to see if she was wearing panties. He had the spaced-out kid to thank for making him aware that that was even a possibility. His glance had lasted no longer than the blink of an eye, but it hadn't satisfied his curiosity, as the sheet had covered the lower half of her body. If anything, it had left him even more curious.

And not just about what articles of clothing she did or didn't wear. Now he found himself wondering how she'd look without any clothes on at all. About the texture of her skin and how it would feel rubbing against his. What sounds she would make, as he stroked his hands over her flesh. Would she arch and purr with pleasure, as she had the night he'd watched her stretch her tired muscles at River's End? Or would she hiss and claw at him with need?

Muttering a curse, he smacked a hand against the side vent window, opening it. A rush of cold air swept inside the tractor's cab and hit his hot face like a bucket of ice cold water thrown on a fire. But it didn't come close to cooling the heat the thoughts of Kayla had generated.

He inhaled a long breath and released it. Inhaled another, held it for a beat, then slowly blew it out. Feeling a little more steady, more in control, he turned the tractor for the barn, vowing that, from that moment forward, he was staying away from Kayla and keeping his mind focused on finding the fastest way to get her off the ranch and back to Austin where she belonged.

Spotting Luke's horse up ahead, Ry sped up, wondering what Luke was doing out in this pasture. Luke and the other hands were supposed to be rounding up strays from the south pasture and bringing them in.

As he neared, he saw Luke kneeling beside a downed cow.

He pulled on the brake and hopped down. "What's the problem, Luke? Sick cow?"

Luke stood and dragged off his hat, using it to gesture at the downed cow. "Dead one. Found her a few minutes ago. Looks like she's been lying here a half a day or more."

"Coyote?"

Luke shook his head. "No. Gut shot."

"Gut shot?" Ry repeated and hunkered down to examine the cow himself. Dried blood caked an opening the size of a fifty-cent piece on the animal's right side and formed a dark pool on the ground beneath her rigid legs, where she'd bled out. Their family had lost cattle before from gunshots, but that was usually during hunting season, when a hunter would trespass on their land and mistake one of their cattle for a deer. Occasionally they'd lose one to some nutcase driving down the road, taking potshots at anything that moved.

Frowning, Ry looked around. "This pasture's a good mile and a half from the highway."

"Yeah," Luke agreed. "At least that."

"Anyone passing by, wouldn't be able to see her, much less hit her."

Luke shook his head. "No, I doubt they could."

Sighing, Ry stood, hitching his hands on his hips,

as he took another look around. "Have you checked for tracks?"

"Not yet."

Ry pulled off his hat and dragged his sleeve across his forehead, sickened by the waste, as much as he was angered that someone would purposely kill one of his family's prize cows. "Help me load her onto the back of the tractor, so I can haul her off, then take a look around and see what you can find. Okay?"

Luke snugged his hat over his head and nodded. "Sure thing, boss."

Chapter 7

Absorbed in the chapter she was reading in her statistics textbook, Kayla jumped at the unexpected chime of the doorbell. She glanced at her watch and was surprised to see that she'd been studying for over three hours. Standing, she moaned and lifted a foot that had gone to sleep, massaging it to get the blood flowing again.

The doorbell chimed a second time.

"All right, already," she grumbled and limped for the entry. "I heard you the first time."

She opened the door to find a woman standing on the porch and immediately wanted to hate her. The woman had that sleek, polished look that Kayla envied, but never quite managed to pull off. Her chin-length blond hair was styled in a bob that hugged her jawline and enhanced slashes of high cheekbone. Her makeup—all but invisible to the naked eye—was applied with a skill only mastered by spending hours in front of a mirror, something Kayla had never had time for. To make matters worse, she had on buff-colored suede pants—a fabric Kayla couldn't afford and a color she avoided because she knew she couldn't keep it clean—and a mink jacket she wore with a casualness most people reserved for denim. When the woman only stared, Kayla forced a smile and extended her hand, thinking a greeting of some kind was in order. "Hi. I'm Kayla."

The woman gave her a slow look up and down, making Kayla painfully aware of the bleach spot on the front of her sweatshirt and the hole in the toe of her left sock, then pushed her nose up in the air and breezed past her. "I know who you are."

Her hand still extended, Kayla stared after the woman, stunned by her rudeness.

Letting the mink slide down her arms, the woman turned a slow circle, looking around. "Where's Ry?"

Kayla set her jaw and gave the door a shove, closing it. "He isn't here."

The mink drifted to the floor, as the woman turned away to prowl. "Do you know when he'll return?"

Kayla was tempted to toss the woman out on her ear. But it wasn't her place to do so, she reminded herself. She was a guest in this house herself.

"No," she replied, then tipped her head and eyed the woman suspiciously. "You said that you know who I am, but I can't seem to place you. Have we met before?"

The woman glanced over her shoulder, then away, rolling her eyes. "I doubt we run in the same social circles."

And wouldn't, even if it were possible, Kayla

thought, bristling at the obvious snub. "Then perhaps you should tell me who you are."

Picking up a picture from the entry table, the woman studied it a moment, then glanced over at Kayla.

"Lana Tanner."

She put just enough inflection on each syllable of her name to make certain Kayla understood the connection. But she could have saved herself the trouble. The feline glint in the woman's eyes was enough to let Kayla know she'd just met Ry's ex.

"Really," Kayla said, and smiled sweetly. "I believe I met a friend of yours the other day." When Lana arched a doubtful brow, Kayla offered helpfully, "Adrian Tyson?"

"Ah, yes, Adrian." Smiling, she set the picture down and selected another. "I'm a big fan of her show," she said thoughtfully, as she studied the picture. "In fact, I particularly admired the interview she did with you at the bar where you work. It was clever of her to use me as a tool to get you to confess to having an affair with Ry."

Rage boiled up inside Kayla, but before she could unleash it, Lana angled her head to look at her. "I think it only fair that I tell you that you aren't the first tramp Ry picked up at a bar."

Kayla curled her hands into fists at her sides. "Tramp?"

Setting down the picture, Lana made a tsking sound with her tongue. "Oh, dear. Now look what I've done. I've upset you." She turned up her hands. "But it couldn't be helped. It would've been cruel of me to allow you to continue making a fool of yourself, when I could spare you the disgrace."

It was all Kayla could do to keep herself from clawing at the woman's eyes. "And how am I supposedly making a fool of myself?"

"Why living here with Ry, of course, and having your adulterous activities reported in the newspaper every day."

Kayla set her teeth. "Not that I think it's any business of yours, but how could anything Ry and I do be considered adulterous, when the two of you are divorced?"

Crossing the hall, Lana fluttered a hand. "Oh, that. A lover's quarrel, nothing more." She peered inside the study, then drew back and gave Kayla a smug smile. "You are aware that he always comes back to me, aren't you? He will this time, too."

While Kayla fumed, too angry to think of a civil thing to say in response, Lana glanced at her wristwatch. "Do you think Ry will be much longer?"

Kayla swallowed back the rage that threatened to choke her. "I haven't a clue. If you want to leave him a message, I'll see that he gets it."

Lana turned for the living room. "That won't be necessary. I'll wait."

Kayla stalked after her, mortally afraid that she'd murder the woman if Lana remained in the house one more minute. "But it may be hours before he gets back."

Lana scooped a magazine from the coffee table and sank down onto an overstuffed chair. "In that case," she said, as she crossed one graceful leg over the other, "I'd like something to drink. Orange juice over ice, if you have it." She opened the magazine, then glanced up, arching a neatly plucked brow, when she saw that Kayla hadn't moved. "Is there a problem?"

Yeah, Kayla thought furiously. *You.*

She forced a tight smile. "No. No problem, at all. Would you like anything else?"

Lana fluttered a hand in dismissal. "That'll be all for now."

Kayla turned, struggling to keep her steps slow and her temper under control, as she left the room. But by the time she reached the kitchen, she was stomping and her blood was boiling. She jerked a carton of orange juice from the refrigerator, slammed it down on the counter, then snatched a glass from the cabinet and dumped a handful of ice into it. As she sloshed juice over the ice, the back door opened and Ry walked in.

"Here," she snapped and thrust the glass at him. "*You* can wait on your guest. I'm paid to cook, not serve as your dang butler."

Ry glanced her way, frowning, as he hooked his hat on the rack. "What guest?"

"Your *ex.* She's in the living room."

He dropped his head back. "Oh, God," he groaned. "What next?"

Kayla pushed the glass against his hand and forced his fingers around it. "Why don't you ask her? She seems to know everything else."

As she spun away, he caught her wrist and whipped her back around.

"What the hell is that supposed to mean?"

"It *means*," she returned angrily, "that she told me all about your mistresses."

His fingers tightened on her wrist, cutting painfully into her skin. "Mistresses? Is that the excuse she gave for divorcing me?"

Before she could respond, he gave her wrist a jerk

that brought her up hard against him, his nose inches from her own.

"I never once cheated on my wife," he said through clenched teeth, "and she damn well knows it. But if you want to believe her pack of lies, you go right ahead. It makes no difference to me one way or the other. But if you're as smart as I think you are, you might want to ask yourself why she'd make it a point to tell you that I had."

With a force that sent her stumbling back a step, he shoved her away from him and strode from the room.

"What do you want, Lana?"

Lana glanced up from the magazine she was reading, then laid it aside, hiding a smile. "Now, Ry, really," she scolded. "Is that any way to greet your wife?"

"*Ex*-wife," he reminded her.

Smiling, she stood and folded an arm across her waist, fingering the diamond that hung from her neck. "It's good to see you, Ry."

"Too bad I can't say the same."

He saw the quick flash of temper in her eyes, before she dropped her gaze, concealing it. She trailed a finger along the velvet cording on the chair's arm. "I see that you're still mad at me."

Her voice had enough regret in it for him to know that it was all an act. Lana had never regretted anything in her life.

"Mad?" He snorted a breath. "I hate to disappoint you, but I feel nothing for you, at all."

She snapped up her head and this time there was no questioning the temper that flared in her eyes.

"What do you want, Lana?" he asked impatiently. "And don't tell me you're here because you miss me. I know you too well to believe that."

"Miss you?" She dropped her head back and laughed. But when she lowered her chin to meet his gaze again, there was no humor in her eyes. Only venom. "Hardly. I've come to claim what's mine."

"I can only assume you mean money. If that's the case, you've wasted your time. The divorce decree specified the amount of alimony I'm to pay you, and you won't get a penny more from me than what is legally required."

"Oh, really?" She turned, holding her gaze on his until the last moment, then began to slowly circle the room. "I wouldn't be so sure about that, if I were you."

A sick sense of dread gripped him as he watched her brush a finger over the canvas of a priceless oil painting, then run the tip of a manicured nail over the lip of the cut-crystal candy dish below it.

She picked up the dish to examine it more closely, as if appraising it and placing a value on it. "You know," she said thoughtfully, "I had no idea you're family had such lovely things."

The dish was his mother's, a treasured gift that her own mother had given to her on her wedding day. Seeing it in Lana's hands filled Ry with a blinding rage.

"Get out," he said through clenched teeth. "And if you ever dare set foot on this land again, I'll have you arrested for trespassing."

"Now, Ry," she scolded. "You know you can't

do that. Not when I have a legal claim on your family's little empire.''

''Like hell you do!'' he roared. ''Now get out, before I throw you out.''

Kayla sat in the rocking chair in her bedroom, rubbing thoughtfully at her wrist. The red welt Ry had left there was already beginning to fade.

He hadn't intended to hurt her. She knew that. He wasn't a cruel man. He had a temper, yes, but he wasn't cruel. She couldn't imagine him ever intentionally hurting anyone. Not physically, anyway.

But his ex-wife was both cruel and vindictive, a lethal combination when possessed by a jealous woman.

Kayla planted a foot on the floor, stilling the rocker. Jealous? Lana? Of whom?

…if you're as smart as I think you are, you might want to ask yourself why she'd want you to believe that I had.

Remembering Ry's warning, she slowly pushed a toe against the floor and set the rocker into motion again, mulling over the possibility.

It was feasible she supposed, though she couldn't imagine why Lana would be jealous of her. Did the woman not have a mirror? Lana was everything Kayla wasn't. Beautiful. Poised. Polished.

The only explanation she could come up with for Lana telling her that Ry had had mistresses was that she wanted Kayla to dislike Ry or, at the very least, distrust him. What woman, in her right mind, would trust a man who'd had one affair, much less multiples? But, if that was the case, that meant Lana considered Kayla a threat.

She snorted a laugh at the very idea. Her a threat? If the woman only knew! Ry couldn't wait to get Kayla out of his house and out of his hair!

But for some reason, knowing that saddened Kayla. She wasn't all that bad, she thought defensively. Not normally, anyway. Granted, she'd been a little difficult to get along with lately. But she'd already vowed to change her ways, improve her mood. She felt she was even making headway in that direction.

And it wasn't as if Ry were any prize. He was sullen and moody and stubborn.

And mouthwateringly handsome.

Okay, she admitted reluctantly. So he had a pretty face and a to-die-for body. So what? There were plenty of men around who were equally blessed.

So why are you so attracted to this one?

She shot up from the chair. She wasn't attracted to him! She wasn't attracted to any man. Wouldn't allow herself to be. She wanted her degree, for God's sake! A man would clutter up her life, make demands on her time and distract her from her goals. Her family needed her. Depended on her. She couldn't let them down.

The sound of shattering glass scattered her thoughts and had her spinning to stare at the door. Had Lana and Ry's argument turned physical? she wondered. Earlier she'd heard them yelling at each other, but she'd tried her best to tune out their voices.

Concerned that someone could be hurt, she ran for the door.

She skidded to a stop, just shy of it, turned two circles, then wrung her hands.

"It's none of your business," she told herself. "Even the police are hesitant to respond to domestic disputes."

But someone could be hurt, her conscience argued.

She jumped at the sound of a door slamming, craned her neck, listening, until she heard the rev of an engine. Knowing by the sound that it was Lana's car leaving and not Ry's Navigator, she wrenched open the door and ran down the hall. She slid to a stop two feet from the living room doorway.

It's none of your business, she told herself again.

But Ry could be hurt! Bleeding! How will you ever be able live with yourself, if he dies and there was something you could have done to save his life?

And what if he's not hurt? she demanded of her conscience. Then he'll think I'm a nosy busybody and be mad at me for interfering.

He's always mad. At least this time he'll have a good reason.

"Now there's a comforting thought," she muttered under her breath.

Gathering her courage, she tiptoed to the doorway and peered into the living room. Ry sat on the sofa with his elbows braced on his knees, his head in his hands. As far as she could see, there wasn't any sign of blood.

Still...

"Ry?" she called hesitantly. "Are you okay?"

"Yeah."

She took a step into the room. "I heard a loud crash," she said, feeling she needed to explain her concern. "I was afraid that...well, I was afraid you might be hurt or something."

He lifted his head to look at her, then sagged wearily back in the chair. "No. I'm fine." He gestured at the shards of glass scattered across the floor in front of the fireplace. ''Unfortunately I can't say the same for my mother's crystal bowl.''

Wincing, Kayla crossed the room and knelt down to pick up the pieces of what had once been the beautiful crystal bowl filled with potpourri she remembered seeing on the drop-leaf table. ''Man, that woman's got a mean temper,'' she murmured.

''One of her more endearing traits.''

She glanced over to find him staring at the broken glass, though she had a feeling he wasn't seeing it. His eyes were unfocused, his expression dark.

''What was she so mad about?'' She quickly dropped her gaze and started picking up pieces of glass again. ''I'm sorry. That's none of my business.''

''I'm afraid she's going to make it yours.''

Kayla looked up at him in confusion. ''But I had nothing to do with whatever problems the two of you might have had. I didn't even know you when you were married.''

''True. But she's threatening to take me back to court and sue me for more alimony.''

Kayla paled, realizing how Lana—thanks to reporters like Adrian Tyson—could make her a part of the suit. ''Can she do that?''

''Hell, I don't know,'' he said in frustration. ''But my guess is she can.''

Kayla slowly sank back on her heels. ''But wasn't the amount of alimony the judge awarded spelled out in the original divorce decree?''

''Yes. But now she claims it isn't enough. She says if I can afford to give $30,000 away, then I can afford to pay her more.''

Kayla gulped, staring. ''This is all my fault.''

He shook his head. ''You did nothing wrong.''

"But if you hadn't given me the money, she wouldn't be demanding more from you."

"This isn't about that. It's my father's estate she's after."

"But I thought a spouse's inheritances were protected by law?"

"They are."

"Then you have nothing to worry about, right?"

Frowning, he shook his head. "I don't know. She accused me of hiding assets from her, claiming I did it so that I wouldn't have to give her the half the State requires in a divorce."

"Did you?"

He burned her with a look.

"Sorry," she murmured, then frowned and shook her head. "But why would she question the settlement now? Why not before the divorce was final?"

"It didn't occur to her to question her cut, until she heard the old man had died."

"Your father?"

"Yeah," he said wryly, "though he never deserved the title."

His frown deepening, he pushed up from the chair and crossed to the window, stuffing his hands into his pockets, as he stared out.

"Lana didn't know that your father had passed away?" she asked.

"No. He died a couple of weeks before the divorce was final."

"And you didn't tell her about his death?"

"Why would I? It wasn't as if they had any kind of relationship. She'd never even met him. As far as she was concerned, he didn't exist."

Kayla shook her head in confusion. "I'm sorry, but

I don't understand. You were married for, what, ten years or more? And you never once brought your wife home to meet your family?''

''Nine years and, no, I never brought her here. I don't even know how she found the place. I certainly didn't give her directions.''

''But why didn't you want her to meet your family? I mean, family is family. Even if you had your differences, you can't deny their existence, your birth.''

''If you'd known my father, you wouldn't say that.''

When she started to question him further, he held up a hand. ''Just drop it, okay? I don't want to talk about this anymore.''

Kayla stared after him, as he strode from the room. But his refusal to let her voice her questions, didn't stop them from circling through her mind, seeking answers of their own.

Why would a man cut himself off from his family? Deny his own father? What could possibly have happened that would keep a man from bringing his wife home to meet his family?

And if Ry had truly hated his father, what was he doing here at the ranch, when he could easily afford to go any place in the world?

And why had he brought Kayla here to hide, as well?

As the questions built in her mind, the span of her curiosity increased, drawing other questions for her to ponder.

What had happened to destroy Ry's marriage? Had he really cheated on his wife? Adrian Tyson, the she-devil interviewer, had told Kayla that Lana was the one who had asked for the divorce and had intimated that there was another woman.

Catching her lower lip between her teeth, Kayla worried it, as she considered the possibility of Ry having had an affair—or affairs. The potential was definitely there. As a plastic surgeon, the majority of his patients would more than likely have been women. He was a wealthy man. Handsome. Successful. There were probably hundreds of women who wouldn't think twice about trying to steal him away from his wife.

By his own admission, he was lonely, a detail about his life he'd shared with Kayla the night she'd walked him back to his hotel. A lonely man was easy prey for a woman on the prowl. Kayla had seen evidence enough in the bar where she'd worked to know that was true.

But was Ry the kind of man who would cheat on his wife?

She mulled over the possibility for a good five minutes, before finally throwing up her hands in disgust. How would she know what kind of man he was? she asked herself in frustration. She'd only known him for a couple of weeks.

But she had time to get to know him better, she reminded herself. She didn't know how much longer she would have to stay at the ranch, but she'd take advantage of what time remained. She wanted to find out what had happened that had destroyed his relationship with his family. And it would be interesting, too, to discover why he'd quit practicing medicine. Kayla still found it hard to believe that anyone would willingly quit practicing medicine.

But, for whatever reason, Ry had.

And she intended to find out why.

Chapter 8

Kayla glanced out the kitchen window, as she gathered her hair up into a ponytail. It was still dark out, but the sun pushed at the horizon, striping the sky with muted bands of pinks and lavenders, a sign that it would be light soon. Slipping the elastic band from around her wrist, she wound it twice around the rope of hair she held, released it with a pop, then bent over and touched her fingers to the floor, stretching and warming her muscles in preparation for her morning run.

"You can't go out today. It's not safe."

She straightened to find Ry had entered the kitchen and stood beside the coffeepot.

Biting back a smile, she flipped the hood of her sweat jacket up over her head. "Don't worry. I'll put on my meanest face, so the coyotes won't get me."

She reached for the doorknob, but he caught her elbow, stopping her.

"We lost a cow."

She huffed a breath. "Well, I didn't steal it. Now, if you don't mind." She gave her arm a tug. "I'd like to get my run in before I have to cook breakfast."

"The cow was shot. Luke found her the day before yesterday."

She stared, horrified at the thought of someone shooting a defenseless animal. "But why would someone kill one of your cows?"

He released her arm. "A hunter might have mistaken her for a deer. It's happened before."

She reached for the door, but he flattened a hand against it.

"Didn't you hear what I just said?" he said in frustration. "A cow was shot. It isn't safe for you to go outside."

She gave him an exasperated look. "I run on two legs, not four. I doubt a hunter would mistake me for a deer."

"And if it wasn't a hunter who killed that cow?"

She stared, the blood draining from her face. "Are you saying you don't think it was an accident?"

He dropped his hand from the door and turned away. "We found another one dead last night."

"Another one? But—" She stopped, swallowing back the fear that slicked her throat. "You don't believe these were random shootings, do you? You think someone intentionally killed those cows."

He poured himself a cup of coffee, avoiding her gaze. "I don't know that that's the case. I just think it would be better if you stayed inside the house until we find out what's going on."

She firmed her lips in a stubborn line. "I'm already

a prisoner on the ranch. I refuse to become a prisoner to the house, as well.''

"No one is holding you prisoner here."

She reached for the door. "In that case, I'm going for my run."

He slapped a hand against the door again. "What does it take to get through that thick skull of yours? I'm trying to keep you from getting hurt!"

"And I appreciate that," she said patiently. "But I'm not going to let fear rule my actions. If I did, I'd have to hide in a closet the rest of my life."

He glared at her for a full three seconds, then dropped his hand and stalked away. "Give me five minutes."

"For what?" she asked in frustration.

"To change. I'm going with you."

Dressed in sweats and a pair of worn Nikes, Ry jogged along at Kayla's side, trying his best to keep pace with her. She ran like a seasoned marathoner, her head up, her chest thrust out, her arms pumping like well-oiled pistons at her sides.

And she did it, while keeping up a constant stream of conversation.

He wanted to hate her, and probably could've worked up the energy required to do that, if she hadn't suddenly stopped alongside the path. He glanced back to find her bent over, stripping off her sweatpants, exposing a set of long, tanned legs and a pair of black nylon running shorts, cut up high on her thighs.

In the process of knotting the legs of the pants around her waist, she looked up and caught him staring at her.

"I was hot," she said, as if he had asked for an explanation.

He gulped, then pushed down his own pants and stepped out of them. "Now that you mention it, I am, too."

"What is *that?*"

Praying he hadn't inadvertently stripped off his shorts, along with his pants, he followed her gaze down and saw that she was staring at the pearl handle of the pistol he'd tucked into the waistband of his shorts. He settled the pistol more securely at his waist. "Better safe, than sorry."

"But what if it were to accidentally go off? You could shoot off your—your—" Her cheeks flaming, she curled her hand into fists at her sides. *"Privates."*

Amused by her embarrassment, he couldn't resist teasing her a little. "Are you worried that I'll ruin my ability to sexually perform?"

Scowling, she spun and jogged off, calling over her shoulder, "No, but that might be a solution to our problem."

He frowned after her, unable to make the connection. "How would that solve anything?"

She turned, jogging in place. "Without you having the necessary equipment, the press couldn't accuse us of having an affair any longer. You could even call a press conference to let them know about your loss." She arced a hand through the air. "I can see the headlines now. Former Surgeon Shoots Off His—"

"All right, already! I get your point."

She lifted a shoulder and turned, jogging on. "It was just a thought."

Scowling, he started after her. "If it's all the same to you, I'll keep what I was born with."

They ran in silence, with Ry falling farther and farther behind. When she made a turn for the ranch's entrance, he dug deep for the strength to catch up with her. "Where are you going?" he called in frustration.

She pulled an envelope from her pocket and waved it in the air, as she jogged in place, pressing the button to open the automatic gates. "Putting a letter out for the mailman to pick up. Won't take but a second."

When the gates swung open, she darted through, stuffed the letter into the mailbox, flipped up the flag and jogged back, before the gate closed.

Barely able to breathe, Ry stopped and bent over, holding up a hand to signal her to wait.

"Are you okay?" she asked.

He gulped, nodded. "Yeah. I'm fine. Just a little out of shape. Who's the letter for?"

"My mother."

Straightening, he pressed a hand against his chest and dragged in a breath. "I thought you talked to her on Sunday?"

"I did."

"Then why write? If you had something else to tell her, you could've just called her again."

"I didn't send her a letter. I sent her a check. I try to every week."

He looked at her in confusion. "You send your mother money?"

"Yes. To help out at home. Come on," she said and jogged off again. "If you stop now, you're going to get a cramp."

Stunned, he stared after her. She helped pay her family's bills? What was she? Some kind of saint? She lived in a hovel, worked long hours at a back-breaking, foot-burning job, plus was paying her way through college. And she sent money home to her mother?

The woman was either a saint or crazy.

Personally, he'd place his vote on crazy.

Her eyes burning from staring at a computer screen so long and her mouth feeling as if it were filled with cotton, Kayla pushed away from the desk and headed for the study door, ready for a tall glass of iced tea and a break from studying.

As she stepped out into the hallway, a commode flushed somewhere behind her. She glanced over her shoulder to frown in the direction of the powder room, wondering how Ry or one of the cowboys had managed to slip inside, without her hearing them.

But the man who stepped from the powder room and paused to fasten his belt buckle, definitely wasn't anyone she knew. She clapped a hand over her mouth, to stifle the scream that jumped to her throat, and backed away, thinking only of escape.

Something must have alerted the man to her presence, because he snapped up his head and met her gaze.

He shot her a grin. "You must be Kayla."

His grin didn't dispel her fear any. Didn't most rapists and murderers get some sick sense of pleasure out of stalking their victims? That he knew her name didn't lessen it, either. Who in the state *didn't* know her name, after all the publicity she'd received?

She took another step in retreat. "Who are you and what are you doing here? I didn't hear the doorbell."

He started toward her, his gait long and lazy. "That's because I didn't ring it."

She backed two more quick steps and thrust out a

hand to hold him off. "I'm not alone," she warned. "There are four men here."

"Really? And here I thought I beat the others to the draw." He stopped to peer into the office, then glanced her way. "So where are they?" Chuckling, he started toward her again. "I'll bet they're out in the kitchen."

She took another step in retreat and her back slammed against the closed kitchen door. Trapped, she flattened her palms against the wood panels. "If you so much as lay a hand on me, I'll scream bloody murder!"

He stopped and hitched his hands low on his hips. "Well, now that's downright insulting. I'll have you know, most women beg for my touch."

She gulped, praying that she could keep him talking until Ry or one of the men arrived at the house. "I—I'm not like most women. I—" The door she had her back plastered to opened. She shrieked at the loss of resistance, flailing her arms wildly to keep from pitching over backward. In spite of her efforts, she sat down hard on the floor.

Dazed, she looked up to find Woodrow standing over her. She slumped her shoulders in relief. "Oh, Woodrow," she said, accepting the hand he offered her. "Thank God you're here. That man," she said and aimed an accusing finger at the stranger, "broke into the house. He was going to—" she gulped, shuddered, then finished weakly, "molest me."

Woodrow glanced over at the stranger and frowned. "You didn't break the lock did you? We just had the old one replaced."

Kayla snapped her head around to stare at Woodrow in disbelief. "You're worried about a stupid lock, when I've just told you this man was going to molest me?''

Woodrow pushed out a hand. "Hell, he wasn't going to molest you. That's just the way he is. Thinks he's God's gift to women."

Kayla looked from Woodrow to the alleged molester, then back again. "You know him?"

"Well, yeah. That's Rory. My kid brother."

"Hey!" the man—Rory—interjected, looking insulted. "I'm no kid."

Woodrow gave him a slow perusal. "Can't prove it by me."

Flattening his lips, Rory marched forward to drill a finger into Woodrow's chest. "Step outside, big guy, and I'll show you who's a kid."

"It's good to see that things are back to normal around here."

Kayla whirled to find another stranger had entered the house. This one through the back door.

"Go to hell, Ace," Woodrow grumbled, then asked, "What the hell are you doing here, anyway? I thought you were going to North Dakota."

"I was in North Dakota. Ry called, so I caught a flight home."

Groaning, Kayla clutched her head between her hands. "Would someone *please* tell me what is going on?"

Woodrow looked at her curiously. "Didn't Ry tell you? He called a family meeting."

"Family?" she repeated dully, staring at the man who had arrived via the back door.

"Yeah," Woodrow said. "That's Ace, our oldest brother."

Kayla dropped her face to her hands. "Oh, God,"

she moaned in embarrassment. "I feel like such a fool."

A finger bumped her chin, forcing her face up, and she found herself looking into eyes the same unique shade of blue as Ry's. Only this set of eyes belonged to his brother, Rory, and were filled with warmth and laughter.

He caught her hands and held them out to her sides, looking her over. "You may be a fool, darlin', but damned if you aren't the prettiest fool I ever laid eyes on."

"Cut it out, Rory," Woodrow groused. "The woman already thinks you're a molester."

His gaze on hers, Rory drew her hands up to press a kiss against her knuckles. "Five minutes alone, and I'll not only prove to her I'm not, I'll have her begging for more."

Kayla was afraid that what Rory had said was true. Not that she would be begging him to touch her again. But she could certainly understand why he'd claimed that most women did. He was a good-lookin' man— and definitely a flirt, just as Woodrow had said—and such a tease that Kayla had found herself laughing along with the others, in spite of her embarrassment.

But no one was laughing now.

Sober as judges, they all filed into the study, where the family meeting was to take place. Ace took the chair behind the desk, while Woodrow and Rory seated themselves on the sofa. Whit, the last to arrive and a stepbrother, she'd learned, had driven from Oklahoma to make the meeting and stood by the door, away from the others, his back propped against the wall.

Kayla perched a hip on an arm of the sofa, ready to slip out at the first opportunity. She didn't know why Ry had insisted on her attending the meeting, anyway. She wasn't family.

Ry moved to the front of the room and turned to address those gathered.

"I think all of you are aware of the press Kayla and I have received recently, concerning our purported affair."

Though no one turned to look at her directly, Kayla felt as if she had been stripped naked and thrust center stage for Ry's brothers to all gawk at. It didn't matter that they already knew about the lies being spread about her. She was mortified at finding herself the topic of discussion in a room filled with males.

She rolled her shoulders forward, trying to make herself smaller—small enough to slide between the sofa cushions and hide.

But her humiliation wasn't over yet. Not by a long shot.

Snorting a breath, Ry gestured at her. "But I think it's pretty obvious why I'd never consider hooking up with a woman like her."

Kayla made a choking sound.

Rory reached over and patted her knee. "Tact has never been one of Ry's strong points."

Seething, she glared at Ry. "You can say that again," she muttered her under breath.

Ry continued on, unaware that Kayla was drilling holes through him with her eyes.

"Although Ace is the one who alerted me to the publicity my gift to Kayla drew, it never occurred to me that anyone other than Kayla and I would be affected by what was being printed about us." Firming his mouth, he shook his head. "But it appears I was wrong, as the reporters have tracked down Kayla's mother. I know that I agreed to stay here while Ace was gone, but I think it would be best if I packed up my bags and headed out."

"Why would you want to do that?" Ace asked.

"To protect you," Ry replied, as if stating the obvious. "The longer I stay, the more likely it is the press will discover my connection to y'all. Once they do, no telling what stories they'll start printing."

Rory glanced over at Woodrow. "You got anything to hide?"

Woodrow shook his head. "Nothin' that I can think of."

Rory looked back at Whit. "What about you? Any dead bodies buried under the dirt in your arena?"

Whit shook his head.

With a shrug, Rory looked back at Ry. "That just leaves Ace, but I doubt he'd mind seeing his name in print. In fact, his agent will probably thank you for getting him the free publicity."

Ry ground his teeth. "Dammit Rory. For once in your life, would you be serious? This is nothing to joke about."

"He wasn't joking," Ace said from behind Ry. "That was just his way of reminding you that you're a Tanner. Tanners stick together through thick and thin."

"Damn right, we do," Woodrow agreed.

Ry shook his head. "You might not feel that way when you hear the rest."

He then told them about Lana's visit and her threat to sue him for more alimony.

"If it were just me involved," he said, in summation. "I wouldn't be worried. I'd tell her to go ahead and sue, and I'd take my chances. But there's more at stake here than just me. Your heads are going to be on the line along with mine, as well as the Tanner name."

"How's that?" Woodrow asked in confusion. "We have no ties to your ex-wife."

"I think I know how," Ace said quietly, then shifted his gaze to Ry. "It's the stock each of us were given at birth that has you worried, isn't it?"

His expression glum, Ry nodded. "That's the only loose string out there that I can think of that she can hurt me with. To be honest, I'd forgotten all about it. You know how the old man was. Every time he'd get mad at one of us or we'd disagree with him over something, he'd threaten to take the stock away. Personally, I doubt he ever put any of it in our names, in the first place."

"But he promised Mom he would," Rory argued, then gestured at Ace. "Ace told me about it. He said that the old man promised her that every son she bore for him would receive a percentage of Tanner stock."

Dipping his chin, Ry gave Rory a pointed look. "Have you ever received a dividend check?"

Rory glanced around at his other brothers. "Well, no," he said, then shifted his gaze to frown at Ry. "Have you?"

"Not a penny. If the old man had put stock in our names, don't you think we would've earned at least one dividend over the years?"

His frown deepening, Rory slid his back farther down on the sofa and folded his arms across his chest. "Damn right, we would."

"Just because we haven't received a dividend,

doesn't mean there aren't stock certificates floating around with our names on them," Ace reminded them. "The Tanner holdings are all family-owned and controlled. And, as we all know, the old man was the one who held the controls."

"Which is what has me worried," Ry said. "The only way Lana can win a suit against me is by proving that I hid assets from her in our divorce settlement. That stock is something I never thought to declare.

"She's greedy. Now that she knows the old man is dead, she'll do everything within her power to try to get a piece of the pie. In order to do that, she'll have to request an audit." He shook his head. "I don't know about the rest of you, but the idea of a bunch of lawyers pouring over the Tanner family's financial records scares the hell out me."

"Amen to that," Woodrow agreed.

"So how do we keep that from happening?" Rory asked.

"I don't know that we can," Ry admitted. "I could try buying her off. Offer her a cash settlement of some kind."

Ace shook his head. "No. That would be the same as admitting guilt. Besides, it doesn't sound as if that would appease her for long. A month or so, and she'd be back, crying for more."

"Do you have a better idea?" Ry asked in frustration.

"I say, let it ride. She hasn't brought suit against you, yet. Maybe all this is nothing but a threat to see if she can squeeze more money out of you."

Ry considered a moment, then shook his head. "Maybe that's all it is. But there's been some trouble on the place that has me worried. We've lost a couple of cows.''

"Rustlers?" Rory asked.

"No. They were shot."

Ace looked at Ry doubtfully. "You're not suggesting that Lana had anything to do with their deaths, are you?"

"Hell, I don't know what to think any more. It just seems damn coincidental that two cows turn up dead around the same time she shows up, demanding a part of the old man's estate."

"Do you want us to us to help you guard the place?" Woodrow asked. "We could take turns pulling the night shift."

"No. The ranch hands and I have already set up a schedule." Ry blew out a breath. "Hell, maybe it is just a coincidence. Maybe those cows' deaths had nothing to do with Lana's threat."

"In case it does," Ace said, and stood, snugging on his hat, "I'll pay a visit to our lawyers and accountants, before I leave town, and have them double-up on their efforts to settle the old man's estate. Without leaving a will behind or any one set of books we can trust, the old man's left us one hell of a mess to untangle. One that seems to be getting messier by the day."

By the time the last of his brothers left, dusk was settling over the ranch. Ry headed for the barn, wanting time alone to think. He couldn't believe his brothers were actually going to stand with him on this. That they would even speak to him, after the way he'd treated them in the past, was no less than a miracle.

Tanners stick together through thick and thin.

Ace's reminder of the slogan that had shaped the brothers' boyhood had shamed Ry in a way that little else could. He didn't deserve his brothers' loyalty. He certainly hadn't given them his. At the first opportunity, he'd bailed out on them, putting as much distance between himself and his family as he could.

It didn't matter that he'd left to get away from the old man. In leaving, he'd turned his back on them all.

As he stepped inside the barn, he reached for the light switch and flipped it on.

"Hey!"

He jumped at the startled cry, then peered down the alleyway and saw Kayla sitting on a bale of hay, an arm bent in front of her face, to block the glare from the overhead lights.

"What are you doing sitting out here in the dark?"

She dropped her arm and scooted around on the bale, turning her back to him. "None of your business."

He switched off the light, intending to head back for the house. But his conscience wouldn't let him ignore the tears he heard in her voice.

"Are you crying?"

"No."

The watery sniff that followed her denial was a dead giveaway that she was. Scowling, he strode down the alleyway, knowing, if she was crying, it was probably his fault. Everything else seemed to be.

"Are you upset because I didn't tell you my brothers were coming over?"

She angled her body farther away from him. "No."

"You're not mad at Rory, are you?" Squinting his eyes against the darkness, he craned his neck to see her face. "He doesn't mean anything with all his flirting. That's just the way he is."

"I think Rory's nice."

"Well, what are you crying about, then?" he asked in frustration.

She whirled on the bale. "You, you imbecile!"

He drew back, surprised by her anger. "Me? What did I do?"

She held up her hands and bent two fingers on each, as if forming quotation marks. "'But I think it's pretty obvious why I'd never consider hooking up with a woman like her.'"

It took Ry a moment to realize that she was quoting him. "Now wait a minute. I didn't mean that as an insult toward you."

She folded her arms across her breasts and turned her face away. "It sounded like one to me. Even Rory thought so."

"Rory? Since when have you and Rory become such buddies?"

She snatched up her chin. "We haven't, but we could. He's a nice guy and seems like he'd be a lot of fun to be around."

"And that's to say I'm not?"

"You said it. Not me."

It was all Ry could do to keep from banging his head against the nearest wall. But he wasn't about to argue with her. Especially over something that could easily be misconstrued as jealousy.

"I wasn't talking about you as a person. I was referring to the difference in our ages."

She humphed. "You don't have to explain anything to me. I assure you, the thought of us having an affair is as distasteful to me as it obviously is to you.''

His male pride suffered a fatal blow. ''And what would be so awful about having an affair with me?''

She gave him a withering look. ''You really have to ask?''

''Well, yeah,'' he said indignantly.

Swinging her feet around, she lifted a hand. ''One,'' she said, tapping a finger, ''you're grouchy. Two,'' she said, and tapped a second finger, ''you're about as much fun as a cheap funeral.'' She tapped a third. ''Three, you have a serious drinking problem. Four…''

He held up a hand. ''Wait just a damn minute. I don't have a drinking problem. I rarely drink, much less get drunk.''

She lifted a brow. ''Oh, really? It seems as if I remember we met in bar. In fact, one night I had to practically carry you to your hotel room, because you were so drunk you could barely stand up.''

''I could've made it to my hotel room. I wasn't that drunk.''

''Most alcoholics have difficulty admitting they have a problem.''

When he opened his mouth to argue, she tapped a fourth finger, silencing him.

''And, four, you're an emotional cripple, which I don't have the time or energy to deal with.''

He clamped his lips together. ''And what is that supposed to mean?''

''That dealing with your violent mood swings is exhausting and time consuming.'' She gave him a grudging look up and down. ''It's a shame, too, since I find you physically attractive.'' She turned up her nose. "But earning a living and going to school is much more important to me than what few seconds of sexual gratification I might gain by having an affair with you."

If she'd waved a red flag in his face, she couldn't have riled Ry more. "Is that few seconds you referred to a subtotal or a total?"

She waved away his question. "Really, Ry. As if it matters."

"Oh, but it does." He caught her hand and pulled her to her feet. "You've questioned my virility, my manliness, yet you have nothing to base your allegations on. I think before you make a statement like that, you should know what you're talking about."

Her eyes rounding, Kayla tugged at her hand realizing his intent. "That isn't necessary. I'll take your word for it. I—"

Before she could say more, he had her up against his chest and his mouth on hers. She strained to get free, but he vised his arms around her, making it impossible for her to move. Pressed up against him, she couldn't breathe, couldn't think.

But, oh, man, could she feel. His chest was like a wall against her breasts, impenetrable, yet so warm and soft she yearned to burrow deep. And his mouth. At first bruising, he gradually softened the kiss, sweeping his lips across hers, nipping at them with his teeth, until she surrendered to him on a shuddery sigh. Whether he sensed her acceptance or simply pressed for an advantage at the first opening, she didn't know, but his tongue was in her mouth now, stirring up needs she had no business exploring.

And he'd succeeded in proving his point. She definitely wouldn't consider having an affair with him distasteful. Not on a satisfaction level, at any rate.

But she couldn't let on that he had proved anything. If she did, he'd stop kissing her and she'd somehow have to muster the strength to laugh in his face and say something catty like, "Is that the best you can do?" just to make him angry enough to assault her again.

And that's exactly what this was, she thought, as she tunneled her fingers up through his hair. An assault on her senses. The silky feel of his hair sliding through her hands. The beat of his heart like thunder against her breasts. The need she tasted in him, the heat that seeped from his body into hers. She'd never believed that each man held a unique scent, thought that was something dreamed up by some clever marketing director to push sales of men's fragrances. But she was a believer now. With each breath she drew, she filled herself with him. Sandalwood and leather, a pleasing scent that teased her senses and aroused her at the same time.

She knew she'd never smell the musky scent of a barn or hear the impatient shuffle of horses moving around in a stall, without thinking of Ry, without remembering this moment. The moist warmth of his breath against her skin. The desperate dig of his fingers against her back. The erotic dance of his tongue with hers.

Much too soon, she sensed him withdrawing, heard his low moan of regret, as he dragged his mouth from hers. And then she was looking up into eyes the color of a summer sky before a storm. Dark, penetrating, turbulent. Questioning.

But she had no explanation to offer for what had

just occurred, no words that would come close to describing his effect on her.

She knew only that, from this moment forward, she would never be the same.

She wondered if he would.

Chapter 9

Ry paced his room, his hair spiked high from his fingers' frustrated combing.

What had come over him? he asked himself for at least the hundredth time since leaving Kayla. He hadn't intended to kiss her. Knew from the start that the temptation to become physically involved with her was there. Had even vowed to do everything within his power to avoid it.

If that was the case, then why was he giving serious thought to marching down the hall, climbing into bed with her and kissing her until she was senseless and begging him to take her?

Because he was a masochist, that's why. Why else would he taunt temptation? Thumb his nose at good sense? Ask to have his heart ripped from his chest a second time?

He jerked to a stop, a cold sweat popping out on

his forehead. Wait a minute. His heart didn't have anything to do with this.

Suddenly light-headed, he sagged weakly to the edge of his bed and stared blankly at the narrow strip of darkness beneath his bedroom door. He wasn't falling in love with Kayla, he told himself. He was in lust. He wanted her body, nothing more. An outlet for the pent-up sexual frustration that knotted inside him. It had been months since he'd been with a woman. Years since he'd considered the act anything more than a form of release.

But that was because of his discontent, he told himself. It had affected every facet of his life, including his libido. He'd worried even at one point that he would become impotent. Hell, for all he knew, he was! He couldn't remember the last time he'd felt anything akin to sexual desire. And even then, it hadn't been anything like what he was experiencing now. He was hard as a rock and as restless as a stud who'd caught the scent of a mare in heat. He wanted Kayla. Wanted to hold her. Make love to her. Wanted to feel her heat, her moistness closed around his sex.

He shot his fingers through his hair and fisted them there, trying to squeeze out the images that stubbornly continued to build in his mind. He was crazy. He had to be. To even *think* of sleeping with Kayla was a mistake. Consummating their relationship would only give credence to the lies that had already been printed about them.

Or, worse, give the reporters more to write about.

Besides, he was older than her. Too old.

But not so old that he wasn't giving serious consideration to saying to hell with logic and heading for her room, where he hoped to find her naked, ready and willing.

He fell back on the bed and dragged a pillow over his face.

"You're not going anywhere near that woman," he told himself. "Your life's too screwed up to take a chance on screwing hers up, too."

Ry decided the only way to resist Kayla was to avoid her. He'd settled on the idea shortly after dawn. An uninspired solution to the problem he faced, but what man could think straight at that time of the morning? Especially one, who hadn't slept the night before.

He slipped out of the house early, skipping breakfast, and headed for town, on the lame excuse that he needed to buy oats for the horses. There were plenty of oats in the feed room to carry the horses through the remainder of the winter, but it was the best excuse he could come up with on such short notice.

He had a boot propped on the tailgate, watching the kid who worked the warehouse load the feed sacks into the back of the ranch truck, when he heard footsteps behind him. He glanced over his shoulder and bit back a groan, when he saw Phil Sharp headed his way.

The chip Phil wore on his shoulder was years old, dating back to their senior year in high school, when Ry had challenged Phil's position as quarterback of the football team and won, stripping Phil of the position he'd played for the previous two years. It was enough to piss off any cocky teenager, and have him looking for a fight.

Unfortunately Ry had added insult to injury by

stealing Phil's girl. Not that Ry had wanted Marilyn Roscoe. A blonde with more boobs than brains, Marilyn had slept her way through the starting lineup of every sport their school had played, collecting letter jackets along the way. The evening Ry was named as the new quarterback, Marilyn had dumped Phil, then driven to the ranch, determined to add Ry's letter jacket to her collection. Since, at the time, she'd been wearing a dress cut to her navel in front and to her ass in back, and had a case of cold beer iced down in the back seat of her car, Ry hadn't put up much of a fight.

And Phil had never forgiven him.

"Heard you was back in town."

Ry glanced over, as Phil stopped beside the truck. Phil had put on a good eighty pounds, since Ry had last seen him, which he wore around his middle, like a spare tire. His rummy, bloodshot eyes, told Ry that Phil had continued with the drinking he'd started as a teenager.

Ry dragged his boot from the bumper. "For a while, anyway."

Phil folded his arms along the side of the truck and looked over at the sacks of oats stacked on the bed. "Thought Ace was running your daddy's place?"

"He was. Now I am."

Phil rolled the toothpick that hung from the corner of his mouth to clamp it between his teeth. With his teeth bared, he looked like a Rottweiler who'd hit the end of his chain. Ry figured that was pretty close to the truth.

"Thought you was a big time doctor in Austin?"

"*Was* being the operative word," Ry replied, but couldn't resist adding, "though grammatically incor-

rect. I sold my practice a couple of months ago. What
are you doing now?''

Phil swelled his chest and gave his jeans a swag-
gering hitch, without a chance in hell of getting get
those 34s over his 38-inch gut.

''Ranching. Got me a place about twenty miles
north of town.''

''So you're a rancher, huh?'' It wasn't much in the
way of conversation, but it was the best Ry could do,
considering he had little to say to the man, and cared
less about trying.

The kid shoved a clipboard and pen in front of Ry's
face, giving Ry the excuse he needed to avoid further
conversation. He scrawled his name across the bottom, then tore off his copy and slipped it into his
pocket. Lifting the tailgate, he locked it into position.

''Guess I'd better be going,'' he said to Phil, as he
strode past him, ''or the hands are liable to have a
posse out looking for me.''

''Why's that? They worried you'll run away
again?''

Ry froze, then curled his hands into fists and slowly
turned. ''I didn't run twenty years ago, and I'm not
running now. If you've got a beef with me, bring it
on. I've been primed for a fight all morning.''

Phil darted a glance over his shoulder, as if expecting to find a buddy behind him.

''Nobody's got your back this time,'' Ry told him.
''It's just you and me here.''

With a growl, Phil bowed his head and charged.
His right shoulder caught Ry just below his ribs and
sent him hurtling back against the tailgate, knocking
his teeth together and the breath from his lungs. While
he staggered, trying to stay on his feet, a fist whizzed

past his ear, grazing the side of his head. Before Phil could swing again, Ry led with a right, striking a blow on Phil's cheek, then followed quickly with a left that caught Phil beneath his chin and sent his head snapping back and blood spewing.

The fight was on.

Kayla was a lot of things, but she was no coward. When faced with a problem, she believed in meeting it head-on, preferring to deal with issues as they cropped up, rather than avoid them and let them grow into something larger. But if and when things came to a fight, she believed in fighting fair and rarely gave in to the urge to hit below the belt.

Which explained why she was currently riddled by guilt and had been for two days. Name-calling, in her mind, was the worst form of fighting dirty.

Ry wasn't an alcoholic. She knew that. The drinking he'd done at the River's End he'd done out of desperation, not out of an uncontrollable need for liquor. She'd only accused him of being an alcoholic because she'd wanted to get even with him. To hurt him, as much as he'd hurt her.

The remark about him being an emotional cripple, she'd made for the same reason, although she hadn't considered it an exaggeration. Ry *was* an emotional cripple. But, whether he was or not, didn't matter. It was still name-calling, which she seldom stooped to do. On those rare occasions when she did sink that low, she always felt guilty afterward and was quick to make amends.

But apologizing to a phantom was impossible. And that's exactly what Ry had become. She hadn't laid eyes on the man in two days. She knew, by the evi-

dence he left behind, that he hadn't returned to Austin
and left her at the ranch alone, as she'd first feared.
A pile of dirty clothes mysteriously appearing in the
laundry room. A used glass found turned upside down
in the sink. His hat missing from those hanging on
the hook by the back door, then reappearing, only to
disappear again.

He was decent enough to send messages to the
house along with the men, informing her that one task
or another would keep him from coming in for the
noon or evening meal.

But the man himself remained stubbornly invisible.

And that irritated Kayla. When she had an apology
to deliver, she wanted it said, so that she could put it
behind her, along with the guilt.

But Ry wasn't cooperating, at all, which frustrated
her all the more.

She had a feeling she knew why he was avoiding
her. It was that kiss they'd shared in the barn. But
what did he take her for? One of those silly women
who thought a kiss was the same as a marriage pro-
posal? No way. Especially not when the kiss was only
used to prove a point. She didn't expect anything
from Ry. Not even another kiss.

But that didn't mean that she was going to let him
continue avoiding her. She had an apology to offer
and, by golly, she was going to deliver it and free
herself of the guilt that was distracting her from her
studies.

With that in mind, after putting dinner on the table
for the cowboys, she tugged on a jacket and went to
the barn, knowing that Ry was there grooming the
horses.

Or so the cowboys had told her. Personally, she

figured he was hiding underneath a rock somewhere, like the snake he was.

But—surprise, surprise—he really was in the barn. She found him in one of the stalls, currying a tall black horse, who didn't appear too happy about having the burrs combed from his mane.

She walked up to the stall and lifted a hand to rub the horse's nose. "What's his name?"

Ry angled his back to her, stubbornly refusing to look at her. "Midnight."

Pursing her lips in irritation, she resumed her rubbing, but wrinkled her nose, when the horse rolled back his lips and showed his teeth. "Yuck. When was the last time you saw a dentist?"

The horse tossed back his head and nickered. "Okay, okay," she groused, snatching back her hand. "It's not like I was going to call and make you an appointment. If you want your teeth to rot out of your mouth, that's your business, not mine."

"His ears."

Kayla glanced over at Ry. "What?"

With his back still to her, he tossed down the curry comb and picked up a brush. "He likes to have his ears scratched."

"Oh." Lifting a cautious hand, she scratched the animal between his ears. He nuzzled his nose against the underside of her arm, as if to let her know he'd forgiven her for the catty remark about his teeth.

Which reminded her that she had an apology to offer.

"I'm sorry I called you an alcoholic the other night."

"I know that I'm not. That's enough for me."

"I really don't think you have a drinking problem."

"Then why make the accusation?"

She lifted a shoulder. "An eye-for-an-eye. You know. You hurt my feelings, so I hurt yours."

He snorted and went back to his grooming.

"I'm sorry, too, for calling you an emotional cripple."

He stilled, as if waiting for her to tell him that she didn't believe he was that, either. But Kayla wouldn't lie. He *was* emotionally crippled. She just didn't know if it was a terminal case or one that he would heal from in time.

When she remained stubbornly silent, he began to brush again, his movements short, jerky sweeps over the horse's back.

"If you'd like to talk about it," she offered, "I'll be glad to listen."

"Talk about what?"

"Whatever it is that's bothering you."

"Who said anything was bothering me?"

"No one had to. It's obvious. I noticed it the first night you walked into the River's End."

He tossed the brush into the tack box, then fished out a hoof pick. With his back still to her, he stooped to lift the horse's rear leg and braced it between his knees, as he chipped clumps of mud and pebbles from the hoof. "If I ever feel the need to be psychoanalyzed, I'll call a professional."

"Oh, for heaven's sake," she muttered and shoved open the stall door. "Would you quit acting like a jerk? I'm only trying to help you. To be your friend."

"I don't need a friend."

"I think you do."

"And what makes you think you know my needs better than I do? Are you clairvoyant? A mind reader? Or is this some kind of God complex you suffer from?"

"None of the above. I have eyes, and I can see when a person is hurting."

"Hurting?" He dropped the horse's leg and threw the pick into the tack box so hard it knocked the container over on its side. "I'm not hurting. I'm dying."

She stiffened, panicked for a moment that this was a confession, that he was suffering from some terminal disease. But she knew by the rigid set of his shoulders, the hands he'd curled into fists at his side that he wasn't dying. Not literally. But he was definitely suffering. Whatever it was that was eating at him had him in a death grip.

She crossed to him and laid a hand on his back. "Ry...talk to me. Tell me what's wrong."

She felt the muscles in his back tense beneath her palm.

"I can't."

"Yes, you can. Who knows? Maybe I can even help."

"You can't. Nobody can."

She stepped around him, refusing to talk to his back any longer. But one look at his face and she fell back a step, shocked by the sight. A thin cut sliced from the corner of his right eye to mid-temple, the skin around it swollen and stained a purplish-green. Another cut high on his cheekbone looked deeper, meaner.

"Oh, Ry," she cried softly. "What happened to you?"

Scowling, he turned away. "I got in a fight."

Her mind fixed immediately on the most obvious reason for him to have been in a fight. "Did you find the person responsible for killing the cows?"

He dragged a handkerchief from his back pocket and wiped his hands. "No. When I went into town the other day, I ran into a guy I went to high school with."

Pursing her lips, she folded her arms across her breasts. "And you beat each other's faces in for old time's sake?"

"He started it."

"Well, that's something." Letting out a breath, she dropped her arms and caught his elbow. "Let me see your face." She winced at the sight, then touched a finger gingerly to the cut at his eye. "Have you put anything on this?"

"Ice." He ducked away from her touch. "It's nothing."

She planted her hands on her hips. "I'd expect a stupid remark like that from a man, but you're a doctor. You should know better."

"I'm not a doctor. Not any longer."

"If you believe that, then you never really were one. Not in the way it counts. No true doctor ever loses his desire to help, his need to heal. It's intrinsic. Something he couldn't deny any more than he could his next breath."

"That pretty much sums it up then, because I did."

She sagged her shoulders in frustration, knowing that wasn't true. Ry wasn't without feeling. Hadn't he recognized her need for money and tried to fill it? Granted, being strapped for cash wasn't a medical problem, but he'd responded to it, which, in her mind at least, proved that he cared, that he had a heart.

But something had happened to make him question himself, his vocation, leave behind what she considered a God-given gift, a duty to his fellow man. That was the only rational explanation she could come up with for him walking away from medicine.

"Ry, talk to me. Tell me what it is that's bothering you. I want to help."

"You can't. Nobody can."

Lifting a hand to his cheek, she stroked a thumb beneath his lashes. "Oh, Ry. Nothing is that hopeless."

He covered her hand with his and held it against his face, as if grasping at a lifeline. "I am."

Kayla wanted to gather him in her arms, hold him, somehow make it all better. But she sensed coddling would only make things worse. What he needed was a good shaking up. And she was just the person to do the shaking.

She jerked her hand from beneath his. "You're not hopeless. What you are is emotionally constipated."

He opened his mouth, then closed it to frown. "I'm *what?*"

"Emotionally constipated. What you need is a good flushing. If you were a woman, I'd tell you to put on a flannel nightgown, sit down in front of the TV with a box of tissues and a pound of chocolate and watch about four hours of nonstop tear-jerkers."

"Tear-jerkers being sad movies," he said, hazarding a guess.

"Yes. The sadder the better. But since you're a man...." She caught her bottom lip between her teeth and worried it, frowning. "The obvious solution is sex, but that won't work."

He gaped. "Sex?"

"Yes. Isn't that a man's cure for everything?" Waving him away, she started pacing. "But this requires something more. Something—" She spun, snapping her fingers. "I know just the thing!" She grabbed his hand.

He dug in his heels, refusing to follow. "If this requires a box of tissues, count me out."

"Would you quit your whining?" She gave his hand an impatient tug. "Now, come on! We've got things to do."

Thirty minutes later, Kayla had a bowl of popcorn and snacks sitting on a tray on the coffee table, the lights turned down low and a fire burning in the fireplace.

"I feel like a fool."

In the midst of adding more fuel to the fire, Kayla glanced over to find Ry standing in the doorway. Biting back a smile, she dropped the log over the flames and straightened. "I don't know. I think you look kind of cute."

He held his arms out to his sides, grimacing as he looked down at the raggedy T-shirt and flannel pajama bottoms. "Whose are these, anyway?"

"Judging by the size, I'd say Woodrow's. I found them in the bottom drawer of the dresser in my room."

He made an abrupt about-face. "That's it. I'm changing."

She ran to catch his hand. "Oh, no, you're not." She dragged him back into the den. "That's the closest thing to a flannel nightgown I could find."

Giving him a push toward the blanket she'd spread before the fireplace, she scooped up the tray of snacks she'd prepared and followed. She knelt, setting the tray in the center of the blanket, then patted the spot on the other side of it. "Sit here," she instructed.

Scowling, he sank down, folding his legs in front of him. "Has anyone ever told you that you're bossy?"

"All the time." She wrinkled her nose at him impishly. "But I just tell them I have strong leadership qualities."

She picked up a bowl of popcorn, passed it to him, then settled back on one of the pillows she'd propped against the hearth and waved a hand. "The remote is on the floor on the other side of you. Hit Play, whenever you're ready."

Rolling his eyes, Ry picked up the remote and punched the button, sure that Kayla had chosen some chick-flick for him to watch. But it was the Lone Ranger who filled the screen, sitting astride his horse, Silver. Ry stared, swamped by memories, most of which were centered around his childhood. "Where did you find this?"

"Over there." She pointed at the bookcase across the room. "There must be a hundred videos in there. Did y'all watch these when you were kids?"

He lay back, resting the bowl of popcorn on his stomach. "Saturday nights, rainy days, days too cold to play outside, when we were sick. The Lone Ranger was my favorite."

She gave him a sideways glance, wondering if he was aware of the analogy. "John Wayne was mine."

He glanced her way, then turned his gaze back to the television screen. "Figures."

"Here," she said and offered him her chocolate bar. "Take a bite."

He drew back, eyeing the bar dubiously. "Chocolate and popcorn? No thanks."

"Don't knock it until you try it." She waved it before his lips. "Come on. Just one bite."

Scowling, he bit off a chunk.

"Now eat some popcorn. Quick!" she cried, when he didn't move fast enough.

He popped a couple of kernels into his mouth, chewed, then widened his eyes and reached for some more. "Hey! That's not bad."

Smug, Kayla settled back against her pillow. "Stick with me cowboy, and I'll introduce you to the finer things in life."

Ry lay on his side at the foot of the blanket, propped up on a elbow, an empty bowl of popcorn and a pile of crumpled candy wrappers sitting on the floor in front of him.

As the credits began to roll across the television screen, he heaved a contented sigh, then picked up the remote. "Want to watch another one?"

When Kayla didn't respond, he glanced over his shoulder and bit back a smile, when he saw that she had fallen asleep. Catching the end of the afghan draped over the arm of the sofa, he pulled it down and carefully spread it over her.

Mewling softly, she dragged a corner up over her shoulder. "Is the movie over?" she asked sleepily.

"Which one?"

She opened an eye to look at him. "How many did you watch?"

"Three."

Smiling smugly, she snuggled deeper beneath the afghan. "It worked, didn't it?"

She looked so warm and cuddly lying before the fire, Ry couldn't resist stretching out beside her.

"If you're asking if I cried, the answer is no."

"My goal wasn't to make you sad. It was to make you happy."

He thought about that for a moment. If not happy, he was at least content. Which surprised him. He couldn't remember the last time he'd felt this mellow, this relaxed. "How did you know that I liked old Westerns?"

Her lips curved. "All boys watch Westerns when they're little and dream of becoming a cowboy someday."

Fascinated by the firelight that danced across her face, he eased closer. "What about little girls?"

"Ever heard of Annie Oakley and Dale Evans?"

Chuckling, he reached to wind a lock of hair behind her ear. "Which one was your favorite?"

"Depended on my mood. Annie was full of spunk. I admired that in her. And Dale...." She lifted a shoulder. "Well, she always managed to get Roy to do what she wanted."

"Ah-h-h. So it was her womanly wiles you admired."

"That, too. Plus, she was darn good with a gun."

"So you dreamed of becoming a cowgirl and shooting all the bad guys."

"Nope." She picked up a kernel of corn that lay on the blanket between them and tossed it over her shoulder into the fire. "I always wanted to be a nurse."

"Never a model? A movie star?"

She gaped, as if stunned that he'd even think such a thing. "Me?" She laughed and shook her head.

"Hardly. I've never wanted to be anything but a nurse."

Ry remembered a time when he was that certain about what he wanted to do with his life.

"How about you?" she asked. "Did you always know that you would be a doctor?"

"I didn't even consider it until I was in junior high."

"Really?" She pushed up to an elbow and propped her head on her hand. "What made you decide then?"

He hedged, not wanting to think about the events that had turned him toward medicine. "It was a mixture of things, I guess. What about you?"

She laughed again. "I can't remember a time when I didn't want to be a nurse. There's a doctor in my hometown. Dr. Andrews. I hung out at his office all the time, making a pest of myself I'm sure. He finally offered me a job, just to get me out from under his feet and out of his hair. I did menial tasks, like vacuuming the waiting room and running errands for him. That kind of thing.

"Then his staff started letting me do some of their filing, straightening the closet where they kept their medicine samples. Before long, I was passing Dr. Andrews alcohol-soaked cotton balls to prep an arm or hip before he gave a shot and handing out suckers to the kids who got them. One time, I talked him into letting me go into surgery with him. Badgered him, really. A tonsillectomy. I'm sure he thought I'd take one look, faint dead away and he'd be done with me. But I didn't faint. I was fascinated." She laughed again, then added, "And hooked. From that moment on, I was determined to find a way to get to nursing school.''

"And you did."

"Yep," she said proudly. "Took me a little longer than I had expected to save the money to get started, and it'll be awhile yet before I earn my degree, but every new day puts me a little closer to my goal."

"Why a nurse? Why not a doctor?"

She chuckled, as if at a private joke. "You know in high school yearbooks where they usually print a person's nickname under their given name? In mine it says 'Doc.' That's what everybody called me. I was even named 'Most Likely to Become a Doctor' at our Senior Awards Banquet."

"Are you planning to go on to medical school?"

"Do you have any idea how long that takes?" she asked incredulously, then snorted a laugh. "Well, I guess you do, since you did it. But it would take me forever! At the rate I'm going, I'll be lucky if I have my nursing degree by the time I'm thirty. If I went on to medical school, I'd be so old when I graduated they'd have to roll me across the stage in a wheelchair to give me my diploma. No," she said, shaking her head, "I'll stick with nursing. I can accomplish what I want in that field."

"And what is it you want to accomplish?"

"Help people. Particularly those who can't afford health care. Do you know the statistics on the number of people who die because they can't afford to go to the doctor?"

"I suppose you do."

She frowned. "Well, no. Not the exact number, anyway. But it's a lot. Children and senior citizens are affected the most, but it's a problem in all age groups. And the worst part is, the numbers are climbing every day.''

She stopped and smiled sheepishly. ''Would you listen to me? I'm preaching to the choir. You, of all people, would know the problems associated with health care.''

Ry wasn't about to tell her that he rarely gave a thought to health care. The patients he'd seen were more worried about their physical appearance than they were about dying. And how they were going to pay for the nips, tucks and embellishments he performed for them, was never a concern. Not for Ry, anyway. His policy was cash up-front or no surgery—though checks and credit cards were accepted. With prior approval, of course.

But Ry wouldn't think about now. Didn't have to any longer. He'd sold his practice. He was a rancher now. For the time being, anyway.

But what then?

He shoved the thought aside, not wanting to think about that, either.

''Thanks for bullying me into watching the movies. I can't remember the last time I binged on Westerns.''

''You should play more often. You're way too uptight.''

He gave her a warning look. ''You're not going to start psychoanalyzing me again, are you?''

She laughed. ''Even if I wanted to, I wouldn't know how. My licensing only allows me to dispense bandages and hugs.''

''I don't need bandaging, but I could sure use a good hug.'' Ry wasn't sure why he'd said that, but he wasn't taking it back. Not now. Not when they were all cozied up in front of a fire. Not when he saw the surprise in her eyes, as well as the flicker of anticipation.

He tried a smile. "Think you could spare me one?"

She wet her lips. "Maybe."

He pushed himself up to his knees and opened his arms. "Give me your best shot."

With her gaze on his, she moved to kneel in front of him and slid her arms around his waist. Turning her cheek against his chest, she closed her eyes, squeezed.

Her arms were slender, and the pressure from them was barely enough to crease his shirt.

Yet, she stole his breath.

Oh, God, he thought, gulping. He hadn't realized how much he'd needed this, how much he'd missed the warmth of a woman's embrace, the sense of caring a simple hug could give. Wanting to absorb all he could, he folded his arms around her and gathered her close, resting his cheek on top of her head.

He wasn't sure how long they knelt on the blanket, their arms wrapped around each other, their bodies pressed close, before he became aware of the slow, languid stroke of her fingers along his spine. There was something different in the movement of her hands. A difference his body had picked up on and responded to, before his brain had registered the change. Aware now of the tightening in his groin, the heat that pumped through his veins, he lifted his head and looked down at her.

If he hadn't already been kneeling, what he saw in her eyes would have brought him to his knees. Tenderness. Understanding. And a need so sharp its prick was like a knife in his groin. Individually, he could have resisted the first two. But woven with the third, they created a force so strong he crumpled beneath it.

Lowering his head, he touched his lips to hers.

And found sweetness.

Swept his tongue along the crease.

And found heat.

He skimmed his hands down her back, cupped her buttocks and drew her up to hold against him.

And found the fire.

It swept over him, through him, a red-hot flame that sizzled and hissed, destroying all thought, all reason. There was no turning back now. No time to worry about regrets or tomorrows. Stabbing his tongue into her mouth, he ground himself against her, letting her know her effect on him.

Her response was everything he'd hoped for, dreamed of, needed. She melted against him, mating her tongue with his in a sensual dance that stoked the heat higher, brighter. She smoothed her hands lower and lower on his back, until she found the hem of his T-shirt, then slipped them under and opened her fingers over his flesh. With them, she urged him closer. Closer still. Tearing her mouth from his, she dropped her head back, gasping for breath.

Fueled by a heat and a need that had simmered for weeks, Ry took the opening she offered. He trailed his lips over her chin, down the graceful slope of her throat, then lower to open his mouth over a breast. He flicked his tongue at the fabric-covered nipple, teasing it into a tight bud, and felt the dig of her fingers into his back, heard the low moan of pleasure that slid past her lips, and knew that she wanted him as badly as he wanted her.

Finding the hem of her T-shirt, he dragged it up

and over her head, pulling her arms up with it, then sank back on his heels and stared, awed by her beauty. *Hard body,* he remembered thinking, while he'd watched her sashay around the bar. She was certainly that. Firelight licked at her skin, turning her breasts a burnished gold, her nipples a dusty rose. Unable to resist, he opened a hand over one, felt her tremble, and pushed back up to his knees to close his mouth over the other, while kneading the first.

She gasped, tensing, then clasped her hands at his head and arched back, holding him against her. He suckled deeply, greedily, even as he fought her pants down her legs. No panties, he thought, and almost laughed, when he remembered the spaced-out kid had told him she didn't sleep in panties.

But the thought of the spaced-out kid brought other reminders. Reporters and age differences and a life too screwed up to ask anyone to share it. He drew back, intending to end it now before it went any further. But she caught his hands, stopping him.

She lifted a brow in warning and drew his arms around her waist. "If you think I'm going to let you stop now, you're crazy."

He shook his head. "But this is—"

Before he could tell her this was a mistake, explain why they couldn't do this, *shouldn't* finish what he had foolishly started, her hands were flattened against his chest and she was pushing him back.

He blinked once and she was on top of him, sliding her body up the length of his. He blinked again and she had her mouth on his, pulling greedily at his lower lip, while she pushed her hands impatiently at the elasticized waist of his flannel pajama bottoms. She managed to get them to his knees, then dropped her forehead to his chin with a groan, and ground her hips against his erection.

"Love me, Ry," she begged and brought her mouth to his again. "Please love me."

Her breath was like a blow torch on his face, her lips clever weapons of persuasion, her fingers merciless as she curled them around his sex and drew him to her. Powerless to resist her, he thrust his tongue between her parted lips and drove his hips up, burying himself deep inside her. She arched high, gasping, her nails scoring his buttocks...then sank down on a shuddery groan and took him deeper.

While he struggled to remember how to breathe, how to move, she lifted her hips slowly. Lowered. Again and again and again, until his skin was slick with sweat and his blood racing. She rose a last time, held herself impaled on the tip of his sex for one, long heart-stopping moment, then plunged and sent them both shooting up high and over the edge.

His legs limp with exhaustion, his chest heaving, Ry cupped a hand behind her neck and pulled her mouth down to his. "You were right. I should play more often."

Her mouth curved against his in a smile. "And why is that?"

Holding her hips between his hands, he shifted to a more comfortable position beneath her. "To build up my stamina. That was over too damn quick."

"You think so? I suppose, if you wanted, we could start working on improving your stamina now."

He opened his eyes fully to look at her, then slammed them shut, with a groan, when he saw the mischievous glint in her eyes. "A couple of hours of recovery and maybe I'll take you up on that offer."

She squeezed her thighs around him and the walls of her sex clamped around him.

He opened one eye to look at her, as he felt himself beginning to harden again. "Or maybe I'll take you up on that now."

Chapter 10

The fire burned low in the fireplace, red-hot embers that pulsed and glowed with heat.

Unable to sleep, Ry brushed a lock of hair from Kayla's cheek and threaded it behind her ear. She lay curled next to him, one fist tucked loosely beneath her cheek, her lips lax in sleep, her knees bumped against his. Her hair, a flaming swirl of blond in the firelight, draped the pillow he'd tucked beneath her head and fell to curtain one bare shoulder. The swell of a breast peeked from beneath the afghan they shared, its rhythmic rise and fall sensual, hypnotic.

Lashes, thick and dusted with gold, brushed cheeks stained a healthy pink. Her eyebrows, shades darker than her blond hair, arched naturally above brown eyes that, when open, could dance with laughter or smolder in anger, depending on her mood. A light sprinkle of freckles lay across the bridge of her nose, and her upper lip peaked in a tight bow at the center of her mouth.

Ry wanted to believe it was her beauty that held him captive, making sleep impossible. But Kayla wasn't beautiful. Not in the traditional sense of the word. She was the All-American girl, the girl next door, exuding a natural kind of beauty that couldn't be imitated or bought. Her unawareness of her appeal made her all the more intriguing.

He remembered the startled look on her face when he'd asked her if she'd ever dreamed of being a model or a movie actress, normal aspirations for a young girl, and the wry ''hardly'' she offered in response. He supposed her reaction could've been for effect, one of the many feminine wiles a woman used to squeeze a compliment out of a man. But Kayla didn't seem the type for games. She was the more the what-you-see-is-what-you-get-and-to-hell-with-anyone-who-expects-more kind of woman.

But Ry didn't expect or want more from Kayla. In fact, he wondered if he could handle what he'd gotten. He'd discovered in her a seemingly insatiable appetite for sex, a spontaneity and freeness about her that he found both arousing and comforting.

He'd never known anyone quite like her before.

Snorting a laugh, he glanced over at the pile of clothes on the floor. Flannel, for God's sake. How in the world had she ever persuaded him to put on flannel? And how had she talked him into trying popcorn and chocolate, a combination he'd have never considered mixing, much less sampling? And how had she known that watching old Westerns would have such a cleansing effect on him, making him forget about his troubles for a while?

Because she was Kayla. There was no other explanation.

"Ry?"

He glanced down to find her looking at him sleepily. Smiling, he trailed a finger down her cheek. "What?"

"You okay?"

"Yeah. I'm fine. Why?"

She closed her eyes and snuggled close. "You're awake. You should be sleeping."

"I slept."

She opened one eye to frown at him. "A couple of hours isn't sleep. That's a nap." She took his arm and draped it over her waist, then nestled against his chest. "Pretend I'm your teddy bear and cuddle up and go back to sleep. You need the rest."

Chuckling, he nuzzled his nose against hers. "I've never slept with a teddy bear, not even when I was a kid."

"A blankie?"

"No."

She bussed him a sympathetic kiss, then rooted closer and wove her feet with his. "That's probably why you're so messed up. You were deprived." Yawning, she gave his hand a distracted pat. "Don't worry, though. I'll loan you mine."

"You have a teddy bear?"

"Mmm-hmm."

"And you still sleep with it?"

"Only when I'm feeling sad or lonely." She pressed a finger against his lips. "Shh. No more talking. Sleep."

And, to his surprise, Ry slept.

* * *

Her brow furrowed in concentration, Kayla read through the question a second time. She hated multiple choice tests. There always seemed to be just enough truth in each answer, to make choosing the correct one impossible. Heaving a sigh, she pressed her pencil in the circle, indicating answer B, and begin to shade it in.

"Are you sure?"

She glanced up to find Ry standing opposite the desk, watching her.

"Well, yeah," she said. "B makes more sense than A, C or D."

When he angled his head, as if questioning her response, she scowled and erased the mark she'd made. Dusting the rubbings away, she placed her pencil on the circle beside C.

"You had the answer right the first time."

She tossed down her pencil in frustration. "Would you stop! You're driving me crazy. This is supposed to be an anatomy test, not a test of my patience."

He lifted his hands and turned away. "I just wanted to make sure you were confident of your answer."

"You're supposed to *monitor* my test, not challenge every answer I write down."

He sat down on the sofa. "I won't say another word." Pressing a thumb and finger together he dragged them across his lips, as if zipping them closed, then folded his arms across his chest.

Rolling her eyes, Kayla shifted her gaze back to the test and read the last question. She frowned, read it a second time. "This doesn't make sense. Listen." She picked up the test and read the question aloud to Ry, then lowered it to look at him. "What does it mean?"

He pointed to his sealed lips, then lifted a shoulder, as if to say, "Sorry. I'm not allowed to talk. I'm just the monitor."

"Jerk," she muttered and slapped the test back down on the desk. She read through the question a third time, shaded in B, then threw down her pencil and shoved the test across the desk. "That's it. Right or wrong, it's done." She pushed back from the desk and stood, stretching her arms above her head. "And so am I," she moaned wearily. Dropping her arms, she looked hopefully at Ry. "Is it time for recess yet, teacher? I've been studying for hours."

When he pointed at his still sealed lips, she huffed a breath and rounded the desk. Straddling him, she made a show of unzipping his lips, then dropped a kiss on his mouth. "Sorry I snapped at you. I get uptight when I take tests."

He drew his head back to look at her. "Really? I never would have guessed."

"You'd snap, too, if someone was breathing down your neck while you were trying to think."

He hooked a finger in his collar and stretched it out. "Go ahead. Breathe on me. See if I snap at you."

Hiding a smile, she curled against his chest. "You just want me to turn you on."

He shifted her hips more comfortably on his lap. "Too late. I'm already there."

She walked her fingers up his chest. "Really? I thought you had a problem with your stamina?"

"Some wild woman proved to me it wasn't a problem."

She shivered as he slipped a hand under her shirt and closed it over her breast. "Any chance you'd

want to join that wild woman for a well-deserved recess?''

He opened his mouth to answer, but the phone
rang, and he closed it to frown.

"I'll get it."

He locked an arm around her waist. "Let it ring."

Laughing, she wriggled free. "But it could be important." She snagged the portable from the desk.
"Tanner residence." Her smile brightened. "Hey,
Luke! What are you doing calling me? I thought you
were supposed to be moving a bull."

Ry watched her smile fade.

"Well, yeah," she said and glanced at Ry, "he's
here. Just a minute." She held the phone out to him.
"He wants to talk to you."

He rose, his brows drawn together in question. She
lifted a shoulder and passed him the phone. "Beats
me."

"Luke? What's the problem?"

He listened a moment, his frown deepening, then
said, "Stay where you are. I'll grab some supplies
and meet you there." He tossed the phone to the sofa
and strode for the door.

Kayla ran after him.

"What's going on? What happened?"

"Fence is down in Pasture Three, the one that runs
along the main highway. Cattle are out. One's already
been hit by a car. Luke's trying to round up the rest
and get them back into the pasture."

By the time he finished the explanation, he'd
plucked his jacket from the rack by the back door,
shrugged it on, and was reaching for his hat.

He opened the back door. "We probably won't

make it back in until after dark, so don't wait dinner on us."

Kayla grabbed her jacket and followed him out. "In that case, I'm going with you."

He turned to block her. "You'll just be in the way. Stay inside where it's warm."

"While y'all freeze your rear ends off?" She zipped up her jacket and pushed past him. "I don't think so."

There was chaos, then there was chaos. The scene that Kayla and Ry met upon arriving at the downed fence was chaos on speed. Traffic was backed up a half-mile in either direction, with cattle darting in and out between the stalled vehicles. Luke raced his horse up and down the far side of the highway, trying to herd the cattle back across the road and through the opening in the downed fence. People had abandoned their vehicles and were waving their hats and arms, trying to help, but were spooking the cattle even more and defeating what progress Luke managed to make. The sound of horns blaring mixed with the bawling of the cattle and the country Western music blaring from some young cowboy's truck stereo. That same young cowboy stood in the bed of his truck, swinging a rope over his head and yipping like a cowboy riding drag on a cattle drive down the Chisholm Trail.

A rodeo couldn't have drawn a bigger crowd or provided more hair-raising entertainment.

"Damn," Ry swore. "Don't these people know they're only making it worse?"

He shouldered open the door. Kayla grabbed his arm before he could hop down. "What are you going to do?"

"If I had a gun, I'd start shooting." He dropped to the ground and scowled at the chaotic scene. "And I wouldn't be aiming at cattle," he added bitterly, before slamming the door.

Kayla climbed down from the opposite side and hurried to intercept him at the hood of the truck. "Tell me what I can do to help?"

He waved a hand at the crowd. "Get as many people as you can back into their cars. Then move the truck over there," he said pointing. "Luke and I will gather the cattle and herd them your way. Your job will be to keep the cattle headed toward the fence and stop any that try to run past you."

Kayla watched a steer dart between two parked cars and take a swipe at a man with its horns. Thankfully, the man leaped out of the way in time, missing being gored by inches.

Kayla gulped, realizing that, in order to get the people back in their cars, she was going to have to wade into the confusion, which would put her in direct line with the cattle.

But she'd insisted on coming, she reminded herself. And she'd offered to help.

"Okay," she said to Ry, then forced herself to take that first terrifying step into chaos.

Kayla filled mugs with hot steaming coffee and carried them to the table, placing one in front of each of the men, before setting one in front of Ry. Closing her fingers around her own mug, she sat down at the opposite end of the table.

"The fence was cut," Ry said to the men. "There's no doubt about that. The question now is, who and why?"

Their expressions somber, all three men stared into their mugs.

"It could've been a prank," Luke offered. "Some kid who was bored and hopin' to scare up some excitement."

Ry's frown deepened. "I'd probably agree with you, if it weren't for the two cows we found shot."

Luke nodded grimly. "Does make a person wonder."

Ry looked around at the men. "Y'all worked for the old man for years. Was there any trouble on the ranch before he died?"

Slim scratched his chin. "Hard to say. There's always things happenin' on a ranch."

"Yeah," Monty agreed, then added, "But before, they seemed more random. We've been hit three times in the same week. Makes you wonder, if there ain't more goin' on here, than meets the eye."

Ry gulped down a swallow of coffee. "That's what worries me. Which is why I asked if there had been trouble before. Y'all know, as well as I do, that the old man had his share of enemies."

The three men shared a glance, but said nothing.

Luke glanced over at Ry. "Think we ought to call the sheriff?"

Shaking his head, Ry picked up his mug and crossed to the sink, to look out the window. "I don't know that it would do much good. We don't have anything to offer him in the way of evidence. Two dead cows and a cut fence aren't much to go on."

"Three dead cows," Slim reminded him. "One was hit by a car."

Ry glanced back, then turned back to frown out the window. "Right. And the guy who hit it has already informed me that he expects the Bar T to pay for the damage to his car. Since there isn't a question it was our cow he hit, we'll pay." He turned back to the men. "That cow's death was an accident, but the cut fence wasn't. If the fence hadn't been down, that cow, as well as the others, wouldn't have been out on the highway. We're damn lucky more weren't killed or somebody hurt."

"Amen to that," Monty murmured.

"So what do we do now?" Luke asked.

"We continue with the night patrol schedule we've already got in place. Tonight's my night for duty. Tomorrow we'll start moving the cattle closer in. As far away from the highway and country roads as possible. We need them close to the house, so we can keep an eye on them."

"But that land's already been grazed," Slim argued. "There's nothing left of the winter grass for the cattle to eat."

"Then we'll feed them," Ry replied. "How are we fixed on hay, Monty?"

Monty pursed his lips thoughtfully. "If we're careful with it, we've got enough left to carry us another month."

"What about liquid feed?" Ry asked. "If we move all the liquid feeders to the pastures where we relocate the cattle, how much more time will that buy us?"

"Another couple of weeks. A month at the most. We've got range pellets we can put out, too."

"And we can buy more, if we have to," Ry added. "As far as I'm concerned, war has been declared on the Bar T and we're going to do everything we can to put an end to it, before any more livestock are lost."

*   *   *

War, Kayla thought, then shuddered. It was such an ugly word. Scary, even. But it did appear that the Bar T was under attack. Three dead cows. A fence cut. Random acts that became threats when occurring in such rapid succession.

She glanced down at the opposite end of the sofa, where Ry lay propped up on a pillow, a book held before his face, his feet tangled with hers. Positioned as they were, they looked like a couple of lovers, snuggled in for a quiet evening at home.

Which was close enough to the truth to have Kayla squirming uncomfortably.

They were going to have to talk about what had happened between them the night before, she told herself. She didn't want Ry to get the wrong idea. They weren't having an affair. They'd slept together once. Big deal.

Or, at least, it wouldn't become a big deal, if she made her expectations clear from the start. She'd simply tell him that she wasn't interested in a relationship. Nothing long-term, anyway. They'd enjoy each other's company while they were together at the ranch, then, when it was safe for her to return to Austin, they would say their goodbyes and go their separate ways. Kaput. Fini. The end.

And she'd tell him that right now.

But first, she was going to have to get that scowl off his face. He might be pretending to read, but she knew better. The deep furrow between his brows was a dead-giveaway that he was brooding, not reading. That, and the fact that he hadn't turned a page in over fifteen minutes.

Fortunately she'd discovered a way to distract him

from his troubles. But popping in an old Western video for him to watch wasn't what she had in mind this time.

Setting her book aside, she eased down the sofa, tipped his book back and leaned to press her lips to his. Startled, he jerked, then melted, letting the book fall to his chest, so that he could wrap his arms around her.

She drew back to smile at him.

"What was that for?" he asked.

She pressed a finger against the faint line that remained between his eyes. "You were frowning, so I decided to give you something to smile about."

He lifted a brow. "Kind of sure of yourself, aren't you?"

She ran a finger along his lower lip, tracing its upward curve. "It worked, didn't it?"

He hooked an arm behind her neck and drew her down. "I don't know. Maybe you better try again."

But he didn't wait for her to kiss him. He lifted his head and kissed her, with a slowness, a tenderness that stole her breath. Before she could draw another, he took the kiss deeper, hotter.

When he released her, she gulped a breath. "How do you do that?"

Biting back a smile, he hooked a finger in the neck of her T-shirt and tugged her back to tease her lips. "Do, what?"

"Go from candlelighter to arsonist so fast."

"I was an altar boy when I was a kid."

She shoved at his chest. "You know what I mean. You start out with a little kiss and all of a sudden fire alarms are going off in my head."

He trailed a finger down her stomach. "Fire alarms,

huh?'' He slid his hand between her legs and cupped her.

She dropped her head to his chest, groaning, as heat shot through her, then snapped it back up. ''See!'' she cried. ''You did it again.''

Laughing, he withdrew his hand to wrap his arms around her. ''I'm sorry. I promise to behave.''

''Oh, I wasn't complaining,'' she said quickly. ''I just want to know how you do it.''

''Here. I'll show you…''

When he lifted his head to kiss her again, she pressed a hand against his mouth.

He drew back to frown. ''What?''

''Maybe we should talk first.''

''About what?''

''This.''

Ry didn't need her to explain what she meant by *this*. He had a feeling he knew. Wary, he laid his head back on the arm of the sofa. ''What about it?''

''We need to set some parameters.''

''Parameters?''

''You know. Share our expectations.''

''I don't know that I have any.''

She sagged in relief. ''Good. I don't, either.''

When she would've kissed him again, he held her back. ''Wait a minute. I didn't say I didn't have any. I said that I don't *know* that I do. I haven't given this any thought.''

It was Kayla's turn to frown. She crawled off him and stood. ''Well, maybe you should.''

''Why do we have to have expectations?''

''Because we do.''

He tossed up his hands. ''Well, that certainly explains things.''

"It's a safety factor, okay? A way to keep either of us from getting hurt."

He swung his legs over the side of the sofa and began to pace. "And what if our expectations change? What happens then?"

"They can't change. That's the whole purpose of making our expectations known. I tell you what I want out of the relationship and you tell me what you want."

He swung back to glare at her. "Doesn't that sound a little premeditated to you? A little cold-blooded?"

"Well, no," she said, wondering what he was getting so worked up about. "I consider it prior planning."

He hitched his hands on his hips. "Do you know what your problem is? You're a control freak."

Her mouth dropped open. "I am not! Just because I prefer to enter a relationship with my eyes open, doesn't mean I have to be in control of it."

"Tunnel vision," he shot back at her. "Your eyes may be open, but you see only what's right in front of you. You don't see all the potential hazards lurking in the peripheral, because you refuse to acknowledge that they're there." Pushing out a hand, he turned away. "Forget it," he muttered. "I don't even know why I'm arguing with you about this. I'm going outside to have a look around."

Kayla stared after him, a lump rising to her throat. She wasn't a control freak.

Was she?

There was no question now that Ry had lost his mind. He expected the men in white to arrive at any moment with a straitjacket custom-made to fit a man his size. Arguing with Kayla, after she'd just given him a thumb's up for a relationship with no strings attached, no expectations? He had to be crazy. If he'd kept his mouth shut, he could be kicked back and enjoying himself right about now.

But, oh, no. He'd had to let his male ego go and ruin what had promised to be a relationship made in heaven. No expectations. No commitments. No demands. What man could ask for more than that from a woman?

One who wanted a woman to have a few expectations, one who wanted a woman to care a little more than a no-commitment kind of relationship required.

He kicked at a tumbleweed that blew across the path in front of him. No. He wasn't crazy.

He was a damn fool.

Because that's exactly what he wanted from Kayla.

He wanted Kayla to care.

Kayla allowed herself an hour to sulk. She figured she was due at least that much time, since Ry had called her a control freak.

Which, by the way, she wasn't.

She was careful. Cautious. Independent. Ambitious. But those were attributes, not failings.

But now that she'd had her sulk, she was ready to get things square between them again. She didn't know why he had blown up the way he had, but she wasn't going to sit around sucking her thumb, waiting for him to apologize.

Thinking a cup of hot coffee might smooth the way a bit, she filled a thermos, tucked it under her arm and headed outside.

A stingy, quarter-moon offered little illumination

against the darkness, but Kayla could see well enough to resist the urge to run back inside for a flashlight. Unsure where she would find Ry, she started down the path that led to the barn, thinking that was as likely a spot as any to begin her search. Her journey took her past the bunkhouse, where a shadowed figure stood on the porch.

"Slim?" she called, sure by the length of the shadow the man cast, it had to be Slim on the porch. "Is that you?"

"Yeah." He took a last drag on the cigarette he held, then tamped it out on the heel of his boot and flicked the butt away. "What are you doing out so late?"

"Looking for Ry. Have you seen him?"

"He passed by a while ago, doing his rounds. Probably at the barn by now. Anything wrong?"

"No." She held up the thermos of coffee. "I just thought he might need something to keep him warm."

"I 'magine a hot cup of coffee would go down good about now. Might help him stay awake, too."

"That's what I was thinking. Good night, Slim."

"'Night, Kayla."

She strode on for the barn, hoping that Slim was right and she'd find Ry there. The thought of venturing farther out onto the ranch, considering all that had happened, with nothing but a thermos of coffee for protection, sent a chill skating down her spine. Hugging the thermos tighter against her body, she stepped inside the barn. It was pitch black inside, and she paused a moment, giving her eyes a chance to adjust. Somewhere ahead a horse shuffled nervously in its stall, obviously sensing her presence. Kayla took a hesitant step forward.

The click of metal striking metal behind her had her freezing.

She flung up her hands and the thermos dropped to the floor. "Don't shoot! It's me. Kayla."

Ry swore, then hit the lights. "Dammit, Kayla! What are you trying to do? Get yourself killed?"

She dropped her hands to turn and scowl at him. "No. I was trying to be nice." She bent to pick up the thermos and thrust it at him. "I thought you might be cold, so I brought you some coffee."

Grimacing he took the thermos from her hands. "You didn't have to do that."

"No, but since I was coming, anyway, to tell you I was sorry, I figured I might as well bring you some coffee."

Sighing, he caught her hand and tugged her down to sit beside him on a bale of hay. "You don't have anything to apologize for. It was my fault. I was being a jerk."

"You won't get an argument from me." She tipped her head to peer at him. "What do you say we start over?"

"From where?"

She took the thermos from his hand, set it aside, then shifted to straddle him. "How about from here? I think this is where we were, before things got all confused."

He hooked an arm behind her hips to hold her in place. "I'd say this is pretty close."

Relieved that he wasn't going to make this difficult, she pushed back a lock of hair that had fallen across his forehead. "As I recall, we were talking about our relationship.'' She trailed a finger down the side of his face, her smile fading as she met his gaze. ''I'm attracted to you.''

She waited a beat, waiting for him to say something. When he didn't, she frowned. ''You're supposed to say that you're attracted to me, too.''

Locking his hands behind her hips, he drew her closer, close enough that he could touch his lips to hers. ''I was trying to think of a stronger word. Attracted doesn't come close to describing your effect on me.''

She reached for the top button of his coat. ''Then I think we should enjoy what time we have together and not waste any more of it arguing over things that don't matter.'' She freed the first button, then moved on to the second.

He looked down in amazement. ''What are you doing?''

''I would think that's obvious.''

''Here?''

She dropped her hands in frustration. ''You're not going to start arguing again, are you?''

''No!'' He caught her hands and drew them back to his chest. ''It's just that it's…well, hell, it's cold out here!''

Hiding a smile, she unfastened the third button. ''It won't be for long.''

She released the last button, pushed aside his coat and started on those on his shirt.

Ry sank back against the wall, his mouth suddenly dry. ''No, I guess it won't.''

Chapter 11

Sated, Kayla pressed her lips to the underside of Ry's chin. "Is the hay scratching your back?"

"I wouldn't know. I can't feel anything but my feet."

Laughing, she rolled to lie beside him. "Was that a hint that I'm too heavy?"

"No way." He gathered her beneath his arm to hold against his side. "My body's numb. Feels like someone drilled a hole in my big toe and drained out all my strength."

She stroked her hand down his stomach. "I could get your blood pumping again, if you want?"

Moaning, he caught her hand. "No, please," he begged pitifully. "I'm older than you. It takes me more time to recover."

"Oh, please. You're not that much older."

He lifted his head. "I beg your pardon, but twelve years is quite a gap."

She rolled her eyes. "Excuse me, while I get you a cane."

He placed a hand beneath her chin, forcing her gaze to his. "It's something to consider."

She stared, realizing that he was serious. But his age wasn't a problem for her, and she refused to let it be one for him. She tipped her head, as if giving his warning thought, then dropped a kiss on his mouth. "Okay. I considered. It's not a problem."

Chuckling, he laid back, folding his arm beneath his head. "You're nuts."

"First a control freak, and now I'm nuts."

He stroked a hand over her hair, his smile fading. "I didn't mean that. About you being a control freak."

"Apology accepted."

"You forgive way too fast."

She shrugged. "I could hold out a while, if you'd rather. But I figure, why hold a grudge? It's unhealthy. Drains me of energy I could use doing something productive."

He dropped his head back. "Christ. You amaze me."

"I amaze even myself sometimes."

He laughed and she felt the vibration of it against her cheek, in her heart. Bracing an arm against the hay, she pushed up to look at him. "You should do that more often."

"What?"

"Laugh. It's good for you."

"*You're* good for me."

"You really think so?" She snuggled against him, pleased. "That's the first compliment you've ever paid me."

He shifted to his side in order to better see her.
"Well, here's another one. You're beautiful."

She pushed at his face. "Ah, now you've gone and
ruined it."

He caught her hand and drew it to hold between
them. "It's true. You are beautiful. Inside and out."

Laughing, she tugged her hand from his. "Would
you stop? If you keep this up, I'm going to feel obligated to tell you that you're handsome in return."

"You think I'm handsome?"

"I didn't say that. I said I'd feel obligated to tell
you that you were."

Rolling to his back, he dragged her over on top of
him. "Oh, I get it. It's just my body that appeals to
you."

She drew small circles on his chest with her nail.
"Well…certain parts."

He dropped his head back and laughed. "At least
there's something about me you find appealing."

She wriggled up higher on his chest, enjoying this
playful pillow talk. "There's actually quite a bit I like
about you."

He drew back. "Careful now," he warned. "You
don't want to give me a big head."

Ignoring him, she trailed a finger down between his
brows. "I like this little wrinkle right here. The one
you make when you frown." She pulled the finger
down the slope of his nose. "And I like your nose.
It's very sexy."

"Sexy?"

"Mmm-hmm. So are your lips. I like the way they
feel against mine. They're so—" She frowned, then
leaned to run her tongue across his lips, as if to remind herself what it was about them she liked.

"Cushiony," she decided, then shivered and pressed a finger against them. "Yet, they can be hard. Demanding."

"Is that a good thing?"

"Oh, yeah," she said, on a sigh. "A very good thing. But not all the time. Sometimes I like to be in control. Like I am now."

"You're in control?"

"I'm on top, aren't I? The one on top is always the one in control."

Laughing, he hugged her to him. "I was right. You are a control freak."

Because she was content to let him hold her, she decided to ignore the jab.

"Your eyes are an unusual shade of blue," she said, mesmerized by them. "Your brothers' eyes are, too. Did y'all get the color from your father or your mother?"

"The old man."

Drawing her hand back, she folded her arms on his chest and rested her chin on them. "You always refer to your father as your old man. Your brothers do, too. Why is that?"

"I suppose because it fits. He wasn't much of a father."

"And your mother? I don't think I've ever heard you mention her."

"She died when I was a kid. My memories of her are good ones, but hazy. Sometimes they seem more dreamlike than real."

"I know what you mean. I was sixteen when my father died, but my memories of him seem to fade more and more with each passing year. Sometimes I'll hear a sound or smell a certain scent and I'll think of him." She turned her mouth against her arm to smother a laugh. "Usually it's the smell of burning meat. He loved to grill out, but was a miserable cook. Everything came out looking and tasting like charcoal."

"How did he die?"

Her laughter faded. "In an accident. He worked as a machinist at a lumber mill in my hometown. He was working late one night. Alone. One of the big machines that rips lumber was down and he wanted to get it running before the morning shift arrived for work. His sleeve got caught in a belt and it dragged him beneath the saw blade. He managed to turn the machine off, but couldn't pull himself free. He bled to death before anyone found him."

Ry pressed a kiss to her forehead, regretting having asked. "I'm sorry."

She gave him a watery smile. "It's okay. I don't like to think about how he died, or how much he might have suffered, but I don't mind talking about him. He was a good man. A good father. I miss him. I think I always will."

"You're fortunate that he left you with such good memories."

"And yours didn't," she said quietly, stating the obvious. Reminded of something he'd said earlier, she looked at him curiously. "When you were talking to Luke and the others, you said your father had enemies. Was he a mean man?"

"Depends on how you define mean. He was careless. With his feelings and those of others. Never thought about anyone but himself."

"Do you really think that whoever is responsible

for killing the cows did it in revenge against your father?''

''Maybe. Are you cold?'' He dragged his coat from the hay he'd spread for them a bed and draped it over her. ''But it could be nothing more than a couple of juvenile delinquents with too much time on their hands.'' He stole a glance at his watch, before folding his arm beneath his head again.

''I'm keeping you from your guard duty,'' she said guiltily.

''I made the rounds just before you came out. Everything seemed quiet enough.'' He gave her a hug. ''But you probably should go in, before you catch pneumonia. I'll walk you back to the house, then take another look around.''

After leaving Kayla at the house, Ry began his tour of the outbuildings and the pastures where they'd moved the cattle, looking for anything out of the ordinary. Though it was pitch-black outside, he navigated the terrain easily, as the ground he crossed was as familiar to him as the back of his hand. His first memories were of skipping over it at his mother's side, his hand clasped tightly in hers. As a young boy, he'd raced across it, trying to outrun one or another of his brothers, or burrowed deep in the best hiding places to escape them. As a teenager, he'd ridden across it on horseback, winter and summer alike, searching every gully and thicket for stray cattle.

But even though he knew the land, he'd never felt for it what his brothers seemed to feel. What his father had expected him to feel.

Just one of the many ways in which he'd disappointed the old man.

Frustrated by the thought, he rammed his hands deeply into his pockets and trudged on. He'd hoped that in coming to live at the ranch, he'd finally be able to come to terms with the resentment he felt toward his father, perhaps even make some kind of peace with the old man's ghost. But, if anything, his resentment burned hotter, his memories more bitter.

He supposed he had Kayla to blame for some of that. Though unintentional, he was sure, she had a knack for dredging up memories he didn't want to remember, making him think about things he'd just as soon forget.

She also had a knack for squeezing a smile out of him, a way of making him forget his troubles for a while. She was like a breath of fresh air in a roomful of stale memories, a defibrillator for a heart that had stalled. She was a distraction, a contradiction, a drug for which he feared he was quickly developing an addition. She was so many things, it would take him a lifetime to discover them all.

And he had so little time left with her.

It hit him as he approached the house, after making his last round. She'd be leaving soon. He didn't know when, but the press was bound to give up sooner or later. When they did, she'd be leaving and he didn't want her to go. Didn't want to think about her leaving. It was inevitable. He knew that. Just as he knew that their relationship would end when she did.

…I think we should enjoy what time we have together…not waste any more of it arguing over things that don't matter.

Hadn't she said that just short hours before? A very mature and contemporary attitude for a woman to have toward an affair. One he might've admired a scant two weeks before. Even applauded.

But not now. He didn't want their relationship to end. At least, not yet. He wanted more time to get to know her, more time to spend with her. He wanted to walk through the pastures with her in the springtime, when the wildflowers were in bloom, share with her their beauty, the botanical names he'd learned from his mother. He wanted to sit with her on the pier at the lake in the summertime, drag his toes through the water next to hers, while they fished, the sun warm on their backs. And he wanted her there in the fall, so that he could show her the deer that came to feed on the oats planted in the south pasture, see the delight in her eyes when the deer bounded away, looking as if they were flying, as they sailed over the fences.

But time had never been his friend. It either flashed like a meteor through a night sky when he needed it most or dragged as if weighted with lead when he wished it would fly. It had flown when his mother was sick and he'd wanted more time with her, seemed to crawl like a snail while he'd impatiently awaited the age when he could leave home, without having the law haul him back.

No, time had never been his friend. But he'd take advantage of what he had left with Kayla.

As he passed by Kayla's bedroom door, Ry hesitated, then turned the knob and tiptoed inside, telling himself he wanted only to check on her. Make sure she was safe. He crept quietly to the side of the bed and eased down on the edge of the mattress. She lay curled on her side, one hand tucked beneath her cheek. Unable to resist, he reached out and stroked a hand lightly over her hair. She stirred, mewling softly, then blinked open her eyes and peered sleepily up at him.

"Did I oversleep?"

He shook his head. "No. It's only a little after four. I just wanted to check on you before I went to bed."

A soft smile curved her lips. "That's really sweet." She folded back the covers and patted the space beside her. "Sleep here. My bed's closer than yours."

"You sure?"

She nodded and inched over, giving him more room. "I'll even let you cuddle with my teddy bear."

Ry quickly stripped off his clothes and slid in beside her, drew her close. "I'd rather cuddle with you."

She burrowed against him, hiding a smile, as she nuzzled her nose against his chest. "I was hoping you'd say that."

When Kayla awakened the second time, she was nestled against Ry's side, her head pillowed by his arm. The predawn light that seeped through the sheers at the windows offered just enough illumination for her to make out his features in the darkness. The high slash of cheekbone; the noble slope of his nose; the square jaw shadowed by a day's worth of beard. Lulled by the even sound of his breathing, she gave in to the urge to simply stare.

Relaxed in sleep, he looked almost boyish. A lock of dark hair drooped over his forehead, forming a lazy J that brushed the top of one brow. The scowl he usually wore was absent, the deep grooves it cut at the corners of his eyes and mouth now only faint lines, barely discernible in the pale morning light.

She shifted her gaze to his mouth and lips lax in sleep and shivered deliciously, remembering the night before in the barn the tug of those lips on her breasts, as he'd suckled, the shocks of sensation that had lanced through her body to knot in her womb like a fist. He was an aggressive, yet skillful lover, seeming to know instinctively when and where she wanted to be touched, applying just the right amount of pressure to prolong her satisfaction, until she was burning with need. Yet, he was thoughtful and considerate, as well, offering the perfect blend of passion and tenderness to a woman who required both.

His right arm was crooked, his hand splayed over his stomach and she gently covered it with hers. She sensed the quiet strength, marveled at the long, tapered fingers, the skill she knew each contained. The first time she had studied his hands, she remembered thinking how soft his skin was, how well manicured his nails. That certainly wasn't true any longer. Nicks and scrapes marred his once perfect flesh and grease from the tractor stained the cuticles around his nails.

Such a waste, she thought sadly, lacing her fingers through his. He should be in a surgical suite, wielding a scalpel or suturing an incision, not hauling hay and wrestling cattle. She still didn't know why he'd sold his practice, why he'd given up medicine.

But there was time, yet, to find out.

And maybe enough to persuade him to return to what she considered a calling, not a career.

Ry sat on the sofa in the study, going through the mail he'd picked up at the front entrance, while Kayla sat before the computer looking over the most recent batch of assignments she'd received from her professors.

"There's a letter for you," he said, laying it aside.

She glanced over her shoulder. "Really? From who?"

He picked up the envelope and read the return address. "Jimmy Jennings." He tossed it aside. "Or at least, I think that's what it says. Jimmy needs to work on his penmanship."

She jumped up from her chair and hurried to the sofa, scooping up the letter, then dropped down beside Ry to rip it open. "Jimmy's my brother and only twelve. What's your excuse for bad penmanship?"

"All doctors are known for their poor penmanship."

She gave his hand a distracted pat, as she began to read. "Sorry, but you can't use that excuse anymore, since you aren't practicing." She read a few lines and laughed. "He says he's supposed to be listening to Mrs. Mitchell's lecture on personal hygiene, but decided, since he hears enough of that at home from Mom, he'd write to me, instead."

Chuckling, Ry settled back. "Sounds like a smart kid."

"He is. And get this. He says he misses me."

"What's so strange about that?"

She looked at him in surprise. "He's twelve. Twelve-year-old boys rarely acknowledge their sisters, much less admit they miss them."

"How long has it been since you've seen him?"

"A couple of months. I took two days off in December and went home to spend Christmas with my family."

"A whole two days, huh?"

She pursed her lips and gave him a look. "Unlike someone I know, I have to work for a living."

"Hey," he said, insulted. "I work. Running this ranch is no vacation."

"Uh-huh." Hiding a smile, she pecked a kiss on his cheek, then turned her attention back to her letter. She read a few more lines and her eyes widened. "That is so unfair!"

"What is?"

"This!" she cried, slapping a hand against the page. "Jimmy says that the kids at school are teasing him, saying his sister is a hooker." She pushed the pages down to her lap and scowled. "Those stupid reporters. Now my reputation is not only ruined in Austin, it is in my hometown, too."

"Not that I don't share your opinion of reporters, but do you really think twelve-year-olds read the paper?"

"No, but their parents do. They probably overheard their parents discussing it and were repeating what they'd heard."

Ry draped an arm along her shoulders and hugged her against his side. "This is my fault."

Miserable, she tipped her head over to rest it on his shoulder. "No, it's not. Well," she amended and stole a glance up at him, "most of it is." She gave his knee a reassuring pat. "But your heart was in the right place. It was the media that screwed everything up."

"There's got to be something I can do to rectify this. At least in your hometown. If you want, I'll call the local newspaper. Explain what happened. Demand that they print a retraction."

"That would only make things worse. You know what they say about the lady who protesteth too

much—or, in this case, the man. The more you deny
it, the guiltier we'll appear." Her expression glum,
she folded the letter and slipped it back into the envelope. "Besides, if you denied it now, you'd be lying."

"How's that?"

She gave him a disbelieving look, then rolled her
eyes. "Because we *are* having an affair."

Ry refused to consider what he and Kayla shared
was in any way dirty or scandalous. For those kids to
have teased her little brother, calling Kayla a hooker,
was ridiculous. An out-and-out lie. If he could get his
hands on the reporters who had started this stupid
rumor, he'd teach them a thing or two about ethics in
journalism and freedom of press, among other things.

He supposed it was the masochistic tendency he'd
discovered in himself that had him driving into town
after lunch to visit the public library for a look at the
newspapers that were kept on hand. He'd have preferred doing the search at home, via the Internet, thus
avoiding the resentful looks he knew the townspeople
would send his way. But he'd feared Kayla would
catch him at the computer and would want to know
what he was doing, and he didn't want to upset her
any more than she already was.

As he made the turn onto the square of Tanner's
Crossing, he tried to recall the last time he'd been in
the downtown area and finally decided it was more
than a decade. Since moving back to the ranch, he'd
made only two trips to town; once for gas and another
to pick up feed for the horses. But both trips had kept
him on the outskirts of town and away from the town
proper, which was his plan.

Amazingly the place hadn't changed much in the years he'd been away. Tanner Savings and Loan still sat in the middle of the square, a testament to the prosperity of the Tanners who had first settled in the area. The retail shops and offices that lined the streets that made up the square might have changed ownership, but physically they looked the same. Awnings still stretched from the store fronts to the curb, as they had for as long as he could remember, shading the sidewalks in front of each building and inviting shoppers to linger in front of the window displays. He knew that many of the buildings were owned by his family, but not a one of the retail businesses belonged to them. Traditionally Tanners were ranchers and land barons, not merchants.

Except for Rory.

Ry huffed a laugh, having a hard time picturing his brother behind a cash register…though he doubted Rory put in much time behind one. He couldn't sit still that long. But he was a natural-born salesman. He could sell a bald man a comb and have the man placing an order for more. Though he owned a chain of country western stores, Ry knew his brother would never allow his businesses to tie him down. Not in the way that most sole proprietors were shackled to their retail stores. Rory liked the challenge of the business, the constant change and variety, but was short on commitment.

Which pretty much summed up his attitude toward women, as well.

Ry couldn't remember Rory ever having a serious girlfriend. The *girl* might have been serious, but never Rory. Like a butterfly to a flower, he flitted from woman to woman, taking pleasure from each, before moving on to the next. His lifestyle made it easy for him to move on. With an apartment in each of the five cities where he owned Western stores, he was constantly on the go, never staying more than two weeks in any one place. It was a hell of a way to live, in Ry's estimation, but it seemed to suit Rory just fine.

Spotting a parking space in front of the library, Ry swung his Navigator between two farm trucks and went inside. The library, like the town, hadn't changed in the years he'd been away. Straight ahead was the checkout desk, a relic from the Forties that loomed over four feet high. Ry remembered as a boy, stretching to his toes to place his books on the counter for Miss Mamie, the librarian, to stamp the due date on the inside of the back cover.

Behind the desk and to either side stood row after row of tall, wooden bookcases. Thousands of books lined the shelves, their spines all neatly facing out. Floor-to-ceiling windows were spaced evenly along the exterior walls, with each sill holding potted plants: African violets, bromeliads, and ivies whose long, trailing vines had climbed within inches of the ceiling.

Seeing the plants made him think of Miss Mamie, as she had always loved flowers of any kind and surrounded herself with them, even while at work. He wondered if she was still around, then snorted a breath. Miss Mamie would've retired years ago.

But of all the people he remembered from his hometown, Miss Mamie was probably the only one he really cared about seeing again.

"May I help you find something?"

The voice, whisper-soft and as fragile as fine bone

china, pulled him back about thirty years. Even as he turned, he told himself it couldn't be her. But there she was. Miss Mamie. The librarian who had shared with him the secrets of a world that existed beyond the boundaries of Tanner's Crossing.

Dressed in a simple black dress, with crisp white collar and cuffs, she moved with a quiet grace as she approached him, in spite of the slight limp a childhood accident had left her with.

A wad of emotion clotted in his throat. "Miss Mamie."

She tipped her head and looked at him curiously, then pressed trembling fingers to her lips as recognition dawned. "Oh, my goodness. Ry." Staring, she dropped a hand to her heart. "Why, I haven't seen you…in years."

"Yes, ma'am. It's been a while."

"And just look at you," she said, looking him up and down. "You've grown into such a fine-looking young man."

"Well, at least the first part's true. I've definitely grown some."

Catching his hand, she drew him along with her to a grouping of chairs. "Come and tell me what has brought you back home."

Ry waited until she was seated, then sat opposite her. "I'm sure you know that Buck died."

She nodded gravely. "Such a shock."

"Yes, ma'am, it was. Since his death, Ace has been taking care of the ranch but had to leave for a photo assignment in North Dakota. I'm looking after things until he returns."

"How long will you stay?"

"As long as it takes."

She looked at him in surprise. "Why, I would think, as a doctor, it would be difficult for you to leave your patients for such an indefinite period of time."

"I sold my practice."

"Oh, Ry," she cried softly, obviously distressed by the news. "Please tell me that you've only taken a sabbatical."

"No, ma'am. It's permanent."

"But you had such big dreams. So many plans."

He lifted a shoulder. "Things change."

She reached across the distance that separated them to cover his hand with hers. "People don't change, Ry. Not that drastically. What happened?"

When he only looked at her, she slowly drew back her hand to knot with her other on her lap. "I'm sorry. That was rude of me to pry. Whatever your reasons, I'm sure they are personal."

Chuckling softly, he shook his head. "Miss Mamie, if I were to tell anyone, it would be you." He opened his hands. "But I can't explain it. Not even to my-self."

"I read about your difficulties in Austin. I hope your decision doesn't have anything to do with that unpleasantness."

He choked back a laugh. Only Miss Mamie would refer to the lies being printed about him as difficulties and unpleasantness.

"No, ma'am. I sold my practice before any of that came up."

"Maybe this is just a phase you're going through, then," she suggested kindly. "Most people experience a low point in their lives, at one time or another. Knowing you as I do, I would imagine you've burned yourself out, working too many hours, not taking any time to refresh, to restore. Give yourself some time to think through your decision before you do anything more."

"Well, I've definitely got the time to do that."

She glanced up at a sound, her hearing as sharp as ever. "Oh, dear. That'll be my group of kindergarten students coming for story hour."

Ry rose. "Don't let me keep you from your duties. If you don't mind, I'd like to look through some of your newspapers. Maybe use your Internet, if that's okay."

Already hurrying to the door to greet the students, she fluttered a hand toward a bank of computers in a cubicle behind her desk. "Help yourself. If you need anything, I'll be in the children's section."

Ry spent the next two hours before a computer screen, reading article after article written about him and Kayla. The information was easy enough to find. He'd simply done an Internet search for newspapers in Texas, then placed his name in each of the paper's individual search engines. The number of articles listed was astonishing…and infuriating. Prior to his search, the last article he'd read was the one suggesting foul play. Ace had told him about the later article, the one in which Kayla's mother was interviewed. He'd hoped that was the last time anything had been printed about them.

Unfortunately he discovered that wasn't the case.

Though the number of articles being printed had dwindled in number over the weeks, it was obvious that the story was still very much alive. Along with the lies and innuendoes previously published about him and Kayla, the reporters had learned that Ry had sold his practice and were now questioning his reasons for doing so. The most laughable explanation offered was that he'd botched a facelift and left a woman looking like a monster. Of course, the reporters protected themselves from any chance of a slander suit being filed against them, by stating that this was all purely speculation.

But they'd succeeded in planting the seed of doubt—or possibility—in the mind of every person who read the piece.

As he made the drive back to the ranch, Ry tried to think of some way to get his and Kayla's names out of the news, before the reporters discovered he'd moved Kayla to the ranch—or, worse, dug deep enough to discover Ry's tie to the Tanners of Tanner's Crossing.

But, to his continued frustration, nothing new came to mind.

As he approached the house, he saw Kayla running toward the barn. Wondering why she was in such a hurry, he sped up and gave his horn a short blast. She glanced over her shoulder, at the sound, then stopped and turned, waiting. He knew by the look of distress on her face that something was wrong.

Rolling down his window, he braked to a stop beside her. ''What's happened?''

''One of the horses is hurt,'' she said breathlessly.

Ry glanced at the barn, his stomach knotting with dread. ''Which one?''

''Midnight. Luke is with him now.''

Setting his jaw, he released the door locks. ''Get in.''

Kayla quickly jumped into the backseat and leaned

forward, placing a hand on his shoulder, as he sped toward the barn.

"He thinks it happened some time this morning," she said, then gulped, struggling to catch her breath. "Luke found him a couple of hours ago, then came to the house looking for you."

"Did he call the vet?"

"I did. But the receptionist at the clinic said he's out and won't return until late."

He braked to a stop in front of the barn and jumped out. Kayla followed close behind.

"Luke?" Ry called.

"Over here," Luke replied.

Ry strode toward the sound of Luke's voice and ducked inside a stall, where he found Luke kneeling beside Midnight, holding a compress to the horse's shoulder.

Ry hunkered down beside him. "How bad is it?"

Grimacing, Luke drew back the compress, so that Ry could see for himself. A gaping wound, almost a foot in length, ran from midcenter on the horse's breast and around to his shoulder.

Ry smoothed a finger over the horse's coat above the cut, talking soothingly, as he examined it more closely. "Barbed-wire?"

Luke nodded. "Looks like it."

"But how did he get tangled up in barbed-wire? The fencing in the pastures where the horses are kept during the day is smooth wire, not barbed."

"I know. But see how jagged the wound is? The gouges, where it's deeper in some places than others? If that wasn't caused by barbed-wire, then you can keep my next paycheck."

"Did you see any loose wire lying around, when you found him?"

Shaking his head, Luke dropped a hand to rest on his knee. "No, but I didn't spend a lot of time lookin'. I hightailed it back to the barn quick as I could and hooked up a trailer and hauled him in."

"Have you given him a shot of antibiotic to ward off infection?"

"Yessur. First thing. I flushed the wound best I could, but he's going to need stitchin'."

"Kayla said she'd called the vet."

"Yeah. But he's out at the Lazy J, helpin' the Johnsons vaccinate their cattle. Won't be back till late this evenin'." He lifted his hand to gesture at the horse's wound. "This is going to need closin' 'fore then."

"Can you do it?" Ry asked.

Luke shook his head. "No, sir. Not me. I can tell you what's ailin' an animal and doctor them for just about anything, but these big ol' hands of mine…" He held them up, then dropped them, shaking his head again. "They ain't no good at sewin'."

Ry frowned. "What about supplies?"

"Buck, he kept a fair amount of veterinary supplies on hand for emergencies. I'd imagine you'd find whatever you need in the cupboards in the supply room."

"Keep the compress on him," Ry ordered, as he turned away.

Kayla fell into step with him, as he moved from the stall, her eyes wide, her face pale. "You're going to stitch him up?"

"I can't take a chance on losing another animal." He flattened his lips in a grim, determined line. "Not when there's something I can do to prevent it."

Chapter 12

Kayla had watched surgeries performed before, but never in a barn, and never one where the patient was a horse. She found the entire procedure fascinating. It was made even more so with Ry as the attending physician. Watching him work was like watching a dancer execute a tightly choreographed ballet...on the head of a pin. His movements were graceful, exact, calculated, and performed within a stall reduced to the size of a small refrigerator, with the two grown men and massive horse that occupied the space.

His hands, encased in surgical gloves, had been rock steady throughout the procedure, yet gentle, even tender, as he'd administered the shots necessary to numb the horse's skin, then cleansed and sutured the jagged wound. And when he'd finished, the cut was all but invisible, if not for the narrow band of hair that he'd clipped from around it. In Kayla's mind, Ry was truly gifted.

And he was currently wasting that gift.

Tucked against his side, she gazed into the fire burning in the fireplace, trying to think of a way to broach the subject of that waste, without angering or alienating him.

"Do you think Midnight will be all right?" she asked hesitantly.

"Barring an infection, he'll be fine."

"He's such a beautiful horse. I hope he isn't left with an ugly scar."

"He won't be. If the hair grows back properly, you'll never even know he was hurt."

"I'm amazed at your skill. You placed the sutures so closely and precisely, there wasn't a pucker or dimple in his hide. You're a talented surgeon."

"There are plenty out there as good or better than me."

She hazarded a glance his way, wondering how far she dared push. "But there's always a need for more."

He turned his head to look at her, then away, frowning. "Nice try. But the answer is no. I gave up medicine."

Frustrated, she sat up and angled around to face him. "Why do you refuse to talk about you being a doctor?"

"Because there's nothing to discuss."

"There is! For starters, you can tell me why you sold your practice."

"I wanted out. Is that reason enough for you?"

"No. I want to know *why* you wanted out. What it was that made you throw away all those years of study, turn your back on people who desperately need your help."

"Are you trying to give me a guilt trip? If you are, you're wasting your breath. My patients didn't *need* my help. Most of them were nothing but a bunch of vain women with nothing better to do with their money and time than spend it on ways to improve their looks."

When she would have pushed harder, he held up a hand. "Drop it, okay? I'm tired and just want to go to bed."

Normally, once Kayla set her teeth into something, she was like a bulldog and would snarl and shake, until she'd gotten what she wanted from it. But she could see the shadows beneath Ry's eyes, the weary slump of his shoulders, and couldn't bring herself to compound his misery by hounding him for answers he didn't want to give.

With a sigh of resignation, she stood and offered him her hand. "Come on, cowboy, and I'll tuck you into bed."

They'd made it halfway down the hall, when a knock on the front door had them stopping to share a puzzled look.

Kayla gave his hand a squeeze. "You go on to bed. I'll see who it is."

Ry tightened his grip on hers. "At this time of night? *I'll* answer the door."

She clamped her hand around his, refusing to be left behind. "We *both* will."

With a shake of his head, Ry crossed to open the door, with Kayla hovering at his side.

Luke stood on the porch, his hat in his hand.

"Sorry to bother you folks so late," he said in apology. "But I forgot to tell you something earlier. What with the horse gettin' hurt, it plumb slipped my mind. I remembered it a bit ago and was afraid I'd forget again, if I waited till mornin' to tell you.''

"No problem," Ry assured him. "We were still up."

Luke blew out a breath. "That's good. I know how I hate gettin' woke up."

"What was it you wanted to tell us?" Kayla prodded, hoping to hurry him along.

"Well, a man came by earlier. Said he was wantin' to buy one of the bulls. He left his card." He fished a business card out of his shirt pocket and passed it to Ry. "Said for you to give him a call."

Ry looked down at the card and frowned when he saw Phil Sharp's name. "We don't have any bulls for sale."

"I didn't think we did, either, which is why I thought I should tell you about the guy. Seemed kinda' jumpy. You know. Guilty like."

Ry's frown deepened. "How did he get on the property?"

"That's just it. He didn't. I was ridin' the fence along the highway, making sure there weren't any more breaks, and I saw a truck parked along the shoulder. Considering all the trouble we've had, I figured I'd better check it out."

"Good idea," Ry said, nodding.

"When I got even with the truck, I saw that the cab was empty. Then I spotted this guy up ahead, walkin' and peerin' over the fence, like he was lookin' for somethin'. I figured he was up to no good, so I loped my horse over to check things out. When I asked him what he was doin', he hem-hawed around a bit, then said he was wantin' to buy a bull and heard we had one for sale. Claimed he was just tryin' to get a look at the bull, before he came on up to the house. I told him I didn't think we had nothin' for sale, but that you were the man he'd need to talk to, if we did." He gestured toward the card. "That's when he gave me that."

Ry looked down at the card, then slipped it into his pocket. "I appreciate you keeping a tight watch on things, Luke. I'll give the guy a call in the morning and see what he was up to."

"Probably a good idea." Luke snugged his hat over his head. "Sorry to disturb you so late," he said again, then turned and strode off into the night.

Pensive, Ry closed the door.

"Do you know the man?" Kayla asked.

"As a matter of fact, I do." He pulled the card from his pocket to frown at it again. "He's the one who gave me the black eye."

Kayla blinked open her eyes and frowned at the darkness, sure that it was a noise that had awakened her. Pushing up to her elbows, she listened, then glanced over at Ry. He lay beside her, an arm slung over his eyes, softly snoring. She was tempted to wake him, but hated to. He'd had a hard enough time going to sleep, after Luke had left.

Easing the covers back, she swung her legs over the side of the bed and moved quietly to the window. She pushed back the sheers and peered out at the night. Not seeing anything out of the ordinary, she dropped the sheers and turned for the door. The view from her window was only of the front of the house and she knew she wouldn't be able to sleep until she'd checked the back, as well. Keeping her footsteps as light as possible, she tiptoed to the kitchen.

One step inside and her eyes flipped wide. She ran for the back door and flung it open. The sky glowed a bright red, lit by the flames that leaped from the roof of the barn. ''Ry!'' she screamed, then grabbed a jacket from the rack by the door and ran out into the night.

Ry bolted upright in bed at Kayla's scream, blinked, then vaulted to his feet. ''Kayla?'' he called, grabbing his jeans. He tugged them on as he sprinted for the door. ''Kayla!'' he yelled, running down the hall.

In the kitchen, he saw the open back door, the wall of flames it framed. His heart seemed to stop, then slammed against his chest. He raced to the door, pushed his feet into a pair of boots he'd left there, grabbed a jacket and shot outside.

''Kayla!'' he shouted, his feet barely hitting the ground as he sailed over it. ''Ka-a-ay-la!''

''Over here!''

She stood in front of the barn, her body a dark shadow against the towering flames behind her, waving her arms over her head. Just as he spotted her, a horse bolted through the open barn doors behind her, its eyes wide with fear. With Kayla directly in the horse's path, Ry closed the last few yards that separated him from her, scooped her up and feinted to his left, the horse missing them by inches. Never once breaking his stride, he ran for a group of trees that stood far enough away from the barn that he was sure the fire wouldn't reach them.

His heart pounding, his lungs burning with the smoke that thickened the air, he gripped her face between his hands. Soot smeared her cheeks and chin and the smell of singed hair stung his nose. "Are you hurt?"

"No. But, Luke—"

"God, Kayla," he groaned, crushing his arms around her. "What were you thinking? Why didn't you wake me? You could've been killed."

She wriggled in his arms, trying to break free. "Ry!" she cried in frustration. "We've got to help Luke get the horses out!"

He whipped his head around to look at the barn, then turned and gripped her shoulders hard. "Stay here," he ordered sternly. "I'll help Luke."

A bloodcurdling scream rent the air and they both spun, to see a man streaking from the barn, his jacket and jeans blazing.

"Oh, my God!" Kayla cried. "Lu-u-uke!"

Ry ran, ripping off his coat. He tackled Luke, knocking him to the ground, and rolled with him, struggling to wrap his coat around the man and smother the flames.

"Kayla!" he yelled.

Already at his side, she said breathlessly, "Tell me what to do."

"Go to the house. Call 911. Tell them we need an ambulance, stat."

A long shadow fell over them, blocking some of the light from the fire. Kayla glanced up to find Slim standing above them, his expression grim.

"I've already called," he said. "They're on their way."

Ribbons of smoke curled from the barn's charred remains, while water dripped from fallen beams, spitting and hissing, as it hit the hot ashes below. The

ground around the barn was churned to swamp by the
feet of the volunteers who'd fought the fire. Most still
remained, gathered in tight groups around the barn's
perimeter, their voices pitched low, as they weighed
the loss, debated possible causes, watched for live
sparks to flare.

Kayla moved among them, her feet leaden by exhaustion, her face smeared with soot, refilling empty
cups with coffee she carried in a two-gallon insulated
jug. Beyond the barn, in a trap used to pen cattle, the
horses stood, their heads hanging low, their heavy
winter coats soaked with water and streaked with
mud.

Thankfully, no horses had been lost in the fire. A
few had received minor burns, others cuts and scrapes
from trying to kick their way out of their stalls. But
the vet had already treated their wounds and left
again, shaking his head at the close call. But Luke,
the man who had fought to save the livestock…

Kayla squeezed her eyes shut, swaying dizzily, as
she heard again his almost inhuman scream of pain,
saw him streak from the barn, as if trying to outrun
the flames that ate away at his coat, his jeans. In his
efforts to save the horses, he'd put his own life at
risk.

And Ry….

On a low moan, she squeezed her eyes tighter shut,
seeing his hands. His beautiful, talented hands, swollen, red, his palms covered with blisters. She wanted
to be with him, had begged him to let her ride in the
ambulance with him and Luke, but he'd refused, in-
sisting that he was all right and would return as soon
as he could.

"Kayla."

She opened her eyes to see Elizabeth hurrying toward her, her arms open. Kayla fell into them on a sob.

"I know, I know," Elizabeth soothed, stroking a hand over Kayla's tangled hair, as she held her. "It's awful. Just awful. Woodrow and I came as soon as we heard."

"Ry. He was hurt." She hiccuped a sob, clinging to Elizabeth. "He w-wouldn't let me go w-with him to the hospital."

Elizabeth pushed Kayla back and teased her with a smile. "Isn't that just like a man? They always think they know what's best for a woman. But don't you worry. I'll have Woodrow call the hospital and check on him." Shifting Kayla to her side, she turned her toward the house. "Now let's get you inside and out of these wet clothes, before you make yourself sick."

Craning her neck to see behind her, Kayla stretched a hand back as if to anchor herself to the tragic scene. "No. I have to serve the men coffee. They've worked so hard. They're so cold. And the horses. They'll need feed. Blankets."

"The men and the horses will be fine," Elizabeth assured her, then looked up and sent a silent signal to Woodrow, who stood with a group of men in the distance, assessing the damage, what needed to be done.

He quickly left the group and scooped Kayla off her feet and into his arms, as if she weighed no more than a child.

She struggled valiantly, but finally went limp, knowing she was powerless against Woodrow's greater strength, and tucked her head beneath his chin and gave in to the tears.

"That's it, honey," he said, his voice gruff with emotion. "Let it all out. You deserve a good cry."

By the time Kayla climbed into bed, shooed there by Elizabeth, the sun was blazing high in the sky.

"Promise me you'll wake me when Ry gets home."

Elizabeth nodded and pulled the covers up over Kayla. "I promise. The moment he arrives, I'll personally come and get you, myself."

Kayla grasped Elizabeth's hand, tears blurring her vision. "His hands," she said, then gulped. "He burned them when he was trying to put out the flames on Luke."

Choked by tears, Elizabeth could only nod. "I know. But Woodrow has talked to the ER doctor and he assured him that the burns Ry sustained were minimal. Luke...."

Kayla squeezed her eyes shut, trying to block the image of Luke's blackened hands, the stench of his burning flesh. "I know," she said, gulping back the nausea, the horror. "His were worse. So much worse."

Elizabeth leaned over and pressed her lips to Kayla's forehead. "Don't think about that now. Focus your thoughts on getting some sleep, so that you'll be rested and can take care of Ry when he gets home."

"Elizabeth?" Kayla asked hesitantly

"Yes?"

"Would you mind sitting with me for a while?"

Her smile tender, Elizabeth sank down on the edge of the bed and gathered Kayla's hand to hold in hers. "No, I don't mind."

"I know I should sleep, but I can't."

"That's because you're worried about Ry, but he'll be fine. He's receiving the care he needs."

She nodded, swallowing back tears. "This is all so unbelievable."

"Yes," Elizabeth agreed, with a sigh. "It's difficult to imagine why anyone would want to harm the Tanners."

"Maybe the target isn't the family, per se, but only one member."

Elizabeth looked at her curiously. "What do you mean?"

Kayla sighed wearily. "I don't know. But while I was in the shower, I kept trying to think why anyone would do this, and I remembered something Maw Garner said."

Elizabeth chuckled. "I wouldn't put a whole lot of faith in what Maw says. She's a bit of a gossip."

"That's what Ry said. But while Maw was here delivering groceries, she said something about Ry having a lot of nerve coming back to Tanner's Crossing. I didn't think much about it, at the time, but now I'm wondering if all of this isn't somehow directed at Ry."

"Oh, I don't think so," Elizabeth assured her. "Ry has never done anything to harm the people of the town. Not as a whole and not individually. Heavens. It's been twenty years since he lived here."

"Then why would Maw say that?"

Elizabeth hesitated a moment, as if reluctant to respond, then let out a breath. "Normally I would tell you to ask Ry, but it isn't as if it's a secret. I've heard the stories several times myself, since moving here.

"It's all fairly complicated and dates back years and years, but I'll make my explanation as brief as

possible. I think you're aware that Ry and his father
didn't get along.''

"Yes. Ry told me they didn't."

"Buck had plans for each of his sons, for their
futures, and expected them to go along with his plans
without argument. All of them fought with him over
this, but none more than Ry. I think Ry was a soph-
omore in high school when he announced that he
wanted to go to college and become a doctor. From
what Woodrow has told me, Buck pitched quite the
fit, swore that he'd never pay a penny toward Ry's
education, thinking, I'm sure, that with no money to
back him, Ry would give in and do what Buck wanted
him to do. But Ry didn't.

"Mrs. Tanner, Ry's mother, left a trust for each of
her sons when she passed away. It was more than
enough to pay for Ry's education, but he wouldn't
receive the trust until he reached the age of twenty-
one. He tried to borrow against the trust, in order to
raise the money he needed, but Buck had enough in-
fluence in the area to keep Ry from getting a loan.

"There was a doctor in town, at the time. Dr.
Rivers. He's gone now. Passed away about twelve
years ago, I believe. At any rate, Dr. Rivers agreed
to loan Ry the money, on the condition that Ry would
return to Tanner's Crossing after he completed his
medical training and set up his practice here.

"Everyone in town knew about the agreement Dr.
Rivers and Ry had made, and they were furious when
Ry remained in Austin, after graduating from medical
school, and set up his practice there, thus failing to
uphold his end of the bargain. Tanner's Crossing
needs more doctors and has for years. By failing to
uphold his end of the bargain, the townspeople felt as

if Ry had let them down, ignored a very real need, for his own selfish gain.'' She smiled sadly. "I know that seems petty, but that's why the people here resent Ry."

Ry sat at the kitchen table, his forearms braced against its edge, holding his hands aloft. Gauze bound his wrists, stretched upward to circle his thumbs, then wound higher, forming loose mittens that covered his hands.

"I've called the others,'' Woodrow said quietly. "They'll get here quick as they can. Slim is taking care of the livestock. Monty was so upset by it all, he was pretty much useless, so I sent him back to the bunkhouse."

Ry nodded grimly. "I appreciate you stepping in and taking over."

Woodrow shook his head. "This isn't yours to deal with alone. We've all got a stake in what happens on Tanner land."

With a weary sigh, Ry sank back in the chair. "I can't help but feel this is my fault. Everything was fine until I came back."

"Don't start claiming responsibility for things out of your control. Besides, what affects one Tanner, affects us all."

Ry looked over at Woodrow, wondering how his brother could say that, *feel* that way with all the years of silence and indifference that lay between them. "I left y'all," he reminded him. "Packed my bags and hauled ass, as soon as I was of an age the old man couldn't call the law and have them drag me back again."

Woodrow hid a smile. "You always were running away."

"And you didn't." Suddenly angry, Ry pushed back the chair and stood. "None of you did. I was the only one who was too weak to stand up to the old man, too cowardly to fight back, when he demanded that I walk the line he drew for each of us to follow."

Woodrow shook his head. "You weren't a coward. "Not then and damn sure not now."

"Dammit, I was!" Ry cried, and caught himself before he slammed a fist down the table. Rubbing a hand over the fist he'd made, he scowled and turned away. "I ran, when I should have stood with the rest of you."

"We all ran, Ry. You were just the first to make the break."

Ry glanced back over his shoulder.

Woodrow lifted his hands. "It's true. Ace left not long after you. I imagine he would've left sooner, if he hadn't felt obligated, as the oldest, to stay and look after the rest of us."

Grimacing, Ry turned and sat down at the table again. "He always did think he was our boss, ordering us around like we were nothing but a bunch of snot-nosed kids."

Woodrow choked a laugh. "That's because we were." He sobered slowly and fixed his gaze on Ry's. "But he did it because he loved us. Because he cared." He looked away and shot an arm beneath his nose, as if embarrassed by the sentimentality, before continuing.

"With Ace gone, I wasn't about to hang around. I pulled out a few weeks after my high school graduation. Rory stayed until Whit graduated, then they both hightailed it, though in opposite directions. None of us stayed, Ry,'' he said in summation. ''We all ran, same as you.''

''I hate to interrupt, but Ry needs to get some sleep.''

Woodrow and Ry both glanced over to find Elizabeth standing in the kitchen doorway.

She offered them both a regretful smile. ''I promised Kayla that I'd wake her when Ry got home. I wouldn't want her to think I'm not a woman of my word.''

Ry pushed back his chair. ''I'll tell her. Y'all go on back home and get some rest. We'll deal with whatever needs taking care of when the others get here.''

Ry showered first, wanting to rid himself of the stench of smoke before he woke Kayla. Bathing himself was awkward, what with the plastic bags he had to place over his hands, to keep the bandages dry. But he was able to wash off the worst of the soot and smell that clung to his body and hair.

With a towel wrapped at his waist, he went to Kayla's room. He stood at the side of her bed, for a moment, staring down at her. When he thought of the danger she'd placed herself in, the risk she'd taken in trying to help Luke....

He swallowed back the emotion that clotted in his throat. She'd grown to mean so much to him. In the short weeks he'd known her, she'd wormed her way into his heart, planted herself firmly in his life. The thought of her suffering harm, the possibility of

him losing her, made his knees weak, his head spin
dizzily.

He loved her. He realized that now. Could finally
admit it. He'd probably fallen in love with her the
moment he'd first set eyes on her. Why he'd fought
those feelings, denied the reality of them, found a
hundred excuses why a relationship with her wouldn't
work he didn't know. He knew only that he loved her
and always would.

Shaken by the enormity of his feelings for her, he
sank to the edge of the bed and stroked the back of
his bandaged hand across her brow, needing to touch
her, to prove to himself that she hadn't suffered any
harm. Her lids fluttered up and her gaze met his. Tears
brimmed in her eyes.

"Oh, Ry. Your hands."

He gave her a small smile. "The bandages make
them look worse than they are. I suffered some minor
burns, is all. The bandages are to keep the wounds
clean."

She gently curved her fingers around his hand and
drew it to cradle against her cheek. "All that matters
is that you're home and safe." She opened her arms
and he leaned into her embrace, letting her hold him,
wishing like hell he could hold her. He satisfied himself by catching the tears that leaked from her eyes
with his lips.

"I'm okay, Kayla. We both are."

She drew back to look at him and combed his damp
hair back from his brow. "Yes. We were lucky." She
gulped and fresh tears filled her eyes. "Luke?"

Ry lowered his gaze, unable to face the question,
the dread he saw in her eyes. "He wasn't so lucky.
He has third degree burns on portions of his face and

neck. Lesser burns on his legs, chest and back. But his hands...they suffered the most damage.''

"He won't lose them, will he?"

He shook his head. "No. I don't think so. Though it's too early to know for sure. They Care-Flighted him to Dallas to the burn unit at Parkland. He'll require surgery. Skin grafts. Months of rehabilitation to regain the use of his hands.''

"Oh, Ry." Choked by tears, she drew him down to hold, her cheek pressed to his, a hand cupped at his nape.

"We'll take care of him, Kayla. The Tanners will see that he has the best doctors money can buy.''

"I'll help, too," she promised tearfully. "He'll be frightened, I know. Won't want anyone to see his disfigurement. Depression is as serious a threat to burn patients as their injuries. But I won't let him get depressed or start feeling sorry for himself. I can do that for him."

Ry drew back to look at her, his heart filled with his love for her. He'd never known a woman who was so unselfish, so caring.

"I love you, Kayla," he said softly. He watched her eyes widen, her lips part and pressed his mouth to hers. "No. Don't say anything." He angled an arm beneath her head and shifted to lie down on the bed beside her, draping his bandaged hand over her waist. "Just hold me," he whispered, brushing his lips across hers. "I need you to hold me. Feel you beside me. Know you're here with me."

As she slipped her arms around him, he closed his eyes, comforted by her nearness and her warmth, as she nestled close.

And slept.

* * *

He'd said he loved her.

Kayla pressed a hand to her stomach, unable to believe he'd actually said the words to her. But he had. It wasn't a dream. If he'd told her the day before, she would've shouted the news from the rooftop, wept with joy that he shared her feelings, because she loved him, too.

But today she could only worry.

"You okay?"

She glanced over, as Ry stepped from the shower, water dripping from his face and arms and pooling on the tiled floor. Forcing a smile, she crossed to him and pulled a towel from a rack on the wall.

"I'm fine," she said, as she dried his chest and face. "Just thinking."

"About what?"

She stepped behind him to dry his back...and hide.

"About what you said to me this morning."

He glanced over his shoulder to look at her. "That I love you?"

Wincing, she nodded, then squatted down to dry the back of his legs.

He turned and hunkered down in front of her. "Kayla, if you don't feel the same way about me..."

Tears welled and she stubbornly blinked them back. "No. It isn't that. I do love you. It's just that..."

He dipped his head down to meet her gaze. "What?"

"Your timing really sucks," she said miserably and sniffed.

He choked a laugh. "Considering all that's going on, that's probably true, but it's nothing to cry over.

Come here,'' he said and awkwardly wrapped his arms around her and drew her to him.

She sniffed again and turned her cheek against his damp chest. ''I want you to know that, when this is all over, should you change your mind, I'll understand. I will, I promise.''

He drew back to look at her. ''What makes you think I'm going to change my mind?''

''People who survive tragedies together often mistake the emotions they feel for each other as love. I just want you to know that I'll understand, if you discover that's what you've done.''

Laughing softly, he hugged her to him. ''I'm not going to change my mind, Kayla. My feelings for you have nothing to do with the fire. I love you and have since the first time I saw you. It just took me a while to accept those feelings.''

Chapter 13

Kayla and Ry entered the study together, each with an arm wound around the other's waist. Ry's brothers were already there, waiting. Ace. Woodrow. Rory. Whit. They formed a formidable wall of support, as they stood to greet them.

Two other men, strangers to Kayla, hung back from the others, their hats in their hand. Ace moved aside to make the introductions.

"This is Sheriff Akin," he said, tipping his toward the man on his left, then gestured to the man on his right. "And Frank Carter, the fire marshal. We've already briefed them on the trouble we've been having over the last few weeks. What we need to focus on now is finding out who is behind all this."

"What about the fire?" Ry asked, directing his question to the fire marshal. "Do you know how it started?"

His expression grim, Carter nodded. "There's no

question it was arson. We found an empty can of gasoline behind the barn. From what we've been able to establish, it appears that whoever set the fire started at the front, dousing the floor with gas, then put a flame to it and escaped out the back. With all the hay stored in the barn, the fire spread quickly. Though our response time was fast, there was little my men could do to save the building, since it was constructed of wood.''

''That barn was more than a hundred years old,'' Woodrow interjected. ''Built by our great-great-grandfather with timber felled and milled on Tanner land.''

''It might've been old,'' Rory added, ''but it was strong. Tanners build to last. Always have.''

''I won't argue that,'' Carter conceded. ''Some of those beams we moved must've weighed half a ton or more.''

Ry shifted his gaze to the sheriff. ''Any clues as to who set the fire?''

''If you're asking about physical evidence,'' the sheriff replied, ''all we have is the burned-out gas can Carter gave us. If the arsonist left any prints on it, the fire would've destroyed them. And the water used to put out the fire washed out any footprints he might've left behind. My men are still out there, and we've widened the search, but so far they've come up empty-handed.''

Ry firmed his lips, thinking of the business card he had in his pocket with Phil Sharp's name on it. ''I have to believe that whoever set the fire is the same person who killed the cows and injured the horse.''

The sheriff dipped his chin, studying his hat. ''It sure appears that way.''

Something in the man's posture made Ry look at him more closely. "Do you know who's behind all this?"

The sheriff looked up and fixed his gaze on Whit. "I have a pretty good idea."

Whit shot out of the chair, his hands balled into fists. "I didn't set that fire!"

The sheriff lifted a brow. "I don't recall saying you did."

His face a furious red, Whit started for the sheriff, but Woodrow quickly stepped in front of him, blocking his way. "Don't go off half-cocked, Whit," he said quietly. "Nobody's accusing you of anything."

Whit flung out a hand, gesturing at the sheriff. "Damned, if he's not. He looked straight at me when he said it."

Ace moved to stand beside Whit and laid a hand on his shoulder. "When you accuse a Tanner of a crime," he told the sheriff, "you better have damned good evidence to back up your claim."

The sheriff snorted. "Whit's not a Tanner. Everybody in town knows that Buck never cared for the boy and only adopted him because Whit's mother wouldn't agree to marry him unless he did.

"The way I've got it figured, Whit resented the old man, and resented the lot of you, too, because you stand to inherit what Buck left behind, while he's left empty-handed."

"So he kills a couple of cows and burns down a barn because he's pissed?" Ry choked a laugh. "Come on, Sheriff. You're going to have to do better than that. Whit would turn a gun on himself before he'd point one at an animal. I know that for a fact, because I had to put down a horse of his that broke a leg when he couldn't do it."

"And you're wrong about Whit being left empty-handed," Ace added. "In our eyes, Whit's a Tanner and has been since the day he moved into this house. Whether it was Buck's wishes or not, Whit will inherit a full share of Buck's estate, the same as the rest of us. And Whit is aware of the inheritance, because I personally informed him of the fact shortly after Buck's death."

Rory moved to the door of the study and opened it. "Here's the door, Sheriff." He shot the sheriff a wink. "Don't let it hit your butt on the way out."

"It's ridiculous, that's what it is," Elizabeth fumed angrily. "Imagine anyone thinking Whit capable of murdering a poor, defenseless animal. Why, the man should be ashamed to even call himself a sheriff!" She slapped her arms over her chest. "I have a good mind to march right out there and rip that badge off his chest."

Sprawled on the sofa beside her, Woodrow gave her thigh a comforting pat. "Don't worry, sugar. He won't be sheriff for long."

She looked at him suspiciously. "How do you know he won't?"

Smug, Woodrow stacked his hands behind his head and reared back, stretching out his legs. "Because election time is coming up and nobody in town is gonna want to vote for him, once they hear that the Tanner boys were the ones who put the arsonist behind bars."

Elizabeth's eyes rounded. "Are you saying you know who set the fire?"

"Not yet, I don't." He looked around the room, meeting each of his brother's gazes in turn. "But we'll find him, won't we, boys?"

"Damn right, we will," Ace agreed.

Rory hooted a laugh. "And have a good time doing it, too."

"I know where we can start."

Everyone turned to look at Ry.

"Phil Sharp," he told them. "He was here the day of the fire. Told Luke he was interested in buying a bull from us. Even left his business card behind, so that I could call him."

Rory scratched his head. "Seems pretty dumb for him to have left a business card behind, if he was planning on torching our barn."

"Phil was never known for his superior intelligence," Ry said dryly.

Ace stood and snugged on his hat. "Then I say we pay Mr. Sharp a little visit."

Single file, the Tanner brothers passed through the gate of Phil's corral, then formed a line, walking five abreast, with Ry in the center as they approached. Their grim expressions alone were enough to have Phil Sharp dropping the feed bucket he held and backing away in fear.

"If y'all are lookin' for trouble," Phil warned, "you can look elsewhere. I've got no beef with the Tanners."

They drew to a stop, as if on signal.

"That remains to be seen," Ry said. "Luke told me that you were by our place yesterday, wanting to buy a bull."

Phil dragged off his cap and wiped at the sweat

that beaded his brow. "I was. There ain't no law that says a man can't shop for a bull when he's in need of one."

"No," Ry agreed. "But there are laws against trespassing, and some pretty serious consequences for arson. Somebody burned our barn down last night."

Phil's eyes bugged and he began backing again, his hands pushed out in front of him. "Uh-uh. No way. I didn't have nothin' to do with burnin' down no barn."

"Seems odd that you were there the afternoon before the fire," Rory said. "Makes a person wonder if you weren't there to case the place."

Phil's back hit the iron pipes of the corral, putting an end to any hopes he might've had to escape.

"I was lookin' for a bull, just like I said. Luke was there. He can tell you. I didn't go anywhere near that barn. I didn't set so much as a foot past the front gates."

Woodrow took a slow look around. "You've got some mighty fine lookin' steers here."

Phil gulped and rubbed his beefy hands nervously up and down the sides of his legs. "Bought 'em cheap. Plan on selling them in the fall for a profit."

A thoughtful frown creased Woodrow's brow. "I don't see any cows. Just steers."

"Steers is all I got. Ain't no money to be made in a cow/calf operation."

Woodrow shifted his gaze to meet Phil's. "Then why would you need a bull?"

Phil's eyes rounded, as he realized he'd been caught in a lie.

Ry took a threatening step closer. "Why don't you tell us the real reason you were at our ranch?"

Phil crumpled, hanging his head and looking like he might cry.

"I didn't do nothin'. I swear I didn't. I was just mad at Ry and thinkin' I might stir up some mischief. Get even with him for whippin' my butt a couple weeks back at the feed store. Had me a can of spray paint in the cab of my truck. Was plannin' on leavin' him a message on the stone wall by the front entrance. Probably would've done it, too, if Luke hadn't happened along."

He looked up. "But I didn't set no fire. I got me a ranch. Nothin' as big as y'all's place. But I know what damage a fire can do. The animals that could get hurt. The cost of replacing a barn. I'd never stoop to nothin' that low-down. I was only wantin' to stir up a little mischief, is all." He lifted his hands in entreaty, begging them to believe him. "I swear. That's all I was wantin' to do."

"I tend to believe him," Rory said.

Seated behind the desk in the study, Ace nodded. "I do, too. Phil may be dumb as a fence post, but he doesn't seem the type to set a barn on fire. Not intentionally."

"I have to agree," Ry said. "But with Phil no longer a suspect, where does that leave us?"

Woodrow stood, scraping his hat off the sofa. "Back at square one. I'm going out to the barn and have a look around. See if the sheriff and his men might've missed something."

Whit stood to follow him out. "I'll go with you."

Ace turned to Ry. "What about Luke? Have you heard any news?"

"Nothing more than what I've already told you.

I'm planning on driving up there tomorrow and talking with the attending physician. I'll drop by the accounting department, while I'm there, and let them know that all of his bills are to be sent to us.''

"Need me to drive you?" Rory asked.

Ry looked down at his bandaged hands. "I appreciate it, but, no, Kayla's going with me. She's planning to stay with Luke.''

"Is that wise?" Ace asked. "There's a chance somebody might recognize her—or you. If that should happen, the media will be all over you.''

Ry nodded, his expression grim. "I thought about that. But Kayla's adamant about going and taking care of Luke. Says she's willing to deal with whatever grief the press throws her way.''

Ace kept his gaze steady on Ry. "And what about you? Are you willing to deal with it, too?''

Ry firmed his lips. "Considering what Luke is going through right now, having my past hauled out for all the world to view seems pretty damn trivial in comparison.''

Kayla stuffed her toiletry kit into the duffel and zipped the bag closed.

"Are you sure you want to do this?" Ry asked, fearing her reaction when she saw Luke. "You could wait a couple of days. They're keeping him sedated. I doubt he'll even know you're there.''

She slipped the bag's strap over her shoulder and hefted it up from the bed. "*I'll* know," she told him firmly. "Besides, you need someone to drive.''

"I can drive.''

She gave his hands a pointed look.

He held them up. "Hey. They may not be pretty, but they still work."

Her face crumpled at the sight of his bandaged hands. Catching them in hers, she brought them to her lips. "Your hands are beautiful."

He laughed. "Is this a case of 'love is blind'?"

Her gaze on his, she let the duffel strap slide off her shoulder and slipped her arms around his waist. "I do love you. You know that, don't you?"

His smile softened. "Yes, though I don't know why."

She tightened her arms around him. "I know, and that's enough for me."

His smile faded. "There's so much you don't know about me."

"What? You leave the cap off the toothpaste? Sorry. I already figured that one out."

When she would've reached to pick her bag up again, he held her in place. "I'm serious, Kayla. You don't know me."

"Ry, really," she said in exasperation. "You act as if my feelings for you will change, and they won't. I love you."

"Kayla—"

She bussed him a quick kiss, then pushed from his arms. "Forget it, Ry. You aren't getting rid of me that easily." She pointed a finger at the door. "Now, move. If we don't get on the road soon, it'll be midnight before we make it to Dallas."

"Dr. Tanner!"

Ry glanced up to see a man striding toward him. Dressed in scrubs and holding a set of charts tucked beneath his arm, he was obviously a physician at the hospital. Ry frowned, trying to place him.

"Scott Taylor," the man said, extending a hand as he reached Ry. "We met a couple of years ago at a medical conference in Phoenix. You were there to speak on a technique you had used successfully on breast reconstruction. Very informative presentation, I might add, and a technique I've used on patients of my own."

Ry lifted a hand, revealing the bandage and his inability to respond to the greeting. "I do remember you, Scott, though it took me a minute. I'm glad you found the seminar helpful."

He widened the circle to include Kayla. "This is Kayla Jennings. Kayla, Dr. Taylor."

Smiling, Kayla shook the doctor's hand. "It's nice to meet you."

"The pleasure is mine," Dr. Taylor replied, then turned his attention back to Ry. "So what brings you to our part of the world?"

"We're here visiting a patient. Luke Jenkins. He's in the burn unit."

The doctor nodded grimly. "Yes. I heard about his case. Suffered severe burns to his hands." He stole a look at Ry's hand. "Are your injuries related?"

"Luke works on my family's ranch. There was a fire in the barn. Luke was injured, trying to get the horses to safety." He lifted the hand. "I was burned trying to put the flames out on Luke. Nothing serious," he added. "The bandages are merely to keep the wounds clean."

The doctor nodded soberly, then looked at Ry curiously. "Is your visit here of a professional nature?"

Ry shook his head. "No. Personal. I'm no longer practicing medicine."

The doctor lifted a brow, obviously surprised to learn this. "That's a shame. Luke could use a skilled plastic surgeon like you. Not that we don't have superior surgeons on staff," he added quickly, then smiled. "But you're the best there is. I doubt there's a surgeon here who would challenge me on that."

Uncomfortable with the conversation, Ry hooked an arm behind Kayla's waist and gave the doctor a nod, acknowledging the compliment. "If you'll excuse us, we're anxious to see Luke."

The doctor lifted a hand in farewell. "It was a pleasure seeing you again, Dr. Tanner."

"I'm sorry, Dr. Tanner, but Mr. Jenkins can't have visitors today."

"Has his condition worsened?" Ry asked in concern.

"No," the nurse replied. "But he became extremely agitated earlier this morning. The doctor increased his medications and left an order for no visitors."

"Agitated?" Ry repeated. "When I spoke with the doctor this morning, he said Luke hadn't regained consciousness."

"He hasn't," the nurse said. "Not totally. But he became restless, moaning, mumbling words over and over again."

"What words?"

"Mostly names. Yours for one," she added. "And the word slim." She lifted a shoulder. "Nothing he said made any sense. The pain medication is strong and he's probably a bit out-of-his head, if you know what I mean.''

"Yes, I do,'' Ry said, slowly. "But Slim is a man he worked with. He's probably concerned about Slim's welfare. If he should regain consciousness, you might tell him that Slim is safe. That we all are.''

The nurse smiled. "I'll do that. Sometimes putting a patient's mind at ease helps them rest better.''

After checking into a hotel, Ry called the hospital and left the number with the nurse on duty, requesting that he be called if there was any change in Luke's condition. Of course, he had to have Kayla's help to place the call, which irritated the hell out of him. He didn't like feeling helpless, but with his hands still bound in bandages, helpless was exactly what he was.

Deciding to put an end to his helpless state, he sank his teeth into the strip of gauze at his wrist and gave it a tug.

"What are you doing?'' Kayla cried, dropping her bag and hurrying to him.

He spit out a piece of string that clung to his teeth. "Taking off my bandages.''

She grabbed his arm and pulled it down, before he could catch the gauze between his teeth again.

"You certainly are not! The doctor put those on for a purpose and they're going to stay on.''

"He put them there to keep the wounds clean, which was what he should have done. But wounds need air to heal, too. I'm giving mine some.''

When he tried to lift his arm, she held on, refusing to let go. "Don't force me to fight you, Ry,'' she warned. "In your condition, I might win and you'll only embarrass yourself.''

"Come on, Kayla," he wheedled, and nudged his knee against hers, forcing her to back toward the bed. "Help me take them off. I'm sick of having my hands wrapped."

"I'm not going to—" With a yelp, she fell back on the bed.

Ry followed her down, stretching himself out over her. "Do you have any idea how frustrating it is not to be able to touch you or hold you?" He stroked the back of a bandaged hand over her cheek. "I want to feel your skin against mine. Hold you in my arms, without having two balls of gauze between us." He brushed his lips over hers. "Please, Kayla? Won't you help me?"

Groaning, she gave his chest a push. "All right, you big baby. Get off me, so I can get my scissors out of my bag."

Pleased, Ry rolled off and sat on the side of the bed to wait. When she returned with the scissors, he held up a hand. "Start at the bottom and work your way up," he instructed.

With the tips of the scissors already poised at his wrist, she stopped to narrow an eye at him. "Would you rather do this yourself?"

He gave her a sheepish look. "Sorry. Habit."

"Doctors," she muttered, as she slid the tip of one blade beneath the gauze. "You think you know more than anyone else."

"I'm not a doctor."

"Yeah, that's what you keep saying. But we're going to talk about that."

"Kayla," he warned.

Frowning, she kept snipping, carefully folding back the gauze, as she worked her way up his hand. "You can 'Kayla' me all you want, but we *are* going to talk about this.'' Reaching the tips of his fingers, she set the scissors aside and carefully removed the gauze. "Oh, Ry," she moaned, and drew his hand to her lips to press a kiss against his palm. "You poor baby. Does it hurt?"

He flexed his fingers. "A little stiff. Some soreness. But not too bad." He offered her his other hand. "Take this one off, too."

She picked up the scissors and began to snip at the gauze. "If you don't want to be a doctor, I can accept that." She gave him a hard look. "I won't like it, but I can accept it. But before I can accept it," she said, and went back to her snipping. "I have to understand why you don't want to be one any longer."

"How can I explain something that I don't understand myself?" He lifted a shoulder. "I just reached a point where I didn't want to do it any longer. I had to force myself to go to the office every day."

"Were you bored? Had it lost its challenge?"

"No. Surgery is always a challenge."

She set the scissors aside and eased off the gauze. "Do you think the breakup of your marriage had an effect on how you felt about your work?" She glanced up at him. "If that's too personal, you can simply say yes or no."

Chuckling, he shook his head. "It's not too personal. And, no, it didn't have an effect. The divorce happened *after* I sold my practice. Lana liked the idea of being married to a surgeon, especially one who was raking in the money. Once I told her my plans, she filed for divorce."

Holding his hand in hers, she eased down onto the

bed beside him. "Were you having problems before?"

"Not problems, really. No major fights or anything like that. But neither of us were happy in the marriage. Personally I think she was relieved when I sold the practice. It gave her the excuse she needed to divorce me."

"Why did you get married in the first place?"

"Lust." He glanced over at her. "Not a very strong basis for a marriage, huh?"

"No, but I'm sure you weren't the only couple to marry for that reason."

He leaned to bump his nose against hers. "At the moment, I'm having very lustful thoughts about you."

She wove her arms around his neck. "Are you trying to change the subject?"

He pressed his lips to hers. "Uh-huh." His smile spreading across hers, he eased her down to lie on the bed with him. "Is it working?"

"Mmm-hmm."

He drew back to smooth his knuckles across her cheek. "You might have to help me with my clothes."

She closed her fingers over the first button on his shirt. "It'll be a hardship, but I suppose I can suffer through."

He shaped a palm over her breast. "Take yours off first. I want to touch you."

Smiling, she pulled her sweater up over her head and tossed it aside. "Better?"

With a sigh, he leaned into her, nuzzling his nose in the valley between her breasts. "Much." He carefully rested his palm in the curve of her waist, testing the sensitivity of his skin, before molding his fingers there.

"Does it hurt?" she asked.

"A little raw in places, but not bad." He wedged his knee between hers and cupped a hand on her buttocks, urging her hips closer to his. "I love your butt. Slim, but firm. Fits perfectly—"

She sat up straight on the bed. "Slim!"

Ry looked up at her in confusion. "What?"

She spun around on the bed to face him. "Slim! The nurse said Luke kept saying Slim's name over and over. He might've been trying to tell her that Slim is the one who set the fire."

He sat up, shaking his head. "I don't know, Kayla. That's a stretch."

"But it's possible. Think about it," she said. "Who found the first dead cow?"

"Luke."

"Who found the second one?"

"Luke."

"And Luke was the one who had guard duty the night the barn caught on fire. Don't you see?" she cried. "It had to be Slim."

Ry shook his head. "I'm not following you."

"Remember the night of the fire, when you told me to go call 911 and Slim said he'd already done it?"

"Yeah. So?"

"He appeared out of nowhere, Ry! When I saw the fire from the house and ran out to the barn, Luke was the only one there."

"If that's what you're basing your opinion on, then it could just as easily be Monty who's guilty."

"No!" she cried in frustration. "Don't you see? I

was on my way to the bunkhouse to get Slim and Monty, when you came to the barn. Then Luke comes running out of the barn on fire, you tackle him and tell me to call 911. Then, *Poof!* Slim appears out of nowhere, fully dressed, and cool as a cucumber and tells us he's already made the call. There's no way that he could have seen the fire, dressed, called 911 and made it to the barn before you did. He was already there! Probably hiding.''

Ry frowned, considering the possibility. ''But why would Slim burn the barn?''

''I don't know *why*,'' she said in frustration. ''But he did! He's the only one who could have done it.'' She grabbed her sweater and jerked it over her head, as she shoved off the bed. ''We've got to go home,'' she said, as she pushed her arms through the sleeves. ''We've got to stop him before he does something else.''

''Whoa,'' Ry said, catching her by the arm. ''You're not going anywhere. I'll go. You need to stay here and take care of Luke.''

''But you can't drive!''

''I don't intend to. You're going to take me to the airport and I'm going to catch a flight to Austin. Rory can pick me up there and drive me to the ranch.''

The urge to go in with both guns blazing was strong. But Ry knew that was the surest way to give Slim a chance to escape, if he was, in fact, the one responsible for all the trouble at the ranch. Before they could approach Slim, they'd need enough evidence to put him behind bars and keep him there.

In a meeting held at Woodrow's house, he shared Kayla's suspicions with his brothers. Though not a one of them was thoroughly convinced of Slim's guilt, they all agreed it was worth checking out. It would be a slow process to do so, but thoroughness, rather than speed, was required to gather the evidence needed for a conviction. They all agreed not to include Sheriff Akin in on their investigation. No one had forgotten—or forgiven—Akin for accusing Whit of the crimes.

The second night after his return from Dallas, Ry called the hotel to talk to Kayla.

"Have you found anything yet?" she asked anxiously.

"Nothing substantial. Woodrow dug the bullets out of the cows that were killed, and they're the same caliber that Slim uses in his rifle. To prove anything, we'd need to have a ballistic test run and that would require involving the sheriff, which we don't want to do at this point."

"I don't blame you."

"How's Luke?"

"Holding his own. The doctor said today that he thinks Luke might lose two fingers on his left hand. Luke doesn't know that, yet, though. He's still pretty much out of it. But his heartbeat is strong, and he woke up enough this afternoon to recognize me. I didn't mention Slim, because I was afraid it would upset him."

"That's probably best. We'll find what we need at this end. There's no sense in upsetting Luke by letting him know that we suspect Slim."

"I miss you."

Ry smiled. "I miss you, too. Want me to come back to Dallas?"

"Yes and no. Yes, because I miss you and, no,

because I want you to stay there and get the evidence you need to nail Slim. We owe it to Luke to see that he pays for what he did.''

''We'll get him, Kayla. I promise you, if he's guilty, we'll get him.''

Ace sat in the middle of the floor, surrounded by boxes, searching for anything in his father's records that mentioned Slim. Ry sat behind the desk, going through drawers, looking for the same. So far they hadn't found anything.

''Why in the hell the old man didn't have a pool of secretaries is beyond me,'' Ace grumbled. He held up a fistful of bound documents. ''Would you look at this? These are deeds to land he bought more than forty years ago, and they're stuck in this box with old bank statements.'' He slapped the documents back into the box and slammed down the lid. ''If it weren't for Luke, I'd tell you to forget it, that this is waste of our time.''

''Maybe if we could settle on a year,'' Ry suggested. ''It seems as if everything in the boxes is associated with the same year. Do you remember when Buck first hired Slim?''

Ace leaned back, bracing himself up on his hands. ''A helluva long time ago. I know that much. We were all still home, as I recall.''

''Wasn't Slim first hired on as a wrangler?'' Ry asked. ''Seems as if I remember watching him break horses in the corral, when I was a kid.''

Ace puckered his lips thoughtfully. ''Yeah. Seems like he was. Jessie was the foreman who hired him. You remember Jessie, don't you?''

Ry snorted a laugh. ''Who could forget him. He

had skin like rawhide and a tongue that cut like a whip. He blessed me out so many times, I started playing sick, just so I wouldn't have to work with him.''

"You and me both. Wonder whatever happened to him?"

"Beats me. Slim took over as foreman after Jessie left, didn't he?''

"Yeah, I believe he did, though I can't be sure there wasn't another foreman between him and Jessie. Jessie was still here when I left. And that was a good fifteen years ago.''

"At least," Ry agreed. He picked up an invoice from inside the box in front of him and looked at it. "We've got to be getting close. The files in this box are all dated eight years ago.''

Pushing off the floor with his hands, Ace sat up again and dragged another box in front of him. "Let's keep going then. No sense in quitting now.''

They'd worked for another hour, when the telephone rang. Ry picked it up and tucked it between shoulder and ear, so that he could continue digging through the box. "Tanner residence.''

"Ry. It's Kayla.''

Frowning, he caught the receiver in his hand, giving her his full attention. "Is something wrong? You sound upset.''

"I'm not upset. I'm out of breath. I'm at the hospital and I had to run downstairs to find a pay phone that wasn't in use.''

"I should have left you my cell. I didn't think about you having to use a pay phone.''

"It doesn't matter. Listen. I remembered something. About Slim. The night we were all at dinner and we were talking about the different ways we learn, Slim said he liked to read.''

"Yeah," he said slowly. "I remember him saying that."

"And Monty said Slim liked to write, too, and Slim came up out of his chair like he was going to attack Monty and accused him of prying in his bunk."

"Yeah, but what does that have to do with anything?"

"It means he probably keeps a diary or something!" she cried in frustration. "Otherwise he wouldn't have been so upset with Monty."

"Okay. I get now where you're going with this. You're thinking if we can find this diary, we'll find something in it that will help us convict Slim."

"Yes," she said, obviously relieved that he'd finally understood. "It's worth a try, at least."

"I'll do it right now."

"Ry?"

"What?"

"Be careful. If we're right about Slim, and he catches you going through his things..."

"Don't worry. I'll be careful."

"Ry?"

"What?"

"I love you."

He smiled. "I love you, too."

As he stretched to hang up the receiver, he caught Ace looking at him. "What?" he grumbled. "You think you're the only Tanner who can fall in love?"

Ace chuckled. "No. Just surprised that you made the fall." He picked up a file to thumb through and added, "Especially, since I distinctly remember you referring to Kayla as a kid."

Scowling, Ry stood. "She's not that much younger than me."

Ace held up his hands. "Did I say that there's anything wrong with marrying a younger woman? Hell, Maggie's a good bit younger than me, and I can tell you there's a lot to be said for a May and December relationship."

"When I've got more time," Ry said dryly, "you can tell what those things are. At the moment, I've better things to do. Kayla seems to think Slim keeps a diary of sorts. I'm going out to the bunkhouse to see if I can find it."

"Want me to go with you?"

Ry glanced at his watch. "No. Woodrow and Rory should be back any minute now from picking up Whit. You can show them what boxes still need going through. Hopefully ya'll can finish up here, by the time I get back."

"Aren't you worried he might catch you at it?"

Ry shook his head. "I sent him and Monty out to the south pasture to work on a well pump. They won't be back for hours, yet."

Chapter 14

"This is about as much fun as having a tooth filled," Woodrow grumbled.

"You had a tooth filled lately, Woodrow?" Rory teased.

"No, but I'd rather sit in a dentist's chair than dig through these files." He tossed down the folder he held in disgust. "Hell, I don't even know what I'm looking for."

"None of us do," Ace said. "But whatever it is, it's going to have Slim's name on it."

"What is his name, anyway?" Rory asked. "I've never heard him called anything but Slim."

"Now that you mention it," Ace said. "Neither have I."

"His last name is Granger," Whit said.

Ace, Rory and Woodrow all turned to look at him.

"How do you know his name?" Ace asked.

Whit held up a piece of paper. "It says it right here

on his job application." He glanced at the page and read, "Stewart L. Granger. And then in parentheses, it says Slim."

"Let me see that," Ace said.

Whit passed him the application and Ace read it through, then huffed a breath. "Well, I've read it, and I still don't know a damn thing more than I did before."

"I bet I know who could tell us about him," Rory said.

"Who?" Ace asked.

"Maw Garner. She knows the skinny on everybody that's ever lived in this town."

Ace hung up the phone.

"Well?" Rory said impatiently. "What did Maw have to say?"

His expression grim, Ace stood. "Plenty. She said that Buck ran Slim off six months before he died."

"Why?" Woodrow asked.

"She didn't know. But she said that she'd never trusted Slim. Said he gave her the spooks. She told me that when Buck fired Jessie, there was talk around town that Slim had something to do with Jessie getting fired. Nobody knows exactly what. Just that Jessie ended up at a bar in town that same night, got himself good and drunk and started spouting off about how he was going to get even with Slim for stealing his job."

"Did he?" Woodrow asked.

Ace shook his head. "No one ever saw Jessie again. Maw said that, when he stopped at the bar, he had his gear packed in the back of his truck and was on his way out of town, so nobody ever thought much of it.''

''Obviously Maw did.''

''You know Maw,'' Woodrow groused. ''She could put the spin on an ice cream social and have you thinking you were listening to a soap opera drama.''

''Just the same,'' Ace said and stood. ''I think we better head down to the bunkhouse and check on Ry. He's been gone a good hour.''

One by one, Ry replaced the items in Slim's trunk, careful to put them back in the order in which he'd found them. He still couldn't believe what he'd discovered. They'd trusted Slim, sweated with him, shared meals with him, when all along Slim was planning to destroy them.

Picking up the worn journal, he stood and slipped the book into the inside pocket of his jacket. As he turned for the door, it opened.

Slim stood in the opening, a rifle held against the side of his leg.

His gaze on Ry's, Slim slowly used the gun's barrel to nudge the door closed behind him. ''What are you doing in here?''

Ry considered lying, but didn't figure there was much point, since he was standing beside Slim's bunk. ''Why did you do it, Slim?'' he asked. ''Luke was your friend. You worked with him for years. How could you stand there and watch him burn?''

''If a man doesn't have the good sense to stay out of a burnin' barn, I'm not riskin' my neck to save his.''

"He was trying to save the horses. Your horse was in there, too."

"I wouldn't put my life on the line for no horse, mine or anybody else's."

"No, I guess a man who would kill a cow, wouldn't think twice about watching his horse burn to death. What did you hope to gain, Slim? You weren't going to get the ranch, no matter how many cows you killed or how many barns you burned down. This is Tanner land and always will be."

Slim curled his nose in a sneer. "And what have you done to earn it? Huh?" He spat a stream of saliva at Ry's feet. "Nothin'. That's what. You don't know what it's like to work a place. Risin' before dawn to scrape a livin' out of land a goat couldn't survive on. Workin' 'til your fingers are nothin' but blood and bone. Crawlin' into bed at night, so tired you don't know if your butt made it back to the house with you, then crawlin' back out the next mornin' and doing it all over again. And just when you think you're beginnin' to get ahead a little, along comes some high roller who offers you what sounds like a fortune for what was a shitty piece of land to start with, and you take it, only to find out later that high roller has parked himself an oil well on that land and has hit himself a nice black river of oil."

"I suppose what you're telling me is that Buck is the high roller who bought your land."

"Not *my* land. My daddy's land."

"So what are you doing here? If you hated Buck so much, why did you come to work for him?"

"To kill him."

He said it so flatly, so emotionlessly that Ry knew Slim was cold-blooded enough to do it.

"But after I was here for a while," Slim went on. "I saw me a better way to get even with him. One-by-one I watched you boys leave. Stood by and watched you let him run you off, with his meanness. Each time one of you left, I could see me gettin' a bigger piece of the pie. Buck liked me. Trusted me. I made it my job to see that he did. He told me that he was going to give the ranch to me. Promised me he would name me in his will, if I'd stick with him and run the place for him. Like a fool, I believed him."

"There was no will," Ry told him. "Even if he had left one, I doubt he would have made good his promise. Buck used people to get what he wanted out of them, but rarely gave anything in return."

"I know there was no will. About six months before he died, I called his hand on it. Asked him to show me where he had it written that the place would be mine."

"And he couldn't."

"Hell, no, he couldn't! He never intended to give me the ranch. He used me. Then he fired me."

"So why did you come back after he died, when Whit put out the word that we were wanting to hire all of the old hands back?"

Slim slowly raised the rifle to point it at Ry's chest. "To make your lives a living hell. To make you wish you'd never heard of Tanner land. You didn't do nothin' to deserve it. I'm the one who worked it, stuck by the old man. I deserve to own it. Not you or any of your damn brothers."

As Ry stared down the length of the rifle's barrel, a trickle of sweat worked its way down his spine. He had no weapon. Nothing to protect himself with. And no chance of escape, as Slim stood between him and the only door. His only hope was his brothers. If he stalled Slim long enough, maybe Ace or one of the others would come looking for him.

"Did you think that you could run us off? Scare us so bad, that we'd all turn tail and run?"

"No. I planned to kill you."

"Surely you don't think you can get by with killing us all? Someone is bound to get suspicious, if my brothers and I are all found murdered."

"It won't look like a murder. It'll look like an accident. I've thought it all out."

Ry arched a brow. "Really? You must be really smart, to plan something as big as this. Tell me how you're going to do it."

The door flew open, letting in a rush of cold air and striking Slim on the back and knocking him forward. Ry lunged, clamping his hands around the barrel of the rifle and pushing it up. He felt the charge, before he heard it, the buck of the gun as it discharged the shell, the heat that raced through the barrel like fire on his raw hands. The blast deafened him, his ears ringing with the resounding shot, as if the gun was fired again, again and again.

A fist hit his jaw, knocking his head back and a knee came up to ram his groin. Fighting back the pain, he set his teeth, the muscles in his arms and legs quivering, as he fought to remain upright, to keep his hands closed around the barrel in a battle for control of the weapon.

And then Slim was crumpling, his face a blur as he slumped to the floor. Ry blinked to clear the sweat from his eyes and saw Woodrow standing where Slim had stood, a piece of firewood gripped in his wide hands.

Dropping the stock of the rifle to the floor, Ry sagged weakly over it, using the gun to hold himself upright. "Damn, Woodrow," he gasped. "What took you so long to get here?"

When the sheriff arrived, Ry and his brothers had Slim hog-tied and waiting on the front porch, a lump the size of an orange on the back of his head. They quickly related their findings, pointing to Slim's guilt, the jealousy and resentment that had pushed him over the edge into madness. As the sheriff loaded Slim into the back of his cruiser, Ace suggested the sheriff might check on a man by the name of Jessie Parker, the former foreman of the Bar T. If Jessie couldn't be traced, Ace told him that Slim probably knew where he was buried.

After watching the sheriff drive off, Ry had Rory drive him to the airport and caught the next flight for Dallas, anxious to return to Kayla. Though it was almost nine o'clock when he arrived, he figured she would still be with Luke, and he hailed a taxi and instructed the driver to take him to Parkland Hospital.

The nurse on duty directed him to the cubicle assigned to Luke, telling him that he'd find Kayla there. He stepped quietly into the narrow space and stood a moment, looking first at Luke and all the equipment hooked up to him, then at Kayla, who sat beside Luke's bed, a hand on his arm, lightly stroking.

Sensing his presence, she turned, then slowly rose, her eyes filled with questions she didn't dare ask.

"It's over," he said quietly and opened his arms. Kayla fell against him, winding her arms around his waist. "Thank, God," she whispered tearfully. "I've been so worried. So scared. Oh, Ry." She squeezed her arms tighter around him, her cheek more closely against his chest. "You have no idea how good it is to see you. Hold you. I was so afraid."

"Not nearly as much as I was." He drew back to look at her and tipped his head toward the bed. "How's Luke?"

"Better, I think. He's waking up for longer periods of time. The pain must be awful, though. He moans a lot. Moves around as if he's trying to get up."

"I'm afraid that's the way it's going to be for a while. The healing process is slow. But even before it can began, he's going to suffer more pain as they scrape off the damaged skin."

She shuddered and tightened her arms around him. "I hate to think that he has to suffer any more. He's been through so much already."

"We'll be with him every step of the way."

A wistful smile curved her lips, as she angled her head to look at Luke. "He asked about you today."

"He did?"

She nodded then tipped her head up to smile at him. "His doctor was here and was explaining to him the procedures he would be undergoing. I'm not sure how much of it Luke understood. He was pretty much out-of-it. But he told the doctor that if anybody was going to be cutting on him, it was going to be you, because you were the best."

Ry stiffened. "Kayla. When I said we'd be with him, I didn't mean I'd be involved in his treatments. I meant in a supportive role. I'm not a surgeon any more."

Her smile slowly faded. "But, Ry. This is Luke

we're talking about. He wants you to perform his surgeries. He trust you. Needs you.''

He forced her arms from around him. "I'll do everything I can to help him. But I won't be his doctor. That I won't do. I can't.''

Kayla lay on her side in the bed next to Ry, but she might as well have been in the next room. Her back was turned to him, her shoulder hunched to her ear, the sheet hugged close to her chin. She hadn't spoken more than three words to him since they'd left the hospital. He knew she was angry with him, disappointed. But he wasn't knuckling under. He wouldn't agree to perform what surgeries Luke required, simply to please her. He'd given up practicing medicine. She knew that. It wasn't fair of her to expect him to start again, when he'd made it clear that he had no intention of returning to medicine.

But he didn't want her to be angry with him. He wanted to hold her, feel her warmth, see her smile. He loved her. And right now he desperately needed to know that she loved him, too.

He placed a hand on her shoulder. "Kayla. I know that you're mad at me.''

"I'm not mad.''

He heard the tears in her voice and felt an almost irrepressible urge to cry, too. "Honey, please,'' he begged. "Try to understand.''

She rolled to her back to look at him, her face streaked with tears. "And how am I supposed to understand something you refuse to talk about?''

Frustrated, Ry sat up and dug the heels of his hands against his eyes. "Kayla, I've told you. I don't understand it myself. I just know that I can't do it any more. Whatever desire I had to be a doctor is gone. I lost it.''

She sat up, too. ''But why, Ry? What made you lose it? I told you I can accept it if you choose not to be a doctor. But I can't accept you not trusting me enough to share your reasons with me.''

He dropped his hands to fist them in his lap. ''It isn't a matter of trust. I can't share something I don't have an answer for. I lost what it takes to continue, and I don't know why.''

If possible, his answer seemed to hurt her even more.

''Feelings don't change, Ry. Not the important ones.'' She balled a hand and held it against her heart. ''I love you. Deep inside me, I know that, and nothing will ever change my feelings. I feel much the same way about nursing, what I'd think you would've had to feel to go through the years of study to become a doctor. But if your feelings for your profession can change, how can I know that your feelings for me won't change, too? Can you imagine what kind of hell that would be to live with? To never know from one day to the next that the person you love might stop loving you?''

She pushed from the bed. ''I'm sorry, Ry. But I won't live that way. When I give my heart to someone, I give it wholly and with a lifetime guarantee. If you can't offer me the same, I don't think we should pursue this any further.''

''Is that a threat?''

She curled her hands into fists to hold on to her temper, to keep from throwing herself into his arms. ''No. It's the truth. I've opened my heart and allowed you to see my insecurities, my needs, my feelings. In doing that, I've given you the power to hurt me. You can love me, Ry. You can trust me enough to share your fear, your insecurities, your needs, or you can walk away. The choice is yours.''

He vaulted from the bed and grabbed his jeans, yanked them on. ''That's not a choice. It's an ultimatum. You're taking your beliefs and trying to force them on to me, make me conform to some twisted set of rules you've dreamed up.'' He snatched his shirt from the back of the chair and shrugged it on. ''Well, let me tell you something, Miss Know-it-all. People do change. Feelings change. You may not want them to or even be aware they are, but it happens. Believe me it happens. I know it does, because it happened to me.''

''Kayla?''

Kayla snapped up her head to find Elizabeth hurrying down the hospital corridor toward the waiting room. She stood, tears filling her eyes.

Elizabeth wrapped an arm around her and pulled her head to hold against her shoulder. ''Oh, honey. What happened? Ry came home in the middle of the night, madder than the dickens, but won't say a word to anybody. The most Woodrow could get out of him was that he'd left you here in Dallas with Luke, and if Woodrow wanted to know anything, he'd have to talk to you, because you were the one with all the answers.''

Kayla squeezed her eyes shut, as the crack in her heart opened a little wider, then lifted her head to look at Elizabeth. ''He's wrong. He's the one with the answers, but he won't share them. At least, not with me.''

Her forehead creased in concern, Elizabeth drew Kayla toward the stairwell and the privacy she felt they needed. "Perhaps if you told me what was said, what happened, I can make sense of all this."

"If you can," Kayla said miserably, "then you're a better woman than me."

A half hour later, Kayla and Elizabeth still sat on the stairs. Kayla held the tissue Elizabeth had given her, balled in her fist.

"And that's exactly what happened," Kayla finished wearily.

Elizabeth stroked a hand over Kayla's hair. "You love him, don't you?"

Kayla sniffed back a fresh wave of tears. "Yes. That's what makes this so maddening. Why it hurts so much that he won't talk to me, share with me whatever it is that's bothering him."

"Do you think you might be asking him the impossible?"

Fisting her hands, Kayla made a growling sound low in her throat. "You sound just like Ry. He keeps saying he doesn't know why he left medicine, he just did."

Elizabeth laid a hand over Kayla's. "I can't pretend to know what's in Ry's mind or heart, but I know what I see, what I have seen from the moment I first met him. He's a very unhappy man. Confused. Discontented. At least he was, before he met you. But since you came into his life, I've seen a glimmer of something else inside him. A warmth that I think he believed he'd lost.

"Like you, I don't understand why Ry left medicine. But I do believe, if his profession was what made him unhappy, he would have experienced some kind of a relief after leaving it behind. He would have found the peace and happiness that he was searching for, when he made the decision.''

"What you're saying is, I was wrong to give him an ultimatum.''

Laughing softly, Elizabeth hugged Kayla to her side. "No. If I were in your place, I probably would've reacted the same as you. We women are nothing, if not emotional. Especially where our hearts are involved.'' She wove a strand of hair behind Kayla's ear. "All I'm suggesting is that you think about what you've asked of him. See if you can find it in your heart to give him the time and understanding he needs to discover what ails him himself. It's a woman's nature to push, when what she should do is stand quietly by and offer her support.''

"Not all women push. You certainly don't. But thanks for lying and saying they do. It makes me feel a little less like a witch to think I'm not the only one who's screwed up a relationship.''

Elizabeth dropped back her head and laughed. "Oh, you aren't alone, believe me. Sometime you and Maggie and I will have to get together and compare stories. I think you'd feel a lot better, after hearing how we almost screwed up our relationships with Ry's brothers.''

Kayla dropped her chin on her hand. "Now I don't know what to do,'' she said miserably. "Leave him alone to work things out on his own or go and apologize and pray he'll forgive me.''

Elizabeth reached into her coat pocket and pulled out a set of keys. "You can pray while you drive. My Mercedes is out front. I'll stay here with Luke.''

* * *

Ace slapped a hand across Ry's rump. "Are you going to stay in bed all day or are you going to get up and tell me what the hell is going on?"

Groaning, Ry rolled to his back and pulled his pillow over his face. "Go away, Ace. I don't need any big brother lectures."

Ace dropped down on the side of the bed. "I believe you do."

Ry dragged the pillow from his face to frown. "Well, you're wrong. Get lost."

Chuckling, Ace stood and began to prowl the room. "Woodrow tells me that you ran off and left Kayla in Dallas."

"I resent your use of the phrase 'ran off.' I haven't run away from anything or anybody since I was eighteen and left home for the last time."

"Excuse me for differing, but I believe you have. You not only ran away from Kayla, you ran away from your job."

Ry sat bolt upright and hurled the pillow at the wall. "What is it with you people?" he asked furiously. "So I decided to try something different. What's the big deal? People change jobs all the time."

"Not the ones who love what they're doing."

"I gave women face lifts and boob jobs. What's to love about that?"

"Maybe it wasn't what you were doing that you didn't like. Maybe it was where you were doing it."

Ry rubbed a hand over his hair, mussing it even more. "Sorry," he muttered irritably, "but I haven't had my morning caffeine. You're going to have to explain that one to me."

"When I first started out as a photographer, I

worked for one of those outfits that travels around taking portraits of kids. You talk about hating a job.'' He shuddered. ''Try getting about fifty screaming kids to smile for the camera one at a time and do it eight hours a day. It would test the patience of a saint. I finally got a stomach full and quit. Loaded up my all my photography equipment and headed north. I didn't know where I was going and didn't particularly care. I just wanted as far away from those kids as I could get. Ended up in Colorado, where I camped for a few days. It took me another couple of days before I could even bring myself to hold a camera in my hands.

''From Colorado, I headed farther north, then west over into Oregon. Since I planned to spend a couple of days there, I decided to have the film I'd shot developed.'' Chuckling, he shook his head. ''Pardon me if I sound like a braggart, but those prints nearly took my breath away. I'd taken pictures of deer, antelope. Even managed to get a few shots of trout swimming upstream. After looking at them, seeing the beauty in them, the talent, I knew then what I wanted to do with my life. But I had to go through hell before I found my niche.''

''So you think I should take up wildlife photography?''

Ace sent him a sour look. ''What you should do is ask yourself if where you were is where you truly wanted to be. Maybe you shouldn't be in private practice. Maybe you should be in a hospital. An emergency room doctor or something.'' He tossed up his hands. ''Hell, I don't know enough about what you people do to even offer advice.''

He scooped the pillow from the floor and tossed it

back to Ry. "But you might want to give it some thought. I'll bet it won't take you long to figure out where you belong."

He crossed to the door, stopped and looked back. "And you might want to think about where you want to be with Kayla. She seemed like a nice kid."

He leaped through the doorway and closed the door, letting the pillow Ry threw at him hit it instead of his back.

Ry heard his laughter all the way down the hall.

Ry showered and dressed, then headed for the kitchen, where he found Ace sitting at the table, reading the paper.

"Don't you have a wife and kid somewhere who need you?"

Ace calmly turned a page. "That I do. I'm waiting on Rory to pick me up and take me to the airport, so that I can fly back to North Dakota and join them." He lowered the page. "And what do you have planned for the day?"

Avoiding his gaze, Ry headed for the coffee pot. "I don't know. Help Monty, I guess."

"You might want to check on the horses. Monty doesn't have the knack that Luke does in caring for them."

"Good idea." Ry filled a mug and turned for the door, grateful for the excuse to avoid Ace's all-seeing-all-knowing eyes.

His walk to the holding pen where the horses were being kept, took him by the burned-out barn. Black, charred timbers lay like an abandoned game of pick-up-sticks, where the building had once stood. They would rebuild, he knew, but knowing that didn't lessen the loss he felt, as he stared at the churned earth, the rubble and ashes that remained in its place.

Though he tried to block out the memory, he saw Kayla as she'd stood that night, a dark shadow against the wall of leaping flames behind her, her arms lifted and waving, as she'd waited for him. The loss that squeezed at his chest at the thought of her outweighed whatever sadness he felt for the loss of the barn. He'd loved her, still did, but he couldn't give her what she wanted, what she demanded. It was a crazy reason to end a relationship. A foolish one, and one totally out of his control.

Depressed by the thought, he walked on, pausing only long enough to open the gate to the holding pen. Talking softly to soothe the horses, he moved through them, looking them over, checking for any sign of a wound that needed tending. When he reached Midnight, he stopped and set his coffee mug on the top of a fence post, then hunkered down to examine the wound he'd closed.

"Lookin' good, Midnight," he murmured, stroking a hand over the horse's coat. As he admired the incision, a sense of accomplishment, of pride in what he'd done settled over him. He'd taken an injured animal faced with the possibility of an ugly and possibly debilitating scar and made him whole again. It was what he'd dreamed of doing as a boy. Taking what life or another human had rendered useless or damaged and making it right again, making it whole.

As he knelt, his palm smoothing over the horse's flesh, understanding came to him in a flash of insight so bright, so sharp, he wondered why he'd never seen it before. Shaken, he stood, a hand braced against the horse's side to steady himself. He had to see Kayla.

Talk to her. Tell her what she'd demanded that he share with her, the one screw-up in his life that he'd never understood until that moment.

Even as the need rose in him to see her, to hold her, anger chased on its heels. She'd turned her back on him, all but pushed him away from her. He wouldn't go crawling back to have her stomp on his heart again.

"Ry?"

He closed his eyes against the sound of her voice, sure that his thoughts of her were what had conjured it.

"Ace told me that you were out here."

He hadn't conjured her. She was there. Behind him. All he had to do was turn and he would see her. Could hold her.

His pride kept his back turned to her.

"What do you want, Kayla?"

"To tell you I'm sorry."

Keeping his hand on the horse's side, he moved farther away from her, fighting the pull, the need to go to her. "You always were one quick to deliver an apology."

"It doesn't make it any less sincere."

He glanced over his shoulder, before he could stop himself, and saw her standing with her hands rammed deeply into her pockets, the wind whipping strands of her blond hair across her face. Dark circles shadowed her eyes, telling him that she hadn't slept any better than he had, that she had suffered as much as he.

"You didn't trust me," he said, unable to stop the words she'd used to slash at his heart. "You didn't trust me enough to give me your heart."

She dipped her chin. "I was wrong to say what I did. Elizabeth helped me see that."

"Elizabeth?"

"She came to the hospital this morning, and we talked."

She lifted her head and Ry's knees nearly buckled when he saw the tears that filled her eyes. The regret.

"You have my heart, Ry. You'll always have it. I was so wrong to ask of you what I did, to expect you to share with me something that you didn't have to share. But I did it because I love you, Ry. I did it because I know that whatever it is that has made you unhappy is still there inside you. I want so badly for you to find what that is, to help you make it right."

She dipped her chin and shook her head. "You were so right about me. I am a control freak. I thought I could fix you, make you happy, when you are the only one who can do that." She looked up at him, tears streaming down her face. "But I didn't do what I did to be mean or to hurt you. I wanted only to help you, because I love you so much."

He could see that love in her eyes, on her face, in her tears. He opened his arms and she ran into his embrace, flinging her arms around him and holding him tight.

"I'm so sorry, Ry," she sobbed.

"No," he said, and drew back to look at her. "I'm the one who's sorry. You opened my eyes, Kayla. You and Ace." He swept her hair back to hold it from her face, so that he could see her, the features he'd grown to love. "If you hadn't pushed me so hard, I don't know how long it would've taken me to figure everything out. I know now what was wrong, what

Peggy Moreland

younger brothers and sisters, so bossiness is deeply ingrained in me.''

''I think I can handle that.'' Smiling, he dropped his arms to loop them loosely behind her waist.

''Let's go to the house and tell the others.''

When he started to turn away, she held him back.

''Ry? Would you do me a favor?''

''What's that?''

''Call a press conference.''

He choked a laugh. ''What for?''

''I want everyone in Texas to know that we're getting married. I'll even take part in it. We're going to set the record straight once and for all. We can even offer to do a segment on Adrian Tyson's trashy television show. When we're done, there won't be a person in Texas who will doubt that I love you for who you are and not how much you're worth.''

Smiling, he tugged her hips close. ''You really like me, huh?''

Laughing, she gave him a hard kiss on the mouth. ''Cowboy, I don't just like you. I'm crazy in love with you.''

* * * * *

Look for the next book in the
Tanners of Texas Saga,
THE LAST GOOD MAN IN TEXAS,
coming in May 2004
from Silhouette Desire!

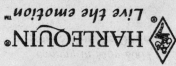

all he did. Not only to me, but the others, as well. In a way, I even owe him my thanks.''

''Why?''

''Because, without knowing it, he was the one who pushed me toward medicine. I'd seen all he'd done, the people he hurt, the lives he'd ruined, and I wanted to give something back, somehow make up for all the wrongs he'd committed. Becoming a physician offered me a way to do that.''

She tightened her arms around him. ''You can make a difference here. I know you can.''

''I hope to. Tanner's Crossing will be my base. Our base,'' he added, ''if you'll agree to marry me.''

When she opened her mouth, he pressed a finger to her lips. ''I know that finishing your nursing degree is important to you. I want that for you, too. We can lease an apartment in Austin for you to use while you're in school, and you can spend your weekends here with me. And I know you'll want to continue to help your family, and that's fine, too. We'll help them together. We can even move them here, if they want.''

She threw her arms around his neck. ''Oh, Ry. Yes. Yes!''

He hugged her tight, swaying with her in his arms. ''I love you, Kayla,'' he whispered against her hair. ''More than I ever dreamed possible.''

She drew back to frame his face between her hands. ''And I love you. We're going to make a good team, you and I.''

''I have no doubt we will.''

She wrinkled her nose. ''I'll probably drive you crazy, bossing you around. I won't be able to help myself. As the oldest, I helped take care of my made me give up my practice. I wasn't where I needed to be.

"But I do now," he added. "I'm going back to medicine, but this time I'm going to do it right. Surgery wasn't the cause of my discontent. It was the kind of surgery I was doing that I found unfulfilling. I want to help people, take a face scarred beyond recognition and give the person behind it, the features he or she remembers, the will to live, hope for a brighter future. If he still wants me, I intend for Luke to be my first patient."

"Oh Ry," she whispered tearfully. "Luke will be thrilled when he hears that you'll be his doctor. You were the one he asked for, the one he trusted to perform the surgeries he'll require."

"I want to set up my practice here, in Tanner's Crossing. Not solely. I haven't thought it all out, yet. I'll probably do some pro-bono work in Austin. Maybe travel to other countries in need of medical care. But here is where I belong. In Tanner's Crossing. I know that now."

"The townspeople will be happy to hear that you're coming home, that you're finally going to uphold your end of the bargain."

He lifted a brow in surprise. "You knew about that?"

"Yes. And I know why you wouldn't come back here. It was because of your father."

He dropped his gaze. "Yes. I knew that if I came back he'd make my life a living hell, would do everything he could to ruin what I hoped to accomplish." He lifted his head to meet her gaze. "But I'm free of him now, in a way that I never could be before. And I've come a long way in forgiving him for